I'M DATING A HOLLYWOOD STAR

❧

BERNICE BLOOM

Bernice Bloom

Published by Gold Medals Media Ltd

DEAR READERS

Hello,

Welcome to the world of Bernice Bloom novels.

This is a gorgeous, funny and heartwarming romp through the chaos of celebrity love, with added danger, baddies, shopping, pills, diets, broken friendships and a dead stylist.

Because - after all - what heartwarming romp would be complete without a dead stylist?

Kelly is an ordinary girl with an extraordinary secret - she is dating Rufus George—the swoon-worthy millionaire star of countless Hollywood blockbusters.

Life is perfect as long as no one knows. But when they decide to go public, Kelly is thrust into a whirlwind of paparazzi, scandal-hungry journalists, and jealous admirers who would love nothing more than to steal her Hollywood hunk.

As Kelly navigates the madness of fame, she discovers that living a normal life is nearly impossible when your boyfriend is a movie star.

Her struggles and triumphs will resonate with anyone

who has ever been in love. Only they are doubly difficult when the world's press is on your doorstep, and you're always worried that Heat magazine will show close-ups of your cellulite.

With her relationship under siege, can Kelly stay true to herself and keep her love alive, or will the pressure of the spotlight tear them apart?

Packed with wit, charm, and laugh-out-loud moments, *I'm Dating a Hollywood Star* is a sparkling tale of love, fame, and the price of both.

"A must-read, beautifully-written story that you won't want to come to an end."

"The new Bridget Jones" (D*aily Mirror)*

"I started reading and couldn't put it down."' *Kelly Brook*

"Girls, leave space in the Miu Miu beach bag for this deliciously dark cautionary tale of what happens when dreams come true." Shari Low, *Daily Record*

CHAPTER 1: THE ARRIVAL OF
HOLLYWOOD'S LEADING MAN

$\mathcal{I}$t's 3:30 pm on a Thursday afternoon, and I'm on my hands and knees applying clear nail varnish to the back of Katie's tights in the hope that I can prevent a ladder from spreading up her leg. The key to getting this right is to apply just the right quantity: too little and the ladder will grow, too much and the tights will stick to the back of her legs, creating a hard lump, and tights that are impossible to remove without seriously damaging her skin. I'm not saying it's like major surgery or anything - just that a degree of precision is required in order to prevent Katie from needing a skin graft.

It was probably unwise to attempt this procedure at work, because I'm at the crucial point of delicately dotting on the varnish when the door swings open, and Anthony Blunt, the manager, walks in with Geoff Cooper. They stand there, hands behind their backs, surveying us critically.

'Let me introduce the girls,' says Anthony, as Geoff shakes hands with Katie and Jenny.

We all work at Richmond Fringe Theatre, and have never met Geoff Cooper before; he's the director of the entire Sentina Theatre group: the big cheese, the name on all the booklets, the website and on press releases. To be honest, I'd never thought of him being a real person - just this glamorous figurehead photographed at celebrity parties,

I put down the nail varnish as surreptitiously as possible and hope he doesn't notice the pungent aroma in the air.

When he reaches me, he shakes my hand, then smiles broadly and holds his hands like a steeple under his chin. I notice he's wearing one of those rings on his little finger that posh people wear. He asks me whether I enjoy my job.

'Oh, I love it,' I tell him. 'The theatre's a wonderful place to work – there's a real buzz here: all the excitement of the actors, costumes and set designers arriving. It's a creative atmosphere, and I work with such lovely people...' I sweep my hands towards Katie and Jenny as I speak, and they give nervous giggles.

'Very good,' he replies, stepping forward, and just missing the pot of clear nail varnish discarded on the floor.

'We've come to tell you that a new artistic director is starting. His name is Sebastian Waters. He will be here tomorrow morning and is planning big changes, so get ready for some unusual productions and get ready to work harder than you ever have in your life; he'll need lots of support.'

We all nod and murmur that – yes, of course - we'll work very hard. Then, as quickly as they came, they turn around and leave.

'God, what was all that about? Do you think we'll all get the sack?' asks Katie.

I confess that I'm worried, too. Why would he need to come in and see us in person unless the new appointment was going to affect us? And why on earth was Cooper there? He's like the king of theatreland.

'I bet there will be redundancies. This new guy will want

to bring in his own marketing and admin people. That's why he came in here, to forewarn us,' says Jenny.

I sigh, deeply.

'You'll be OK, Kelly – everyone fancies you; they won't get rid of the office pin-up girl, but I better start sprucing up my P45,' says Katie.

'Ha ha. Thanks for the compliment, but I think I'd better start doing some sprucing, too. This doesn't look promising at all.'

By the time I get home from work that evening to the flat I share in Twickenham with my two best friends – Mandy and Sophie, the misery has settled in, and I've convinced myself I'm about to be sacked. Even the sight of Mandy and Soph trying to entertain me with drunk gymnastics doesn't raise a smile. They have been drinking since lunch and can't stop giggling.

'What will I do?' I ask as Mandy falls into the side table and smashes her phone.

'You don't know that you're going to lose your job,' she says, standing up and surveying the damage. 'It's pointless to start worrying about it now when it might never happen. Think about it logically – you're good at your job, well-liked, never take sickies, and are more or less on time every day. I mean – why would they get rid of you? I wouldn't get rid of you if I were them; I'd promote you and make you the boss of the whole world.'

I wish my drunk flatmates were running the theatre; I'd be OK then. I know Mandy's right; I've given them no reason to get rid of me, but I'm worried.

'Come on, have a glass of wine, and stop making that frowny face,' says Sophie, but I'm just not in the mood, so I call it a night and leave them watching our favourite reality show, 'At home with Zadine' and discussing the fact that Mandy's phone is now completely broken, while I lie on my bed, and think about alternative careers.

I'm so worried about impending unemployment, that I'm in the office early the next morning. Jen and Katie are early, too. We all find ourselves sitting at our desks, smartly dressed and raring to go at 8.30 am; this has never happened before.

We then set about working hard and not messing around, fearful that the new creative director would come in and sack us all on the spot if he caught us chatting.

It's 10 am when Sebastian makes his entrance and our fears turn to delight. He is completely lovely – tall and proud with a mop of sandy-blond hair that is so dishevelled it looks as if he's got it on backwards. His confidence fairly bounces off the walls and his enthusiasm fills the theatre from floor to ceiling. We love him from the moment he walks in – all bubbly and excitable like a puppy, but with this incredibly loud voice you can hear from the next room.

'Lovely to meet you all,' he booms, smiling from ear to ear like he genuinely means it. He is wearing a ridiculous ensemble; it looks as if he borrowed clothes from a friend who is completely different in shape and size. He wears fawn-coloured cords that sit just above his grubby white socks so that when he sits down and crosses his legs, we are treated to the sight of four inches of pale, freckled shin covered in strawberry-blond hairs. On top he wears a creased white shirt (too big) and a mustard-coloured jacket (too small).

Despite all that, though, there is something charming and erudite about our cuddly new boss; he is bursting with ideas for adaptations and alterations and ways in which we can make improvements that will secure the theatre's future.

Our first impression of Sebastian lasts, and he announces a few weeks later that he is keeping us all on. His effervescent nature attracts backers who bring new funding to the theatre, meaning big plans are afoot. Suddenly, the future is looking very bright. I am promoted to head administrator and given much more responsibility. No more money, of course; we lowly theatre administrators do it for love, not financial remuneration.

Every day at work is filled with optimism as we look forward to a future more magical than we'd ever thought possible.

One bright, sunny morning, a few months after Sebastian's arrival, Katie and I are sitting in the office comparing suntans when Sebastian calls us in and announces that a Hollywood heart-throb will be joining the cast of *Only Men* – a new play set to start with us at our little theatre for a month before moving to the West End.

'Who?' we ask, imagining Chris Hemsworth setting himself up at the desk next to us.

'You'll have to wait and see,' says Seb enigmatically as he sweeps out of the office, leaving us to speculate wildly.

'That's it then,' says Jenny with a weary shrug. 'It's going to be someone old and distinguished, who we've never heard of.'

There are nods all around. It will be some dull Shakespearean actor with very little hair and a collection of brightly coloured cravats.

But the next day, as we are guessing which octogenarian will appear before us, Seb discloses that the actor is Rufus George, the sexiest man ever to walk the earth (and that's official – he's come top of the *Cosmo* list for the past two years).

'Google him,' I say to Katie, and we all gather around her computer and watch, entranced, as a million or more articles about him decorate her screen. We begin clicking through them one by one. By lunchtime, there is nothing we don't know about him.

He was 8lbs. 8oz. when he was born. His mother is an interior designer with high cheekbones, large earrings and a wardrobe which appears to consist entirely of expensive beige separates. From the photos, she seems like one of those women who always looks like she's just walked out of the hairdresser. 'We all know the type,' I mutter to Katie and Jenny.

Rufus's career started because of his mother. She wanted to be an actress herself, so when she left Rufus's father (breaking the poor man's heart, by all accounts; he died the next year), she took her six-year-old son to live in L.A. so she could pursue her dreams of making it big in Hollywood.

Rufus was dragged along to auditions and screen tests and forced to attend drama classes while his mother fought to be taken seriously as an up-and-coming actress. Ironically, though, it was Rufus who made it 'big in Hollywood' when he was picked out of his drama academy and given a role as a young boy who had to be rescued by Michael Douglas after being cast adrift on a fishing boat. His mother never made it beyond a couple of walk-on parts in minor films. When the ageing process robbed her of any chance of being the starlet she'd so yearned to be, she turned to interior design and worked with some of the biggest names in Hollywood, taking millions from them to deck out their homes.

'I'm kind of glad he made it and not her,' says Jenny. 'She sounds like a right piece of work.'

While his mother cut a dash in the world of soft furnishings, Rufus's career grew. He played an angst-ridden teenage boy in *Tease Me*, a highly acclaimed film loved by critics but largely ignored by audiences, and played a pirate in a *Pirates of the Caribbean*-type epic. Then, when he was twenty-one, he took the lead role in a remake of *Tarzan* and became a huge household name and worldwide pin-up. It was the biggest-grossing film of the year. There couldn't have been a young girl in the land who didn't fall helplessly in love with the tall, dark, handsome young man swinging through the trees, wearing little more than a tea towel.

'God, do you remember that film?' says Jenny, waving her legs from side to side and nearly booting Katie in the shin.

'Gorgeous,' whispers Katie, while I just stare at the apparition on the screen.

After *Tarzan*, came *Tarzan II*, unsurprisingly, in which Rufus looked even better: more manly, less 'cute'. The boyish good looks had been replaced by a rugged handsomeness that left Jen, Katie, and I struggling to stay upright.

'Jeez, he's perfect,' says Katie.

'Mmmm …' Jenny and I respond, both of us having lost the power of speech. Rufus starred in a collection of top box office films after *Tarzan*, including *Dead of Night* and *Justice for James* before playing a psychotic killer in *The Jewelled Dagger*, two years ago – a role that earned him an Oscar.

There isn't much to be found on his private life. He's been linked to a couple of actresses but no one for very long. Most of the references to him away from films feature his charity work.

'He's too fucking good to be true,' says Katie excitedly. 'I mean – looking like that and having no girlfriend.'

'He's probably been concentrating too much on work,' I suggest. 'Or he's gay.'

'No,' says Jenny, decisively. 'He's been saving himself for me!'

'Yeah,' Katie and I chorus.

I should tell you a little bit about the girls in the office. Katie's a real laugh; the sort of girl who's the centre of attention and always cheering people up. I can't think of anyone more fun to work with; she beams all day and makes sure everyone is happy and enjoying life. She's always taking the mickey out of me, and saying that all the men fancy me, and she hates going out in public with me because of it. The truth is that Katie is very attractive, though she clearly doesn't realise. She's good-looking in a very grown-up sort of way; you'd almost call her 'handsome' rather than 'pretty'. She looks like the teacher at school who all the boys secretly fancied.

Jenny's quite a different character; she's less outgoing than Katie, and more formal in some ways. She's very intelligent and always reads the newspapers while Katie and I are scouring *Heat* magazine. Jenny's not what you would call attractive, but she has an incredible figure. She's very tall and slim. She holds herself well, too, and as she walks around the office, with her head held high, her shoulders back, and her arms swinging elegantly by her side, she looks like a ballerina or something. The thing is – she's just not interested in how she looks, and doesn't make much effort at all. She has grey speckled through her auburn, bobbed hair (even though she's only thirty-two), and she wears these really unflattering glasses. I don't think I've ever seen her wearing jewellery or makeup of any kind. I always think that if Gok Wan or one of those other makeover people got hold of her, they'd make her look absolutely stunning in no time.

They're both lovely, and I'm so lucky to be working with them.

It's Tuesday afternoon, a few weeks after Sebastian's announcement about Rufus, and the three of us are very bored, to be honest. It's the end of July, and quite hot in the office. It's also quiet in the theatre over the summer, so the hours drag a bit. To lift the mood, we revert to playing our favourite game, the World Malteser Throwing Championships. This is the one we like most because it involves competitive behaviour, chocolate, and laughing.

I like it for all the above reasons, but also because I'm very good at it, and I frequently come close to breaking the theatre record. This fine day, I am the first receiver and have eight little chocolate balls buried in my cheeks as I stand with my feet shoulder-width apart, ready for Katie to hurl a Malteser from behind the pile of handbags.

'Ready?' asks Jenny (she's chief official for the occasion because she's more sensible than the rest of us – she's in charge of theatre accounts).

'Yesh,' I reply, jiggling the eight Maltesers I have already caught in my mouth. One of the game's rules is that you cannot swallow until you've finished catching. Your turn ends when you miss a Malteser. Eight is the most we've ever done; this Malteser is crucial.

'Five, four, three, two, one,' she says.

Katie tosses the small chocolate ball towards me with a degree of accuracy born of long hours training (most of our salaries go in buying Maltesers). If she put that amount of work into the accounts, she'd be running the theatre by now. I catch the chocolate in my mouth, fair and square, thus setting a new theatre record ... yeeeesssssss! But when I look up – hands aloft, chocolate dribbling down my chin and cheeks full to bursting – expecting there to be cheering and congratulations echoing around the office, there is nothing. Jenny is staring at the door like a mad woman, and Katie has collapsed onto the desk. I follow Jenny's gaze.

Fuck, fuck, fuck.

Sebastian is standing in the doorway, surveying us all quizzically and next to him is Rufus George.

Oh. My. God. He is beautiful. He is flawless. He oozes sex

appeal. It's like he's been carved out of marble. He is even more gorgeous than he looks in his pictures, and let's be very clear about this – he looks bloody gorgeous in his pictures.

'Nice to meet you,' he says, looking directly into my eyes. I return the gaze because, with a man who looks like Rufus, that's what you do. I am well aware, though, of the chocolate-drenched spittle escaping from the corner of my mouth, and I am painfully conscious of the fact that I have to crunch these Maltesers before I can return the greeting. I do that – masticating madly before swallowing the sticky mess and feeling it claw its way down my throat so slowly, that I am forced into making vigorous gulps to help it on its way.

What with the almost choking, mad swallowing and chocolate everywhere, it isn't the ideal position in which to meet a Hollywood heartthrob. I look up at him again, hoping I look adorable now. I no longer have hamster cheeks, but I am all too aware that the smile playing on his lips probably has more to do with the fact that my teeth, lips and tongue are now all brown, than any warmth he may be feeling towards me.

Then, out of the blue, the most amazing thing happens.

'Let's have a go,' he says, walking behind me, gently touching my waist as he does. I feel my hips burst into flames. No, really, I do; I have to look down to check my tight black skirt hasn't caught fire. He takes his position in front of the bags and nods towards Katie.

'Come on!' yells Sebastian. 'You can do it. It's boys against girls.'

Jenny continues in her role as chief adjudicator, as Katie and I battle for the fairer sex, while Sebastian and Rufus do their best for mankind. We win easily.

'You need practice,' I say. 'That was embarrassing.'

'Perhaps you could teach me your technique.' Rufus looks straight at me.

'Sure,' I say, as he leans over and picks up my business card from my desk. 'See you girls later. Nice to meet you.'

Rufus leaves, and the three of us sit down heavily at our desks.

I can't believe he took my business card.

'That was Rufus George,' says Jenny, almost shouting the words. Jenny is not a woman given to emotional outbursts. I don't think I've ever heard her raise her voice before.

I can't believe he took my business card.

'What did he take off your desk?' asks Katie.

'A paperclip,' I reply. For reasons I can't quite articulate, I want to keep quiet about the fact that he took my business card.

CHAPTER 2: THE TEXT

That evening, I float out of work to the bus stop thinking about the day I've just had, and the madness of Rufus's visit. I'm thrown by how much fun he was, how down-to-earth and approachable. He played catch the Malteser for goodness' sake. If I hadn't been there to witness the magical moment with my own eyes, I wouldn't have believed it. I thought he would be handsome, charming and full of the confidence that success and wealth bestow on a man, but I hadn't expected him to be properly good fun.

The bus winds itself through busy traffic, and I look out at all the people scurrying past on their way home in Richmond until the bus moves through St. Margaret's and onto Twickenham. I like living here in this bustling part of the world. I wonder what all these people would think if they knew I'd met Rufus George today. I smile to myself as the bus reaches my stop, and I hop onto the pavement full of warmth and joy.

Now you should know that I'm not someone who goes gooey over men. Not ever. I just don't. I've had lots of boyfriends, and I know I have a few admirers in our local pub, but right now I'm enjoying being single and having the best time with my mates. It's just that Rufus was so lovely. He was lovely, wasn't he? I'm not over-exaggerating; he was properly good fun.

And it's not because he's rich and famous. Christ, no - I've seen enough of rich and famous actors while I've been working in the theatre to know that it's not the route to happiness. I couldn't care less about how much money someone has. I like my men real, solid and down-to-earth.

The reason I'm so thrown, and can't stop thinking about the Hollywood hunk from earlier, is because never in a million years did I expect Rufus to be quite so real, solid and down-to-earth. But he is. And obviously he's staggeringly handsome as well which doesn't hurt.

I'm first home to the flat, and it's something of a relief. For reasons I can't quite put my finger on, I don't want to tell my flat-mates about Rufus. I don't want to discuss him ad nauseam until the lovely little dreamlike encounter becomes like a scientific experiment - prodded and poked until it loses its shape.

So, I tidy up and lie on my bed, holding a book but not quite reading it, until I hear the sound of voices in the hallway.

'Pilates time,' shouts Mandy, rushing in. 'Are you there, Kel? It's time for Pilates.'

Oh God, I'd forgotten about that. 'You should have phoned and reminded me. I might give it a miss today.'

'I couldn't phone: my mobile is all smashed up, remember? I broke it tumbling into the wall. I can't afford another one, so I'll have to do without one for now. And you have to come tonight...Dave's going to be there. I need you to help me talk to him.'

'Help you talk? What - like a ventriloquist?'

'No, you know what I mean come with me and give me

your view. When he talks to me, I want you to tell me whether you think he likes me. Does he look at me in that way? You know what I mean. Get your kit on.'

With an important role like that to perform, I know I have to go, so I slip into my Pilates gear and jump into Mandy's car next to her.

'Just watch what he's doing: does he look at me? Is he glancing at me? That sort of thing. I need to know whether there are any vibes that he likes me.'

'OK, I'm on it,' I promise, as we all file into the Pilates studio and I set my mat up so I have the best view of Dave and Mandy. I feel like a detective stalking a suspect; there is nothing that Dave can do that I won't see. Dave glances up and catches me watching him, and I'm treated to a kiss blown in my direction and a rather grubby wink. He's not the sort of guy you'd ever want one of your best friends to fancy, but for reasons that defy my understanding, Mandy has been lusting after him for ages.

I was completely taken aback when she first said she fancied him and claimed that he was her soulmate and believed it could work between them. 'What do you think?' she'd asked.

I'd shrugged at first, not wanting to upset her but then she made me holy swear that I was telling the truth. This is something we do. When you want the whole, unexpurgated truth, you make the other person say, 'I holy swear on my life.' Then they have to be honest. No bullshit allowed.

'I think you can do better,' I said calmly.

'You holy swore, remember. The whole truth.'

'I think he's a complete knob. I don't like him at all, and I don't understand why you like him. He's horrible and I'm sure he'll end up hurting you.'

'Oh,' she said, but my words did nothing to alter her view, so once I'd said how I felt, I fell into line with her and just told her to be careful, while I assisted her in her efforts to conquer his heart, because that's what friends do. So, here I am, watching him like a hawk.

Dave stretches out in a way that is both effeminate and alpha male. Does that make sense? He's full of misplaced confidence and bluster, but also stretches out in such a pouty, limp and ineffective way, that I want to punch him.

As the class starts, I'm watching Dave so closely it is verging on voyeurism. At no stage does he look at Mandy. He looks in the mirror a lot, and pouts as he flicks his soft, floppy fringe out of his eyes, but he's not watching Mandy. He's really not. She's staring at him at every opportunity, but he doesn't show a flicker of interest in her, not at any stage.

'Well, who was he looking at then?' asks Mandy, I'm clearly not giving her the feedback she wants.

'No one,' I say. 'He was just getting on with the class.'

'Should I just ask him out? Maybe that would be easier than trying to catch his eye in Pilates, or, we could just go wherever he's going to be and bump into him in a more social setting, away from the class.'

'I think maybe just keep seeing him in Pilates for now. You don't know where he's going to be, socially, do you?'

'Yes, I do; I follow him on Facebook.'

'Oh, you're friends on Facebook? I didn't realise that.'

'No, not friends. He didn't reply to my friend request, but I can see a lot of his posts anyway.'

'Oh Mandy, we need to find you someone else, someone gorgeous and lovely.'

'Why? I like Dave.'

'But he hasn't even accepted a Facebook friend request from you. You can do better.'

'We spoke about this, and you said you'd support me.'

'And I will, but it doesn't stop me thinking that you can do better.'

15

We get back to the flat and Mandy disappears into her room. Perhaps I shouldn't have said anything, but I had to. She'll look back in a while and wonder what she saw in him. I don't want her to spend any more time worrying about what he's thinking or dreaming about him when he's clearly not remotely interested in her.

I lie back on the sofa and pick up my phone. There's a message:

'Hey, Rufus here. Nice to meet you today. Can I take you to dinner tomorrow night? No Maltesers involved.'

Holy mother of God.

I sit bolt upright on the sofa and read the message again. In fact, I read it several times before putting the phone down and walking around the room. When I return to the phone, the message is still there.

Rufus George has asked me out to dinner. That's completely ridiculous.

I mean – I'm not unattractive or anything. People are always saying that I look like a young Kelly Brook. A few have even suggested I could model. But I'm not what you would call Hollywood attractive. I'm curvy for a start, not skinny like all the women he is used to seeing.

I check the message again: *Can I take you to dinner tomorrow night?*

And that, ladies and gentlemen, is how the whole thing started. Little did I know, as I lay on the sofa, giggling to myself on that gentle, summer's evening, that my life was about to be transformed in ways that I couldn't begin to understand, and was in no position to deal with.

One simple flirtation over a Malteser would tear through the heart of my friendships, lead to loss of independence, and force me out of a job I love. It would even end with me being arrested by the police and surrounded by people eager for my downfall.

Perhaps, if I'd known how things would turn out, as I lay there, still in my Pilates gear, I would have ignored the bright and breezy text from the Hollywood star.

But I didn't.

Of course, I didn't.

'Would love to,' I replied.

CHAPTER 3: NIGHTS OUT AND NIGHTS IN

❧

*W*hat, in the name of all that is holy, does a girl wear for a night out with a Hollywood super-star? I've looked through my clothes and tried to work out how to make something elegant and sophisticated (and just a little bit sexy) from the clothes I've got, but it's not working; I don't have anything suitable. I've got quite nice work clothes but - be honest - is that the look I should be striving for on a date with a Hollywood star? Who on God's Earth would wear 'quite nice work clothes' on a date with Rufus George?

Not me. Instead, I'm wandering around Richmond, wondering what the hell to buy. I haven't got a clue; what's appropriate? How can I possibly know?

I've seen a dress in New Look, in an emerald-green colour. It is nipped in at the waist, makes my breasts look massive and my legs look long and shapely. It doesn't look expensive though. Do you think that matters? Oh God, I don't know. I am now wandering around helplessly in case I see something better, but anything that looks really expen-sive turns out to be really expensive. Funny that!

That's it; I'm going to buy the green dress. I power walk

through the streets, back to New Look, to claim my purchase.

By the time I get back to the flat, the girls are both out. I confess that I breathe a sigh of relief. I love them to death, but there's nothing like having the flat to yourself when you're getting ready for a hot date, and let's be clear about this, they don't come any hotter than Rufus George.

I run a bath, put on a face pack and sit on the edge of my bed, fretting like mad. I'm completely out of my depth here. Perhaps I should have spoken to the girls? But I'm so sure this won't go anywhere, that I'm reluctant to tell any friends about it, then have to tell them it's all over after one date.

Before long, the bath is run and I manage to get myself bathed, dressed, made-up and out to the side alley identified as the best place to meet Rufus. His PA, a woman called Christine, called to say he can't come to the flat in case there are paparazzi around, which seems a bit extreme. Surely they don't follow him everywhere? She said there was an alleyway just opposite that he would pull into.

I walk towards it and see the large black car straight away, tucked into the side of the alleyway, out of sight. I walk towards it, trepidation running through me with such force I fear I might faint. A man jumps out of the driver's side and I go to embrace him, before realising that it's not Rufus, but an older, portly man with a kindly face and a warm smile.

'I'm Henry,' he says. 'I'm Rufus's driver.' He opens the door for me and I slip in, next to Rufus.

'Hi,' I say as he kisses me lightly on the cheek and tells Henry to head for a restaurant in Barnes. I haven't heard of it before, but - let's be honest - it was always unlikely that I would have.

'You look lovely. The emerald gown really suits you,' says Rufus.

'Thank you. 'You look lovely too.'

There's something quite magical about the way Rufus speaks to me. In the shop, this was a green dress; in Rufus's mind, it's an emerald gown.

'Tell me about your week,' he says, as we ease through the traffic. 'What have you been up to?'

'Well, I met this film star yesterday, and then went to Pilates last night and I've been at work today. That's about it.'

'You've been busier than me,' says Rufus, in a self-depre-cating manner. 'I've just been reading scripts and drinking coffee, that's all. Come on, this is it...'

Rufus points to the restaurant, and Henry opens my door before I've even found the handle. It's so weird that he has a driver. I'm usually impressed if a guy has his own car, never mind his own chauffeur.

Once we get inside, my first thought is how quiet it all seems. There is no one at any of the tables and just a couple of wait-resses who immediately spring to attention when we walk in.

'Please, sit here,' they say, wide-eyed with excitement at the sight of a film star.

'I thought it best to book out the whole restaurant, just to make life a bit easier,' says Rufus.

'Really?? I didn't even know you could do that.'

I'm flattered, but also a bit embarrassed. I'm not used to extravagant gestures. I'm not someone who wants to stand out from the crowd or be treated differently. As pathetic as it sounds, I just like to fit in and feel comfortable. Here I am, way out of my comfort zone.

'I know Annie, who owns this restaurant, so Christine called her and arranged it. It's lovely food, I hope you enjoy it.'

'I'm sure I will,' I say. I feel more nervous than ever now that I'm aware of the lengths he's gone to in pursuit of the perfect date.

'You look very pretty this evening; I love your hair in those waves.'

It's the second compliment of the evening and we haven't even ordered yet. I feel myself flush with embarrassment and look down at the menu.

'May I order for you?'.

'Sure,' I say, but I'm not sure. It feels odd. I want to read through everything and choose because there are so many weird-looking dishes on the menu that I'm worried he'll order me something I won't like.

'Is there anything that you're allergic to?' he asks.

'No, not allergic. I like quite simple food though. I'm not good with spices and things.'

A small stocky lady comes out from the back of the restaurant and greets Rufus like a long-lost friend. They hug and speak in French, and I'm completely at a loss. I don't speak French, so I sit there, discomfort rippling through me as they chat through the menu. I don't have a clue what's going on.

'How are you with rare meat?' he asks.

'I like meat well done,' I say, and I'm sure the chef woman looks disgusted. Oh, Christ.

'But you're OK with garlic?'

'I guess, but not too much.'

'Guinea fowl?'

'I don't know what that is.'

They go back to the menu and I sit, staring at the two of them as they talk flamboyantly in a language I don't speak. I don't understand any of this. I feel like an idiot.

When I thought about this date, I thought of the two of us tucked away in the corner of Nando's, sharing chicken, laughing, and having fun. I know that's unrealistic, but that's my world; that's what I'm used to. This is so grown-up, so otherworldly. I should be loving it, but I just feel like an idiot. I'm scared of being foolish.

'You look worried,' he tells me. 'Do you not like the look of the food?'

'Oh gosh, Rufus, it all looks wonderful, and I'm really grateful that you have brought me somewhere so special; it's just not the sort of place I normally come to. And it's making me feel a little bit weird, to be honest.'

'Right, then we need to unweird this, don't we? What do you normally order in a restaurant?'

'I never come to restaurants like this. When I go out with my friends, I have chicken burgers and pizzas, and I love Sunday roasts. I think they're my favourite. But I know they don't have food like that here, so whatever they have is fine.'

Rufus stands up, and I think for one awful moment he's going to walk out on the girl in the cheap green dress who's trying to avoid getting it dirty so she can take it back (I wasn't going to tell you that bit, but it's true; if I can keep it clean, I can swap it for something else).

But he doesn't walk out. He says, 'I think we can do better than "fine." He goes into the kitchen, where I hear him chatting in French with the owner again, and he walks out clutching a bottle of champagne.

'All sorted,' he says, pouring me a glass. Now we can relax.

We sip the champagne until the food comes: prawn cocktail to start with, which is lovely, and roast chicken dinner for the main course. Only the chicken is more delicious than any chicken I've eaten in my life before. It's wonderful. The vegetables are special, too, cooked in garlic and with walnuts and pine nuts sprinkled onto them.

'This is just perfect,' I say to Rufus. 'I'm sorry I made a fuss. I realise now that anything on the menu would have been great. I panicked.'

'That's fine. Don't apologise,' he says, taking my hands. 'I want you to be happy. It's wonderful to see you enjoying the food. I've never met a woman who eats properly before. It's great to see.'

'Thank you,' I say, wondering whether that was a barbed comment about my weight but deciding that I'm being over-sensitive. 'Thank you for bringing me here.'

'Fancy meeting for coffee tomorrow?' he says, lifting my hands and kissing them gently.

'That would be lovely.'

'I'll get Henry to collect you from the theatre at 11am.'

'Sure,' I say, realising that Henry is going to be a big part of this burgeoning relationship.

We meet for coffee the next day, as planned, and then coffee turns into a drink, which turns into dinner at another wonderful restaurant, which turns into snogging madly like teenagers.

I soon start to feel relaxed in his company. He's captivating, delightful and beautiful. The nerves and anxiety of that first date disappear beneath a veil of reassurances and flattery. I've never met anyone remotely like him before. Our dates are full of fun and laughter. I tell him about my flatmates and all the fun we have together, and he smiles as I recall the mad nights out and inappropriate boyfriends.

The bizarre thing is that it all feels so natural, relaxed and, well, nice. I even get used to the stories featuring Jennifer Anniston and mentions of George, Brad, and Johnny Depp.

We are quite a way into our dating before Rufus suggests that I stay the night. 'Why don't you come round and I'll cook for you,' he offers, and we all know what sort of offer that is. I pack my knickers and a toothbrush and head for Richmond.

I'd been onto Google Streetview and seen what his house

looks like, of course. I mean - who wouldn't? It looks absolutely gorgeous on screen, but nothing could prepare me for the sight of it in real life, sitting at the top of Richmond Hill, imperious and commanding with stunning views across London. Apparently, on a clear day, you can see all the way to St Paul's Cathedral one way, and to Windsor Castle the other.

From the front, the house looks spectacular, with a sort of tower and a series of turrets, some with pointed roofs and others with circular tops. There are windows up the turrets, indicating that there are dozens of bedrooms and bathrooms. The house is set behind a gate, which opens as Henry approaches.

'Gosh, this is wonderful,' I say to him.

'Yes, and especially nice tonight because there is no press outside.'

'Are there usually?' I ask.

'More often than not. It can be a difficult life, sometimes, being as famous as Rufus is. It's a wonderful house, but sometimes, when the photographers gather he's forced to stay inside; I think it's more of a gilded cage. Sorry, that was out of order. My apologies.'

'No, don't be sorry. Honestly. I can see how close the two of you are; you're bound to worry about him.'

But Henry has gone back to being his normal, professional self, as he opens the door and helps me out.

'Where do I go?' I ask nervously.

'I'm sure Rufus will come out and see you now, he knows we are here.'

'How does he know?'

'Cameras are everywhere, and the license plate is registered; it's just a security thing.'

'Okay,' I say nervously, then I spot a woman standing in the doorway with her arms folded and a scowl on her face.

'That's Rosemary, the housekeeper. Watch her,' says Henry, as he gets into the car and drives off. The woman in the doorway doesn't look to have moved. She must be mid-50s, is dressed entirely in black and is painfully thin. Everything about her is bony and angular. She doesn't look as if she's smiled since about 1972.

I approach her and put out my hand. 'I'm Kelly,' I say. She looks at my hand as if she might slap it out of the way, and without returning the introduction, turns to walk inside.

'In here,' she says, opening the door to the sitting room. 'Wait in there until he's ready.'

I walk into the room, and she closes the door behind me. It's a truly beautiful room: two big squashy white sofas (white sofas! I mean - really) face one another, with a gorgeous, artistic table between them. It appears to be made of driftwood with a beautiful glass top. On it, there is a large glass vase teeming with lilies that fill the air with perfume. There are large bay windows through which I can see the driveway and the manicured lawns at the front of the house. But I'm finding it hard to enjoy the beautiful and quiet elegance of the room because I'm so bloody enraged. How dare that housekeeper woman glare at me like that, then shut me in here and close the door. The least she could do is take my coat and give me a cup of tea or something. I'm Rufus's girlfriend, not some ne'er-do-well who's crawled in off the street to try and sell him peg bags and tea towels.

This whole business of having staff to pick me up and welcome me into the house is going to take some getting used to. I'd much prefer it if Rufus came to get me and if he let me into the house instead of the miserable housekeeper in her funereal clothing. I open the sitting room door, planning to storm out and find Rufus, but Rosemary is standing right next to the door as if listening. I jump as I see her.

'Where is Rufus?' I say.

'He's busy.'

'Busy where? I'd like to see him.'

As I speak, Rufus must hear me from deep inside the bowels of the house because he comes rushing out, flour on his hands and face and a tea towel over his shoulder. 'It's you. I thought I heard you. Come through. What are you doing hanging about here?' he says.

I treat Rosemary to one of my most vicious glares as I follow Rufus into a huge and glorious open-plan kitchen. 'Things aren't going brilliantly,' he says. 'I'm going to be honest with you...I'm not altogether sure how this is going to turn out.'

As it happens, Rufus is right. It doesn't turn out well. He is a hopeless cook, but has given the staff the evening off, so we end up eating cheese on toast and drinking Rufus's favourite Pol Roger champagne while candles cast beautiful light across the shadows of his face. Then we go to bed, and it's bloody amazing. Oh, it's fantastic. Well worth the wait.

In the morning, I wake up bathed in light as the September sun flickers through the slats in the blinds and casts dancing shadows across us as we lie. I feel like I'm in one of his movies when I look over at him, sleeping peacefully and looking more handsome than ever. The only problem is that I need the loo, and I don't want to go to the one in the ensuite in case he hears me (I know it's silly, but we're still in the first flush of adoration and he doesn't need to wake up to the sounds of me on the toilet). The trouble is, I've no idea where the other bathrooms are, so I tiptoe into the long corridor outside Rufus's massive master bedroom and head off towards the sweeping staircase, taking stealthy little steps, hoping I won't be heard.

I'm creeping along when I see her: Rosemary: the fierce-looking woman who 'greeted' me when I arrived. She is staring at me as if she loathes every part of me. She has eyes that can suck the joy from any situation. The sight of her makes me jump out of my skin.

'Ahhh ...' I scream, running down the stairs, taking them three at a time, almost tripping over. As I do, all the alarms burst into life. I mean all of them; you'd think a prisoner had just escaped from Broadmoor with the noise they make. I stop dead in my tracks in case there are snipers hidden somewhere and turn to face the woman at the top of the stairs, but she has gone.

Rufus jumps out of bed and comes running after me. 'Where are you going?' he asks, running his hands absently through his hair and leaving it all mussed up and looking incredibly super–sexy.

'To the loo, but then I saw Rosemary, and she made me jump out of my skin, so I screamed and ran down the stairs, and the alarms went off.'

'Yes, the alarms downstairs are activated until the staff start work. Rosemary doesn't start for another couple of hours. You must have seen a shadow or something.'

'No, it was her, definitely.'

'It couldn't have been. Come here...'

'It was, I tell you. She was just outside your door.'

'Come back to bed,' he says, wrapping his arms around me. I follow him back to the room, feeling safe in his arms but still looking for Rosemary. Why was she there? It was her. I know it was.

'She freaks me out,' I say to Rufus when we're back in the bed, and he's stroking my hair. 'There's something odd about her.'

'She's OK,' he says. 'She takes a bit of getting used to, but she's very discrete and hard-working.'

'Mmmmm...' I say, unconvinced. 'She was quite rude to me.'

'OK, I'll have a word with her, but it's the first time she's seen you; she's bound to be sussing you out, working out whether you're going to treat me well.'

Yeah, burning into my soul with her evil eye, more like (I don't say that, though).

We snuggle up in bed for a little longer before he suggests coffee. 'Let's have it down by the pool terrace, and you can swim if you fancy it.'

'Sure,' I say, like everyone has a swimming pool in their home.

Later that day, I leave by sneaking out through the staff doors that run off one of the kitchens (I know, I know, two kitchens). A girl called Julie, who works there and must be about the same age as me, smiles at me as I go past.

'Don't worry: the press won't find you here,' she says. I smile back and mouth 'thank you', properly grateful for the fleeting moment of warmth and friendship in this big, beautiful, strange house with the terrifying housekeeper.

CHAPTER 4: THE ROSE GARDEN

*I*t's so weird to be dating this wonderful man, and experiencing this incredible new life that he lives without telling Mandy and Sophie anything about it. But, having not told them at the start, it would now feel odd to mention him, so I get back and sneak into my bedroom and don't mention the wild nights out with the man in the multi-million-pound house. When the girls ask, I say that I am seeing friends from work as Rufus and I continue to get to know each other in secret. It's perfect. It allows us to spend time together and get to know one another away from the prying eyes of the world. We are in our own, magical little bubble.

'What do you fancy doing at the weekend?' he says, as we're chatting on the phone later that week.

'You choose,' I say. I tend to do that quite a lot with Rufus...leaving him to plan everything, which I know I shouldn't. I'll make sure I plan the next one, and introduce him to my world. He starts the new production at the theatre next week, as part of the Christmas season, so I know we won't have anywhere near as much time together then.

'OK. Leave it to me,' he says. 'I'm going to organise something really English for my lovely English rose.'

The week crawls past until the weekend finally arrives, and I head to the lay-by up the road where we always meet. Sometimes he's by himself; sometimes Henry, the driver, is there. Today, I see the nose of the big black car poking out and realise that he's brought Henry. I say hi to the friendly driver and I jump into the back of the car next to Rufus, and am immediately grabbed for a huge hug.

'Missed you,' he says, as the car winds its way through the streets of Twickenham, heading out of town.

'You have to tell me where we're going,' I say, as the car eases towards a beautiful bridge with boats and canoes sweeping along beneath it. Henry pulls over and Rufus jumps out. He runs round to my side of the car and swings my door open for me. 'Welcome to Hampton Court,' he says.

I have to admit, I am amazed. The place is about twenty minutes from my flat and I've never been here before. Rufus, on the other hand, seems to know the place intimately. We walk through the old Tudor kitchens and down into the giant greenhouses containing the world's largest vine. 'How do they know?' he whispers at every new historical fact. 'Have they measured every vine in the world? I bet they just make this stuff up.'

'Spoken like a true American,' I retort, as we escape through a small wooden door and out into the palace court-yard featuring a beautiful fountain in the middle.

'Make a wish,' says Rufus, digging into his pockets for coins. He hands me enough money to keep a family of six fed for a week and urges me to throw them. I toss the coins into the air and watch them fall and splash in the sparkling water, pennies from heaven.

'OK, my turn.' He throws his money into the fountain and makes a wish that nothing will change between us.

'I want us to stay like this forever,' he says, wrapping his arms around me.

'Me too,' I say, smiling like I've never smiled before.

'I want us to get to know each other, and for us to get closer and closer, but most of all I want the special bond between us to stay like this.'

'Yes,' I reply, almost breathless with joy. 'I want to know everything about you, too.'

'Me first,' he says with a big smile. 'Tell me … what is the naughtiest thing you've ever done? Go on; tell me something about yourself that I don't know.'

Oh shit.

'Go on. It can't be that bad,' he says, sensing my reluctance. 'Can it?'

'I got banned from driving for twelve months once,' I say sheepishly.

'How fast were you going?'.

'No, drink–driving. But I hadn't been drinking. Well, I had, but I didn't know I had. I mean, my drinks were spiked by this guy that Mandy was going out with. He didn't like the fact that I wasn't drinking, so put loads of alcohol into this fruit punch and fed it to me all night. I drove home, was stopped by police and ended up getting banned. Luckily no one got hurt …'

Rufus is silent for a moment and then gives me a hug and a wry smile. 'Wow. I'm dating a convict,' he says. 'Did you have mugshots done, and fingerprints taken and everything?'

'Oh yes. The whole works. What's the worst thing you've ever done?'

'I suppose it would be being unfaithful. I hate myself for it, but - yeah - I haven't been the most faithful of boyfriends over the years.'

My heart sinks as he says this.

Oh God, I couldn't bear it if he was unfaithful to me.

'Why are you looking so sad? Are you thinking about your criminal past? I know what'll cheer you up … I've saved the best till last. Come with me.'

He takes my hand and whisks me away from the courtyard, past the maze and out to a gorgeous rose garden. The smell as we approach is unbelievable, hanging in the air as the flowers smile and bask in the afternoon sunshine. It's September but it might as well be June. I've no idea how they keep these roses blooming.

All I know is that the sun is shining, I am surrounded by beautiful roses and I am in love with Rufus. There, I've said it. In this beautiful rose garden in a palace, on the banks of the river where scents drift through the air, I am sure that I am in love.

Rufus leads me past the benches dedicated from one devoted spouse to another to a bench with no dedication at all. 'This is my favourite bench,' he says, and I almost squeal out loud. A man with his favourite bench! Who'd have thought? 'I call it the bench with no name.' We sit holding hands in companionable silence for a few moments, while I take in the majesty of the place.

'Good morning,' says an old man, walking towards us with a stoop, he's clutching a spade, though he looks far too old to be working in the gardens.

'Frank!' says Rufus, jumping up to greet him. 'Come and join us, and meet Kelly.'

'Ahhh…so this is the mysterious Kelly. How do you do, Ma'am?'

'Hello,' I say, as he removes a flask from his large coat pocket and begins to pour out a drink. 'So, you're the girl who's caught his eye, are you? He told me about your game with the Maltesers.'

'Oh, he did, did he? Did he mention that I beat him?'

'Ha, ha,' says Frank, with a lovely big smile. 'No, he didn't mention that bit. Have you been to the Palace before?'

'No, this is the first time. I only live in Twickenham, but have never visited. Does he bring all his girls here, then?' I tease.

'None. You're the first. You're the only girl he's ever mentioned to me.'

'Oh good,' I say, smiling at the old man as he does up his flask and stands to leave.

'Now, I must be on my way. See you soon Rufus, lovely to meet you, Kelly.'

'You're the first and only,' confirms Rufus, smiling at me. 'You know I've always felt this was a very special place, but now it will be our special place; a place that only the two of us know about.'

We have a special place! Our place, all our own! And it's in a palace and it's full of roses! I look up and see butterflies playing beside us, fluttering their wings as if in courtship. The sentiments of the moment seemed to be reflected in nature all around us.

'It's amazing! I love it. I love...' I break off, scared of what I am in danger of revealing but Rufus kisses me again, giving me the courage to try. 'I mean ... I think I'm falling in love with you ...'

'Good, because I feel exactly the same way. Only you should know what you're getting yourself into, Kelly. My life is crazy. The press follow me most places. I have to guard my privacy where I can. I want to protect you from that craziness, but once the press know we're together ...' He paused. 'Once the press know we're together, life is going to get very difficult. Things will change. Until you live through it, you have no idea how hard it is to cope with the constant intrusion.'

Rufus looks so serious all of a sudden; I am overcome with the need to lift him out of his solemn thoughtfulness.

'Whenever they upset us, we'll come here,' I suggest, looking at the picture of beauty and solitude painted in the brightest colours all around us. 'We'll escape to the Rose Garden and hide in the bushes like squirrels and no one will find us.'

'That's a lovely thought,' Rufus says, flashing me that incredible smile of his and speaking with such love and warmth. 'From now on, this is our rose garden, our refuge. The place we first declared our love to one another, and somewhere we'll always come when things get tough.'

I breathe deeply. 'We'll never, ever tell anyone about our rose garden, Rufus; it's just for us … our special place. I'll never breathe a word to anyone about it, then no one will know.'

I smile then, feeling lost and dizzy in the thrill of the moment.

CHAPTER 5: TELLING THE GIRLS

'I've told Brad and Carl about you,' says Rufus.

'Brad Pitt?' I ask, somewhat astonished, but delighted, obviously, to be the subject of conversation between Hollywood hunks.

'No, Brad Court. I told you about him. Brad and Carl are my best buddies from home. We go back years.'

'Oh yes,' I say. 'Of course. Are they both living in America?'

'Amerecaar,' he responds, mimicking my English accent playfully. 'Yes, they're both in the US. In New York these days, but when I met them, we were at school in L.A. We were all complete sports nuts: basketball, baseball, football, proper football, not your kicking it around rubbish. We were obsessed. Brad's a teacher now, and Carl Deeves runs a sportswear shop in Brooklyn.'

'Just like me, Mandy and Sophie,' I suggest.

'Just like that,' he says warmly.

'So, if you've told Brad and Carl, maybe it's time for me to tell Mandy and Sophie?'

'Do you want to?' he asks.

Over the course of our burgeoning romance, I went to some lengths to hide the fact that I was dating the most eligible man on the planet. I kept it quiet because I didn't want anyone to burst the bubble of adoration, tenderness and love that we had built up around ourselves. We wanted to get to know one another without the eyes of the world on us, locked in our private love.

But whilst I've loved our secret romance, I have always hated the fact that I'm lying to my two close friends. Mandy, Soph and I share everything, we always have. Then, when the most astonishing thing happens, I don't mention it to them.

I've hated lying to the girls in the office as well, and they're clearly suspicious that I keep sneaking off at lunchtime. It's created a distance between us because I can't talk to them properly like I did before. I go into the theatre to work every day: he goes into the theatre to perform in front of packed houses, and no one knows we're together.

'Yes, I want to tell them,' I reply. 'I think I should also tell the girls at work.'

'Let's start with your flatmates,' he says.

So, we do.

It's late September by the time we finally decide to come clean. We've been dating for a few months by then and are getting serious.

'Do it then,' he says one day. 'Tell them tonight. It will make our relationship much easier if we don't have to hide away all the time.'

When everyone's home from work, I stand up dramatically and tell them I have something to say.

'This is going to be a bit weird,' I start. 'but I've got a secret boyfriend.'

They look at me, confused and slightly worried. 'Not Dave?' asks Mandy, imploringly.

'No, not Dave. Gosh - no, of course not Dave. Do you ever think I would do that to you, Mandy?'

'No,' she says. 'But you look so serious.'

'Yeah, I look serious because it's a pretty big deal. I'm going out with Rufus George.'

'Ha, ha, ha,' says Mandy, then adds another 'ha' on for good measure.

'You're obviously joking,' says Sophie. 'Who are you really going out with?'

'Rufus.'

'No, really.'

'Rufus.'

'You're going out with Rufus George?'

'Yes. I met him at work. We've been going on dates and I really like him.'

'And you waited until now to tell us, instead of the very second he asked you out," says Sophie

'Yes. I never thought it would last, but it has. I'm in love with him.'

'Is this for real? I mean - you're telling us that you're going out with Rufus George...the megastar movie guy.'

'Yes.'

I end up having to call Rufus and get him to speak to the girls, as well as showing them some of the pictures on my phone.

They see the ones of me in Rufus's house, and of the two of us at Hampton Court Palace and, finally, they're convinced.

'I knew something was going on because you kept going out and not saying where you were going and being a bit vague, but I thought you must be having an affair or a mid-life crisis or something. I never in a million years expected this,' says Sophie.

'No one else in my life knows about us.'

'No one?' says Sophie.

'No one. You two are the only people who know and Rufus has told his two best friends. Noone else. So, if you could keep it quiet for now, that would be great.'

'Of course,' they both say.

But I know that keeping things quiet will be hard. I realise that people will find out, and then my whole life will be flung up into the air like the pieces of an intricate jigsaw. I don't know what sort of picture they're going to create when they land. All I know is that it'll be different from the picture of my life right now.

'Is his house amazing?' asks Mandy.

'God, yes. You have to come round and see it. You won't believe it. It's completely lovely. The only thing that's weird is this horrible, house-keeper he has, called Rosemary. She's really spooky.'

'Like Mrs Danvers?' offers Sophie.

'Mrs Who?'

'Mrs Danvers...the housekeeper in Rebecca. She's really eerie and scary.'

'What's Rebecca?' asks Mandy.

'It's a novel. I did it for GCSEs, and there's this madly, spooky, housekeeper in it.'

'Yeah, well - Rosemary is just like that. But there are nice people there too: Julie is a kind of junior housekeeper and she's lovely, and so is Pamela, the chef. I like Henry, the driver. I don't see much of David, the butler, but Rufus says he's great, so I assume he is.'

The girls are open-mouthed as I speak.

'He has all these staff?' Mandy says.

'I know. It's crazy, isn't it? And there are more, as well - guys working as ground staff and cleaners, and there's a pool in the basement with staff. We had coffee on the pool terrace when I first met him. It was awesome. You both need to come over and see it. You'll absolutely love it.'

'Don't ever change, will you, Kelly,' says Mandy.

'Of course I won't change. I'll still be me - same friends, same job, same cheap clothes and fat bottom.'

'You promise?' says Sophie.

'I promise. Why do you look so worried?'

'Because you're talking about the staff and the pool terrace like it's all perfectly natural...like you're one of them,' says Sophie. 'Holy swear you won't change?'

'I holy swear on my life.'

'Write it down.'

'What?'

'I want you to holy swear on your life and write it down. We'll put it on the wall,' says Sophie.

I pull out a piece of paper, and I write down that I holy swear on my life that I will never change.

'Add in all the things you just said,' instructs Mandy.

'OK. I holy swear that I won't change. I'll still be me - same friends, same job, same cheap clothes and same fat bottom.'

'Good. Phew,' says Mandy. 'All this talk of staff, and the swimming pool and everything. It's like a different world.'

'Hey, it's not going to change me. I'll still be the same Kelly.'

Sophie takes the note and lays it on the mantelpiece.

'He'd love to meet you,' I say. 'Why don't we make a plan for tomorrow night? I'll get him to come here, and we'll order the biggest takeaway in the world.'

'Oh, I'd love to meet him,' says Mandy. 'That would be fab.'

'Right, then let's do it. I'll get Rufus to come over tomorrow.'

CHAPTER 6: MOVING DAY

'Sorry about tonight,' says Rufus, as we sit in the small snug off the back of his rear sitting room, looking out at the way the gorgeous sparkles from the fairy lights hit the water in the pond in the garden. 'The show ran on, and I was stuck talking to Sir Tom Stoppard. There was a good artistic turnout tonight: Phoebe Waller-Bridge came, and Alan Ayckbourn came. David Hare was there, too: he's a decent chap. They enjoyed the performance. It's all going very well.'

'I wish you could have come to meet Mandy and Sophie: they tidied the flat from top to bottom because you were coming round. They were dying to meet you.'

'I'll meet them soon. Why don't we get them around here one night? Henry can pick them up, and we'll get Pamela to prepare a lovely six-course dinner for them.'

'You don't need to do any of that. They just want to meet you. I'd really like for us to go to my flat and see the girls there?'

'Sure,' he says. 'We can do that. I have to say, though, I don't like it one bit when you talk about "my flat".'

'Why?'

'Because I want this to be your home.'

'I'm here most of the time anyway, it practically is. What I'm saying is that I'd like us to go to my flat to see Mand and Soph.'

'Yes, and what I'm saying is that I don't want you to live there. I want you to live here. I want you here all of the time. I want you to move in with me.'

'Really?'

'Yes - really. Why not? Then we can see one another when I get home from work, and go to bed together every night. It'll make things easier,' he says.

'It'll make things easier? That's not the most romantic way to ask a girl to move in with you,' I say.

'There's also the fact that I love you with all my heart, and don't want to spend another moment apart from you.'

'That's better. I'd love to move in with you.'

Telling Mandy and Sophie that I am moving in with Rufus proves to be quite difficult. Sophie is sceptical since Rufus didn't turn up to meet them. She thinks he might be too busy, too focused on himself and not caring enough.

'I'm sure he's lovely, but is he what you want?' she says.

'He makes me happy,' I try. 'When you meet him, you'll see what I mean.'

'We'd love to meet him,' says Sophie. 'We did try, but he didn't seem that interested in meeting us.'

'No, no, he's really interested in meeting you, it's just that work's a bit full on with the show starting. He's been caught up in doing interviews, photoshoots and press conferences. You'll meet him really soon though, I promise.'

The decision to move in with Rufus means that we are now 'official'. So, I tell the girls at work, then book a week off to give myself time to move, and settle into Rufus' home.

First, though, I need to pack, and I have to confess that I have a lot of stuff piled into my room. I'm slightly hoarder-y, and hate throwing anything away. So, the girls take the afternoon off work and stand next to me as we survey the chaos of my bedroom.

Well, I say bedroom, but I've piled everything onto the bed so it now looks like a huge jumble sale. The theory is that I set it all into boxes to be picked up by some of Rufus's 'people' at 6pm. Rufus said he'd organise a team of packers to come in and do it all for me, but I quite liked the idea of doing it with Mandy and Sophie. Now, though, I'm not sure that I made the right decision.

'You're going to have to throw some of this crap away,' says Sophie. 'Honestly, mate, it needs to go.'

'No, take it. If he loves you, he'll love your stuff,' says Mandy.

'Come on then.' Sophie begins folding and arranging stuff into piles so that when we pack it, it will be orderly, and easy to unpack at Rufus's. Before long, the tip is looking like a clothes store. We put everything into boxes and push them out into the sitting room, ready for collection.

The last thing to be packed away is the only thing I have of any value: a beautiful nineteenth-century porcelain jewellery box that has been passed down through the generations of my family. On its lid there are three simple diamonds in a row. I keep my grandmother's wedding ring in there, and it means more to me than any other possession. I haven't even had it valued, because that seems disrespectful somehow. Why do I care what it costs? I love it, and I'd never part with it. I wrap it in a scarf and lay it in between the folds of my softest sweaters. When I look up, Mandy and Sophie are standing in front of me, as if they are preparing to make a speech.

'It might be a silly thing to have done, seeing how much crap you've got, but we've bought you a present,' says Sophie, her brown eyes looking suddenly very sad. 'It's for you to wear at your fancy parties. We're really going to miss you around here.'

She hands me a white, carrier bag containing a fabulous, fitted, grey dress. It's gorgeous, perfect, ideal. 'Thank you so much,' I say, really meaning it. Rufus has bought me so many things since we've been seeing each other – expensive perfume, jewellery and designer labels. He's introduced me to the sort of restaurants I'd only ever read about before, but there's nothing quite as lovely as your best mates buying you a dress to say they'll miss you, especially when you know how difficult it would have been for them to afford it.

'I love it,' I say, hugging them closely.

'You can wear it to Mandy's birthday party.'

'Of course, that's a good idea.'

'You'll definitely come, won't you? It's on 12th,' says Mandy

'Yes, I wouldn't miss it for the world. Of course I'll be there, and of course, I know what date it is.'

'And lunch on the Saturday afterwards,' says Mandy. 'Don't forget that, will you?'

'Of course I won't. I'm looking forward to both already.'

'Will Rufus come?' they ask.

'He's doing this month-long run at the theatre so I think he'll still be tied up with that, but I'll find out.'

'We'd like to meet him,' says Sophie. 'And make sure he knows what will happen to him if he upsets our girl.'

'I will. And I promise to fix it up for you to meet him as soon as I can.'

'We will never be parted,' says Mandy.

'Never,' I agree.

'Don't change, will you, Kelly? Please don't change.'

'Of course not. I'll always be the girl you know. I made the pledge, remember. I even wrote it down.'

That's when the tears start falling – tumbling from my eyes as we hug each other tightly in this room littered with boxes of clothes, shoes, jewellery and a lifetime's 'stuff.'

CHAPTER 7: BREAKING NEWS

OLLYWOOD STAR SETTLES DOWN WITH HIS BRITISH STUNNER. EXCLUSIVE
By Katie Joseph, Daily Post Showbiz Correspondent
Handsome film star Rufus George, the world's most eligible bachelor, is in love. I can exclusively reveal that the heartthrob star of The Jewelled Dagger and Love in the Summer, is dating Kelly Monsoon, a twenty-eight-year-old, theatre assistant from Twickenham. Last week the pretty brunette moved into George's £8 million house on Richmond Hill and friends of the actor say he's in love for the first time. She has given up her job and the two are practically inseparable.

It's a real Cinderella story for curvaceous Kelly, who met George when he came over to star in Only Men at Richmond Fringe Theatre

Do you know Kelly Monsoon? If you do, call the Showbiz desk now on 020 7765 0064, or email showbiz@daily–post.com.

Noooooo ... I'm lying on the world's largest bed, under a duvet as soft as bunny rabbits' tails, thinking that nothing in the world can ever go wrong for me again, when Rufus drops the Daily Post onto the end of the bed, and I'm greeted by the news that I am, in fact, the news. I've been here two days and I've been rumbled already. Where's all this coming from? And what's all the 'Kelly has given up her job' crap? Just because I take a week off, they think I've left.

'There are photographers all around the house,' says Rufus. 'I was in the kitchen just now and could see them on the CCTV cameras.'

'Sorry,' I say, even though the article has nothing to do with me.

'The press in this country is a nightmare, but we'll survive, sweetheart,' says Rufus. 'Best not to tell Mandy and Sophie everything we're up to, though, then things won't end up in the paper.'

'But I haven't, and they wouldn't. And this stuff in the paper is lies anyway. It hasn't come from Mandy and Sophie. They would never call journalists. Mandy doesn't even have a mobile, for God's sake…she broke it doing drunk gymnastics and never replaced it. The house phone never works, and…'

'It's fine, sweetheart, don't worry. They were probably approached by a journalist who started asking them questions. It's not their fault. This is a whole new world. Maybe we should get them some media training?'

'No. no, we definitely can't do that. Rufus - this isn't them. This is just all made up. I know they wouldn't say anything.'

He smiles at me endearingly, and heads off to find David to request more coffee. Rufus has one of those posh coffee makers in the drawing room that I love; it radiates a smell like a Parisian café. You press the button on the side, and suddenly it's so French you can almost hear the sound of accordions and feel the presence of the Eiffel Tower. The whole place pulsates with the aroma of roasted coffee beans. It's a bit different from the old flat where the mink–lined kettle chugged into action very reluctantly, making more noise than a small factory, as it nudged its way to boiling point. But right now, I think back to that little kitchen, and the girls working out how long they can get the milk to last before they have to buy some more, and I feel tears stinging at the backs of my eyes. I know they wouldn't have said anything to the journalist. I just know it. It annoys me that Rufus would ever dream of saying something like that.

He appears at the bedroom door carrying a tray, and he puts my cup of coffee onto the lovely cream bedside table which was imported from France at great cost. Every time I look round this amazing house, it strikes me that there are pieces of furniture in here that are worth more than my parents' home. And this is Rufus's casual London place. His main house is in Los Angeles, then there's the ski lodge he owns in Aspen and the flat in New York, not to mention, the villa nestling in the Tuscan Hills.

'I don't want to go on about it, but Mandy and Sophie definitely wouldn't have talked to a journalist. Never. Not ever.'

'OK,' he says. 'I didn't mean to upset you. Have you told your parents about us yet?'

'Not really,' I say.

'Might be worth mentioning it,' he suggests, with a shrug. 'I'm sure they'd rather hear from you than from the show-biz editor on the Daily Post.

'Yes,' I say. 'Yes, you're right. Of course I should.'

My family are the very opposite of 'showbiz', they probably don't realise that newspapers have showbiz correspondents.

My family's origins are in the East End of London. They moved out of the area when I was ten years old. I think they realised that if they were going to make the move, they'd better do it before I went to senior school and got settled in.

We moved down to Hastings where Dad was working. I remember it being just as rough as where we'd come from, but somehow so much nicer with a blast of sea air drifting through it. It's amazing how nothing's quite as bad when the beach is round the corner.

I haven't told them about Rufus, because I know they'll worry if I say I'm going out with a Hollywood star. But Rufus is right; I definitely need to talk to them and explain what's going on.

The newspaper's still spread across the bed in front of me. I see Rufus looking over at it as he sips his coffee.

'And what's all this about me quitting my job? I haven't given up my job! I've taken a few days off.'

'You could, you know ...' he says with a lazy smile.

'Give up work and do what?'

'Anything you want. You don't need to work. You could be around here, help me out.'

'What? Turn into a housewife?'

I may not have pictured myself as a madly focused career woman but I'd certainly never seen myself as a housewife at the age of twenty-eight. Sophie would beat me to a pulp if I left the theatre and turned into a domestic goddess.

Rufus just shrugs.

'It will be easier to keep on top of press intrusion if you don't work.'

'I'm not giving up work. That's insane. It'll be fine. I'm going to carry on working and carry on being me.'

Rufus lies down on the bed next to me, leans in close and stares at me with eyes the colour of palest moss. He has the most amazing, thick, jet-black eyelashes, fluttering out from around these astonishing eyes. The fact that everything about Rufus is dark except for his eyes seems to highlight their lightness even more. His skin always looks tanned, his hair is thick, dark and glossy, but those eyes– they lift out of his face, full of laughter, joy and this alluring intensity. God, he's gorgeous. He pulls me towards him.

'I think it will be hard to carry on working,' he says as he pulls the duvet off me, and I feel his eyes travel the length of my body before resting on my breasts. 'But we're not going to carry on talking about that now. I have other plans. Come here,' he growls. I can feel his erection digging into my leg. 'Mmmmm,' I murmur back as he begins to kiss me, and all my worries about work and my lovely flatmates drift quickly from my mind.

We're sitting at the breakfast table in the snug a few days later, enjoying a range of berries, and some fruits I've never heard of before, like goji berries. Goji berries? We only had apples and bananas at home. And, maybe, strawberries if we were feeling flush. Now it's all star fruits, lychees, pomegranates and goji berries (which, for the record, are foul; I don't care if they're a superfood). I munch through the fruit plate, which has been prepared by Pamela – one of the chefs. She's my favourite one, actually; she looks like every great housekeeper ought to, with her large barrel-shaped body, and her light-grey hair fashioned into the tightest of curls on her head. She always wears an immaculate white apron over her long grey skirt. She and Julie have been so lovely to me. Ever since I started coming to the house regularly, all those months ago, they've looked out for me, and they make an effort to come and say 'hi'.

I'd count them as friends, if circumstances were different, to be honest. Not like Rosemary, who completely gives me the creeps. She's been off for the past couple of days, since I arrived at the house with all my luggage, so I haven't had to creep around the place, trying hard to avoid her.

This morning I have a notebook in front of me, onto

which I've drafted out an important list of things to do. First thing on the list is: 'call the girls'. This is proving harder to do than I'd predicted, because there's only one way of getting hold of them, and that's through Sophie's mobile. Mandy broke her bloody phone, of course, and the one in the flat never works properly. One of my main tasks over the coming weeks is to persuade them to mend that phone in their flat so that the three of us can actually talk to each other in the evenings.

I miss them. I guess I never realised how important it would be to be able to call them regularly; I had these ideas of popping round there in the evenings, but, since it turns out that the press are permanently outside since the article appeared in the paper, I can't leave here unless it's under armed guard, and with three decoy cars ahead of me, so 'popping' is not really an option.

'Why would you write 'call the girls' on a list?' asks Rufus in his simple male way. He stands behind me, nuzzling his stubbly chin into the back of my neck. 'Why not just call them?'

'I've tried a million times,' I exaggerate. 'I've put it on the list to remind myself to keep trying. They're very hard to get hold of. Neither of them has a PA! Imagine that?'

'Funny lady,' he says. 'I know people without PAs too.'

'Yeah right,' I respond sarcastically. 'Your milkman probably has a PA.'

He grabs me from behind as if to strangle me. 'You'll be sorry,' he growls. 'I'll teach you to take the mickey out of me.' Just as I start to fear that he might actually start to wrestle with me, he tickles me playfully and wraps his arms around me.

'I hope you don't really think I'm like that,' he says. 'You do know that my two best friends hang out at baseball games trying to get autographs. Deeves spent the whole of last summer selling hot dogs at the Yankees games so he could watch 'em all without paying.'

'Did he?' I ask. 'Why didn't you just buy him a season ticket?'

'Because the man has pride,' Rufus says, shaking his head. 'What can you do? Have to say I love him for it though. I reckon he must have been sneaking himself some free hot dogs somewhere along the line to make it all worthwhile.'

'You are friends with a sausage thief?' I suggest in mock horror.

'I fear so,' he retorts, sounding as British as he can. 'Why don't I send someone round to mend the girls' phone today so you can call them tonight?'

'Oh, that would be great,' I say. 'Can you do that? Really? Thank you.'

'And I have another good idea.'

He pulls me in close to him as he speaks. I love the way he does that: squeezes me so tightly that I can barely breathe and end up sucking in light raspy breaths – it makes me feel all wrapped up and protected. When he hugs me like that, I feel that no harm can come to me.

'I think we should go shopping,' he suggests. 'I'd like to go and buy you the necklace to match it.'

'Match what?'

'Oh, didn't I mention?' he says mischievously. 'I've bought you a bangle.'

'A bangle?'

Have I mentioned that there are times when living with Rufus is a bit like starring alongside Rufus in one of his films?

He pulls out a bag and hands it to me. Inside, there's a Tiffany's box. Oh my God.

'Thank you,' I say, smiling up at him as I pull the ribbon off the turquoise box, and watch it fall softly and gracefully to the floor. Even the disposable packaging is stylish on this gift. I lift the lid, and stand back in sheer delight and amazement. The bangle has three diamonds on it – in a row, exactly like my beautiful, favourite jewellery pot. 'It's exactly the same!!' I say, genuinely awe-struck by the beauty of the piece of jewellery. 'I can't believe it.'

'Neither could I when I saw it,' says Rufus, grinning from ear to ear. 'I'm glad you like it.'

'I do, I do,' I say, trying to fix it around my wrist, as he pulls me into his arms again.

'They have matching necklaces,' he says, squeezing me close to him. 'I ordered one and it's in the store. I was going to ask Christine to collect it, but why don't we go? You can wear it tomorrow night.'

'Can we do that?' I'm aware that going anywhere with Rufus demands an operation of military-style proportions and precision, or the shop will be full of fans. 'Will we have to parachute in under the cover of darkness?'

'We can do it,' he says cautiously. 'And, if we get it right, probably without parachutes. Henry can drive us, and we'll go in by the back door.'

I sit back and watch as Rufus briefs Christine in that gentle way of his, making her feel like the only girl in the world, as he asks her to call ahead to the manager and request that the shop be shut when we arrive.

'Thank you,' I say. 'You're very thoughtful. Oh, and what's tomorrow night?'

'It's a dinner,' says Rufus, taking my face in his hands. 'I should have mentioned it. It's for a top-notch theatre investor, all very dull and boring, but at least, I'll be able to formally introduce them to you.'

'I was thinking of going round to Mandy and Sophie's tomorrow night. You know, because I haven't seen them for a few days, and I can't get hold of them.'

'I'll take care of the phone situation so you'll be able to get hold of them, but I need you at this dinner tomorrow.'

'OK. Well at least I've got the perfect dress to wear. Mand and Soph bought it for me as a leaving present.'

'No need to worry about anything like that. Elodie will come during the day to sort out your outfit. She's a great stylist. You might remember her from a tv programme she used to host years ago, with her ex-boyfriend.'

'Oh blimey, yes. I remember.'

'Now, come on, let's get you a necklace.'

I wish I could reciprocate in some way; I wish I could buy Rufus something that he would adore, and would make him go as mushy and adoring as I go when he buys things for me, but how? What could I buy that he couldn't afford to get himself two million of?

When it comes to purchasing power, our relationship feels so unbalanced. He's only got to say in an interview, at a party, or anywhere else, that he quite likes the look of the new Burberry suits, and the entire winter menswear collection will turn up in seconds. What's the point of me saving up to buy him a tiepin when the manufacturers will give him every tiepin ever made?

'Ready?'

We've arrived at the back door of Tiffany's in Bond Street. Rufus pulls his cap down and his collar up, looking around shiftily, as if he's off to hold up a bank or something. We go darting through the doors that swing open to greet us. Now this is something I've really noticed about Rufus's world: doors are being opened for me constantly. I've only been living with him for a few days but I don't think I have deigned to open my own door once in that time. Everywhere I go there's someone expecting me, and swinging the door open, as I arrive, in greeting. Like magic!

Rufus places the necklace around my neck and it hangs,

sparkling wildly but elegantly, against my skin. I can't speak. I just stand, looking into the mirror, while the sales assistants coo and say 'gorgeous', while clearly looking at my boyfriend. I notice how he doesn't return their admiring glances, though: he keeps on looking at me, like he's absorbing me with his eyes, like there's no one else in the room. He may be the world's most adored film star, and

– yes – I know there are women queuing up to be with him, but at times like this I just know, know, that he would never cheat on me.

'So, you like it then?' he says.

'I love it.'

'There'll be loads more where that came from. I want to make you the happiest girl in the world.'

I want to tell him that my happiness does not depend on necklaces, and that what would make me really happy would be to see my friends, but I know that would spoil the moment, so I smile at him before we rush out to the car, having successfully avoided meeting anyone. I climb in, while Rufus answers his phone.

'Good news,' he says, as he sits down next to me. 'The girls' phoneline will be fixed and working properly by the end of the day.'

'Oh, that was quick. I didn't even have the chance to tell them you were doing it for them.'

'It's OK, I got one of the PAs in London to sort it out. They called and made an appointment with them.'

'Right.'

'Is something wrong?'

'No, no, not at all.' I touch the lovely new jewellery he has bought for me, and think about how kind and generous he's being. 'I suppose it's just all new to me, all these PAs and everything. I guess I'd have liked to have called the girls myself.'

'Ah, PAs can be extraordinarily useful. They can take all the hard work out of your life.'

But they're my friends, I think to myself. They're not hard work. I try calling them on their new landline, but there is still no answer. They're obviously out having fun. I wish I was with them. I wish it was possible to be back in my old life, but still with Rufus. I love him very much, I really do, it's just that this whole life is not what I'm used to at all.

CHAPTER 8: TELLING MUM
AND DAD

'Mum, I've met someone,' I say.

'Who have you met?'

'I mean, I've met a man...a new boyfriend, and I've kind of moved into his house.'

'Moved in with him? Why are you only mentioning this now?'

'Because it was a whirlwind, and it just sort of happened.'

'OK. Well, what's his name? Tell me about him.'

'His name's Rufus and he's an actor. He's quite a famous actor. Rufus George. Have you heard of him?'

'Well, yes, I think so. What's he been in?'

'*Tarzan*,' I say. It's the one she's most likely to have seen.

'You mean Johnny Weissmuller? I thought he was dead.'

'No, Rufus George.'

'Johnny Weissmuller played Tarzan but he's dead. I'm sure he's dead. Is he dead?'

Christ, it shows how long it's been since she went to the cinema.

I hear Mum yelling through the house. 'Tony, Tony, is Johnny Weissmuller dead?'

Dad's frustrated voice booms out in the background. 'How on earth would I know something like that?'

'Your father doesn't know whether he's alive or dead,' says Mum.

'It doesn't matter whether he's dead or alive; I'm not going out with him. I'm going out with Rufus George.'

'Oh, Tony, have a word with her, would you,' she says. 'She doesn't care whether Johnny Weissmuller's alive or dead.'

Oh God. Why is everything like explaining nuclear physics to a terrapin?

'You coming through to the den?' asks Rufus when I've put the phone down on my very confused mother. His enquiry makes me jump. I had no idea that he'd been standing in the corner of the room all the time I'd been talking.

'How long have you been standing there for?'

'Not long. I'll be in the den if you need me.'

'Sure. I'm just going to call the girls on their new phone line, then I'll be in.'

But before I can call the girls, mum rings back. I answer it and she squeals down the phone like a wild penguin.

'I've just had a look online...it says you're going out with Rufus George.'

'Yes.'

'The actor Rufus George!'

'Yes, that's who I'm going out with. I told you.'

'I thought you were joking! I thought you said Johnny Weissmuller.'

'No, I said the actor who played Tarzan...that's Rufus.'

'Oh,' says mum.

'We'll come down and see you for the day on Thursday, shall we?'

'Tomorrow?' asks mum.

'No, tomorrow's Wednesday. We'll come down on Thursday.'

'Lovely,' says my mum. 'That's lovely.'

'Where are you?' asks Rufus, in a whiny voice, like a young child. 'When are you coming in here?'

'I'm just going to ring the girls.'

'Do that in the morning. I want you to come here right now.'

'I can't call them tomorrow; I'm going in to work.'

'Into work?' He sounds quite shocked, and a little angry, so I walk into the snug.

'I'm just going in for a meeting. I'm off this week, but I don't want to drop the girls in it, so I thought I'd join them for the planning meeting.'

'You know Elodie's coming to see you, and we have the dinner in the evening.'

'Yes - I'll just be in work for the morning.'

'OK, make sure you mention it to Christine so Henry's here to take you.'

'I can walk there from here. There's so much traffic on Richmond Hill in the morning, it'll be quicker to walk.'

I'm also looking forward to getting some fresh air and not feeling so hemmed in.

'No, no, you can't walk. Henry will pick you up.'

'Oh, there's something else,' I say. 'I just promised mum that you and I would go to Hastings to visit them on Thursday. We can just go for lunch. Is that OK?'

'Have you checked with Christine?'

'No, of course not.'

'Worth running everything past her first.'

'But, Rufus, I don't want to do that. This is a visit to the parents of the girl you're in love with, not a contractual negotiation with American lawyers.'

'OK, well, I'll check with her then. She manages my diary, that's all.'

'Yes, but I want you and I to make these decisions. I don't want Christine, or Rosemary, or Elodie, or Henry or David always involved in everything. When we were dating, it was just you and me, now there's a whole entourage.'

'The entourage was there before, angel. Christine booked the restaurant out, and made sure we could wander round Hampton Court gardens without hassle. Henry drives me everywhere. It's just how my life is.'

'OK, so can *you* check with Christine?'

'Of course,' says Rufus. 'Now come here.'

The next morning, at 8:30am sharp, I climb into the back of the car, and chat amiably to Henry while we sit in traffic.

'Oh, I've just had a message for you, from Christine.' he says, fiddling with his phone. 'She says that Rufus can make the trip to see your parents tomorrow.'

'Oh good. Thanks, Henry,' I say, though why the message from Rufus had to be relayed via Christine and Henry is beyond me. I decide to try the girls before they leave for work.

'Hey, it's me.'

'Sorry, we don't know a 'me',' says Mandy. 'We used to have a flatmate but she moved out and never contacted us again.'

'No, not true, not true. I've been trying to call you and can never get hold of you.'

'Yeah right. You know exactly where we are - come over and see us.'

'I'd love to,' I say. 'Honestly, I'd just love to, but it's so hard with press, and fans and stuff.'

'Oh, your life must be so hard. There can't be that many press. Just tell them to go away, and come here for wine and pizza.'

'I'll try,' I say. 'But the press follow him everywhere, and they've started following me since I moved in.'

'You're not *that* famous,' says Mandy. I know what she means, and I know how naff I must sound, talking about how hard it is with fans following me.

'I'm not, but Rufus is, and you have no idea how much the press want a story about Rufus's latest girlfriend. They are desperate for something on me.'

'Is that why Rufus wanted a safe line installed in the flat?'

'No, it's not a safe line. What's a safe line in any case? No, that was just to get a line installed so we could all talk to one another more easily.'

'The guy who put the line in said it was a secure line, so no one could tap into it, except Rufus, of course; apparently he can play back calls any time he wants.'

'Whaaaaat? What are you talking about? That's not true.'

'It's what the guy said. Go and ask Rufus.'

'I will,' I say.

'Come round and see us tonight. Let's catch up properly.'

'Oh God, I'd love to, but I have to go to this dinner thing tonight, with Lord Simpkin, some amazing theatre person, who Rufus needs to impress.'

'Come for a drink at ours first?'

'I would, but the stylist is coming this afternoon.'

'The stylist? Bloody hell, Kelly.'

'It's just the way Rufus is,' I try to explain, but I know my explanations are falling on deaf ears. 'It's just a different sort of life. The stylist is Elodie, the famous stylist who had her own show years ago. Do you remember?'

'Yes of course I remember that show. God, she's going to get you into all these fancy new clothes. Didn't she go out with that fashion designer who died?'

'Yes, that's right.'

'Is that why you're having a boob job?'

'A what, now?'

'A boob job.'

'Have you forgotten how massive my boobs are? It's really the last thing in the world that I need.'

'I'd take a look at the *Daily Post* if I were you.'

'Have you got a copy of the Daily Post by any chance?' I say to Henry. We're still sitting in traffic going to the theatre (it *would* have been much quicker to walk), so Henry reaches over and hands me his copy.

'Who are you talking to?' asks Mandy.

'To the driver. Just on my way into the office.'

'Oh, you are so posh,' says Mandy. 'I can't believe how bloody lucky you are, having a driver to take you to work.'

'Yeah, it's not all as wonderful as it seems. You guys get to go out whenever you like, and have fun.'

'Oh yes, I remember now, there are fans following you everywhere.'

'No, come on, Mand, don't be like that.'

'I just thought you'd come back and see us.'

'I find it hard,' I say. 'I never thought I would, but it's hard.'

'Yeah, right, course it is. Listen, on balance, I'll take your life, thank you. If you hate it so much, take the bus.'

'I can't. Really, I can't.'

'We'll see you soon then, yeah?'

'Of course,' I reply. 'I'll be over soon.'

'And take care. Don't let them change you too much. We kind of like you the way you are.'

. . .

EXCLUSIVE: FILM STAR GIRLFRIEND HAS MASSIVE BOOB JOB

By Katie Joseph, Daily Post Showbiz Correspondent

The steamy love affair between the hunky film star, and his knockout English girlfriend, Kelly Monsoon, grows stronger by the day. And Kelly is determined to keep her man by her side: she's planning to undergo a huge breast enlargement operation. The lowly theatre administrator, who already has more than her share of curves, will be bustier than ever in a few weeks' time. Meanwhile rumours still circulate about whether George is set to become the new James Bond.

- *Don't forget to read our exclusive interview with Kelly's former boyfriend Greg Clarke in this Sunday's paper. 'She went like a train,' said Clarke. 'I've never had sex like it.' Lucky Rufus! Read more EXCLUSIVELY on Sunday.*

Do you know Kelly Monsoon? If you do, call the Showbiz desk now on 020 7765 0064, or email showbiz@daily–post.com. We will pay for information and your identity can be kept secret.

When I read the piece, I'm horrified. I can hardly believe my eyes. There, in a national newspaper, read by millions of people (including my friends and family), is a chicane of complete lies about me. I went like a train? I hardly know Greg. He's just a barman who I went out for a drink with once. I never even kissed him, let alone slept with him, so I don't know how he knows that I 'go' like a train. Bloody hell. I'm no virgin, but I definitely never slept with him!

And boob job? I mean – hello – of all the people in the world, I really don't need a boob job. I'm 34E for crying out loud, what would I inflate them to? I'd look like I had two footballs stuffed down the front of my shirt.

'Can we turn round, and go back home?' I ask Henry. I can't face being in the office today.

I text the girls in the office to say I'm not feeling well, and sit back as the car moves through the traffic. When we're at Rufus's place, I jump out of the car and rush inside, brandishing the newspaper in the air.

'Have you seen this rubbish?' I squeal.

Rufus glances at the page and raises his thick, black eyebrows. He looks like a man who's seen this sort of thing time and time again, which, to be fair, is exactly what he is.

'I've got people looking at them,' he says rather enigmatically.

'Looking at what? My boobs – the ones that I've apparently had inflated?'

'No, silly. I've got my lawyer looking at the allegations in the pieces they have been writing. I'm trying to find out where they are picking up all these lies from. Someone must be talking to them and saying all these things. Believe it or not, they don't completely make things up; someone is telling them all this rubbish.'

There's a pause while I stomp up and down the room. 'I couldn't face going in to work for the meeting today,' I tell him. 'Reading lies about yourself is very destabilising.'

'I know. It's horrible. Look, don't worry about work; I'll clear it with Seb when I go in for the matinee.'

'No, I'll sort it out. I don't need you to do anything. I've texted the girls and they'll cover for me.'

'I'll tell the head of the theatre,' he tries, but that's not what I want. I feel like every part of me has been absorbed by him. I've only been in the house for a matter of days but suddenly I don't exist anymore, except as an adjunct to him.

'I've sorted it,' I say. 'I know you're being helpful, but you don't need to sort everything out for me. I feel like I can't exist. I can't breathe.'

He stands there with his hands on his hips, presumably wondering why I'm being so melodramatic. Before I moved in here, I would have thought someone behaving like this was a real drama queen. I'd have thought that having a boyfriend who could click his fingers and make everything happen would be a dream come true, my knight in shining armour. But it turns out that I just feel as if I'm being smothered.

'You didn't install some fancy telephone lines into the girls' flat that you can listen into, did you?' I ask him.

'Not really,' he says.

'How do you mean, not really?'

'We installed a phone line that allows them to speak without anyone being able to tap into the line. I thought that would make it safer for them.'

'So why did the engineer who fitted it tell them that you could listen?'

'I'm not going to listen, Kelly. But if we find information is being leaked, it's possible to check the recordings of calls on the line... just to eliminate them.'

'They are being recorded?'

'No, no. Come on, it's nothing like that. We'll never listen to a word of it, but it protects them if there are issues about people talking to journalists.'

'This is all so weird, Rufus. Honestly, I feel like I'm in some terrible afternoon movie.'

'Come on, angel. I know it's a different life to the one you're used to, but you knew that. You'll get used to it. And at least we're together. That's the main thing.'

'Sure,' I say.

'Now the lawyers are doing everything they can to stop the papers from printing the interview with your ex-boyfriend on Sunday.'

'He's not my ex.'

'Well, whoever he is ... "train man" ... we'll stop him talking about having sex with you.'

'I didn't have sex with him. Can we get this really clear, Rufus: he's not my ex-boyfriend, and I didn't have sex with him.'

Rufus just stands there looking at me.

'I just don't believe it,' I say, largely to myself, but Rufus hears and ruffles my hair affectionately.

'Don't you?' he says. 'Did you think we'd be left alone to develop our relationship in peace? I'm afraid I've had a working lifetime of this. They don't let up; they're always after stories, always wanting to hear more. That's why we have to be careful who we trust.'

'I didn't think it would be like this,' I say. I'm not stupid; I knew the journalists would want to write stories, but it didn't occur to me that the newspapers would be this inter-ested in the minutiae of our relationship. I imagined that once we started going to events and parties together, the journalists would want to write about us, but I just didn't expect this. I didn't imagine for a minute that if they couldn't find a story, they'd make one up.

I guess I thought I could control things; I thought that by not going out and not doing anything wrong, I'd be OK. If I was caught falling out of a nightclub, taking drugs or working in the slave trade, I realise that the story would hold extra interest because of my link to a film star, but I didn't think that by doing nothing I'd still end up in the papers, unable to see my friends and go to work.

I seem to be even more of a target for the media by not doing anything. Heat magazine announced that I was 'oops ... too fat by far' after they got a picture of me clambering out of the car. I nearly cried, and realised, perhaps for the first time, that when you're looking at these pictures as a non-celebrity, they seem harmless and fun. But when you're the target of the pictures, they feel like a real attack. It's all so personal. I never realised before how undermining and cruel so many of the jibes are in magazines.

'I guess I was naive.'

'Listen, I don't want you to worry,' says Rufus in that calm way of his, as his mobile phone rings.

'Courty!' he shouts into the phone. 'How ya doing, buddy?' There's a pause during which Rufus smiles from ear to ear, as he listens to his friend recounting a story of some kind.

'Ha, ha, ha,' Rufus says in reply, his voice rising with every laugh. 'And you had it coming to you,' he adds, pointing abstractly at the wall as he does so. 'You had it coming, bud. Now, hold on, let me put you on loudspeaker so you can talk to Kelly ... Can you still hear me?'

'Sure can, buddy.'

'Kelly, say hi to Mr Brad Court, one of my oldest friends.'

'Hey, less of the 'old', Tarzan,' says 'Courty', adding: 'Kelly, are you there?'

'Hello,' I say nervously. 'Nice to talk to you.'

'Hey, it's great to talk to you too,' he says. 'How's it going with old misery chops?'

'Hey,' Rufus shouts, over my shoulder. 'Watch it.'

'It's going OK actually,' I say. 'He hasn't introduced me to the world of baseball yet, though; I understand you're a real fan.'

'God, I love your accent,' he swoons. 'It's soooo sexy.'

'Enough,' shouts Rufus over my shoulder, taking the phone. 'I need time alone with the accent now, so you, my friend, are history. Talk soon, buddy.'

'Sure thing,' says Courty. 'Nice to talk to you, Kelly. If you're as hot as your accent, then Rufus must be one hell of a –'

Gone. Rufus cuts his friend off in his prime, and tucks the phone back into his trouser pocket, looking over at me.

'Courty's a really nice guy. He's a proper, decent, honest guy. People like that don't worry about what's in the paper. They know the real person behind the headlines, and they take no notice. Don't worry too much about what the likes of Katie Joseph write. She's really not worth worrying about.'

'OK,' I say, cautiously.

'I have to go to the theatre now. I'll get Elodie to come over and meet you at 3:00pm. I'll try and come back here early tonight but I've got a couple of meetings this afternoon so that might not be possible. Look through the notes that Christine has printed out about Lord Simpkins, so you know about him in time for the dinner.

'Oh, OK. What meetings have you got?'

'It's about a new role, and to firm up details for a promo tour. All very dull … but I have to go, sweets. Anyway, you'll have tons to do before the party tonight, won't you? I know what you girls are like. Have fun with Elodie. I think you two could be great friends.'

'Sure,' I say, and I smile at him as he leaves for work in the theatre, and I really wish I was in the meeting I was supposed to attend today. I'm not cut out for hanging around the house by myself, unable to go out, with just a visit from a once-famous stylist to look forward to.

It's nice that she's coming over, so at least I'll know someone other than Rufus at the dinner tonight, but I'm also a bit concerned that he wants to change the way I dress. Why else would he bring a stylist over?

As much as I love the guy, I feel like my life has been 'Rufus-ed' enough.

I decide to walk down to the gym and pool at the bottom of the house, and take a look around. If I'm not going to be going out as much as I used to, then it would be useful if I started swimming every day before work. I walk down the glamorous staircase that would look more at home on the set of *Selling Sunset* than at the back of a house, leading down to the gym, when I bump straight into Rosemary. She gives me such a fright that I jump. I thought she was off this week.

'Are you lost?' she asks.

'No, I'm fine,' I say.

'May I ask where you're going?'

'I'm going down to the gym.'

'Does Rufus know?'

'I'm living here now,' I say. 'This is my home. I don't need Rufus's permission.'

'Fine,' she says.

I give her a half smile, and walk past her, down to the basement which is so well appointed, that I swear it has more gym equipment than the sports centre where Mandy, Sophie and I do Pilates.

'Remember Elodie is coming at 3pm,' she shouts down to me.

How the hell does this woman know everything?

'Yes,' I say. 'I hope she's not too much of a nightmare.'

'She's brilliant. You're very lucky that she's coming. She's a wonderful stylist...she will transform you.'

I walk through the mirror flanked gym and find lots of equipment that I'm comfortable with...the giant inflatable balls that we use for Pilates, treadmills, bikes, rowing machines and rows and rows of weights.

There's a glass wall separating the gym from the pool. I look through it at the sparkling water...a huge pool with no one using it. Christ, I'm so lucky. I really am. But, at the same time I feel ever so slightly guilty. I think of all the children whose parents can't afford to take them swimming, all the people who would love to be able to use a gym and swimming pool like this, and here it is - at the bottom of the house, sitting empty. I think I'm going to struggle to get used to all this luxury...it makes me feel bad that I have so much. I almost feel trapped and tied up by the exquisiteness of it all.

It's 4pm before Elodie appears. I have my grey dress on, so she can see that I have nice clothes. I watch her car pull up, she slides out and walks gracefully, as if on water, towards the house; there's no clumpiness or heavy footfall, just a gentle glide towards the front door. She's dressed all in black and is painfully skinny. One interesting accessory is a water bottle which she grips like a marathon runner as she floats effortlessly towards the house.

There's something charismatic about her...even from a distance. But I'm alarmed that I don't like what she's wearing at all. She's draped in a kind of black cape thing that flies out behind her. Underneath it, a corset–style top clings to her tiny frame. She has skin the colour of freshly fallen snow and tomato–red lips. The whole bizarre costume screams 'trans-vestite vampire woman'. I guess it cost her half a million quid to look like that, so I'm not saying it's not fashionable or desirable or anything, it's just not, well … pretty. Is it old–fashioned of me to say something like that? She looks like a vampire bat instead of a woman and, where I come from, that's not a good thing.

She kisses me on the cheek when we meet and I feel myself hoping she's not going to bite my neck.

'So, you think I'm a bit of a nightmare, do you?' she asks.

'Do I?'

'Darling,' says Rosemary, appearing from the shadows, with her arms extended.

The two women embrace, and it becomes obvious where Elodie heard that I thought she was a nightmare.

'Pretty face,' says Elodie, turning her gaze to me, but

appearing to talk to Rose. Now go and get yourself dressed in your party gear and make yourself utterly fabulous and I'll see if I can help make you look even more gorgeous.' Rosemary looks me up and down with an unnecessary scowl on her face, and I'm so tempted to remind her that I live here and she just works here, and I swear to God, I'll have her fired if she doesn't watch it. But I know that would be a huge mistake. She's an important part of the household. To be honest, I'd hate to have to ask Rufus to choose between us, for fear that he might choose her. So I turn my attention to Elodie.

'I am dressed in my party gear,' I say. I thought this look screamed chic and elegant...apparently not. It screams something different entirely. Something that Elodie is struggling to come to terms with as she moves from one expensively shod foot to the other.

'You're dressed? Dressed for the Lord Simpkins dinner party? You can't be serious.'

'You've got your hands full. I'll leave you to it,' says Rose, backing off with a smile that reminds me very much of Joker in the Batman films.

'Yes, I'm dressed for the party,' I say, with all the confidence I can muster. 'This dress is new. My friends bought it for me.'

'OK, well, you'll look more lovely than ever by the time I've finished with you,' she says, throwing a dart of warmth towards me.

'Now, let's have a proper look at you.' She stands back and lets those scary catlike eyes travel up and down my body. She's stroking her chin and I feel like a piece of meat being sized up by a butcher. 'Lovely décolletage. Good bone structure too. Have you ever thought you'd like to lose weight? If you do, let me know; I can help you lose lots of weight... trust me – I have a very easy way of doing it.'

I look at her with raised eyebrows, both eager to hear her weight loss tips and angry that she thinks I need them, but she's moved on.

'Now then.' She takes one of my hands in hers and looks at my nails in amazement.

'Goodness gracious, was this for a joke?' She is grimacing at the sight of the pale–orange colour on them.

'Don't you like this shade?' I thought I was on pretty firm ground with the pale–peach fingernails.

'Beautiful on an apricot,' she says. 'Not so much on fingernails.'

'But what if I like the colour?'

'Then you should wear it. I'm just here to advise you on style and what people expect from someone in your position. Please ignore me if you don't think I'm right.'

The woman swings from being gentle and helpful to seizing upon an opportunity to criticise. As soon as she realises that she's caused offence, she backtracks by saying it's not a problem and she's here to help, but the offence has been caused by then. Many of her criticisms arrive silently, like a knife in the ribs. Some of them come thundering towards me with all the subtlety of a herd of charging rhinoceroses.

'It must be odd to be so busty,' she says. 'I mean, don't you feel a bit cumbersome?'

'No,' I say, alarmed at the suggestion. 'I've never felt cumbersome. In fact, not until this very minute.'

'Oh sorry,' says Elodie. 'No offence meant; I guess I was just thinking out loud, because I know I'd hate to have big lumps of lard stuck on the front of my chest. Now, what have we here?'

She reaches over and pulls swirls of taffeta and sheets of silk from her bag; they ripple to the floor, a great wave of blues, greens and azures shimmering in the light. 'You'll look gorgeous when I've finished with you,' she says, scooping the dresses into her arms and leading off towards the bedroom. 'Just you wait and see.'

How does she know where the bedroom is?

It takes just ten minutes for Elodie to convince me that she really knows what she's doing when it comes to fashion styling, and that she genuinely wants to help me in any way she can. Despite the caustic words, and the initial doubts I had about her, I have to concede that she's a REALLY good stylist. She makes me feel gorgeous, and by the time she's layered the chiffon dresses over one another, pulled the whole lot in with a silver chain belt, and added earrings, I've quite forgotten my concern about how on earth she knew exactly where the bedroom was.

I look like one of the girls you see in magazines. I look stylish; that's the right word. I look as if I understand clothes, as if I have a great apartment and a super job. I don't just look attractive, I look like I'm bursting with attitude and sophistication, something that I've never really grasped before.

I find myself actually looking forward to the dinner party; looking forward to meeting the host of celebrities who will become my new friends.

'Happy?' asks Elodie.

'Yes,' I say, beaming.

'Good. You deserve to be. You seem nice. And you'll have enough to worry about with Rufus, without wondering whether the clothes you're wearing are appropriate. I'll be around to sort all that out for you.'

'What do you mean - worrying about Rufus?'

'No, I mean - this whole new world, all the fans, the amount of time he's away on set with gorgeous actresses. Just that sort of thing.'

CHAPTER 9: DINNER PARTY
FROM HELL

*R*ufus is at the opposite end of the long table; he smiles lovingly at me, and I wish more than anything that I could be sitting next to him. I had hardly any time to talk to him after his meetings today. He sauntered home much later than I expected, followed by a rather large entourage of men in suits. They trailed in after him as if he were the Pied Piper, taking up residence in the sitting room where their deep voices carried through the house. Their debates ranged from issues like contracts and intellectual property rights to whether Rufus should be willing to do nudity.

'Ass double,' shouted a voice that I recognised as belonging to Rufus's rotund, cigar-smoking agent. 'Tell 'em Rufus doesn't do his own ass work. Not ever.'

'And we own your face,' the agent added. 'Make a note of that too. That's a given.'

It seems inappropriate to interrupt when their high-level talks have strayed into areas as surreal as ownership of my boyfriend's face and discussions about his 'ass', so I retreat to the bedroom instead and ponder the issue of what you have to do in life to own someone's face. Do we not just all own our own faces, or am I being naïve?

If I'm honest, I had hoped that Rufus would sense that I wanted to spend some time with him before the party and join me in the bedroom so we could chat while we got changed. What I was forgetting was that getting changed doesn't mean sticking on a dress while dancing around to Pink and drinking cider any more. It means having a vast army of experts descend on your body and dress it as if it were an abstract concept and not really part of you at all. Being in Rufus's world is almost like going back into the Victorian times when maids rush in and attend to your every need.

So, for the party preparations, a host of people descended and swarmed towards me like a rather terrifying mob of angry wasps. They spoke to each other more than to me, talking about my body and the unique challenge it represented to them as if I weren't there at all. The truth is that my view isn't relevant: they are the experts; they will do the job.

I saw Rufus for about a second, when we passed on the huge landing area. My team and I were heading to the massive floor–to–ceiling mirror at the top of the staircase.

While we were mirror–bound, Rufus and David were going to his dressing room.

'Hey, how did the meetings go?' I asked. 'I haven't had time to talk to you properly.'

'It was excellent, sweetheart,' he said. 'Sorry we haven't had time for a chat but I'll tell you everything later. I'll be going to LA though – that much is definite. This is going to be an era–defining movie.'

There were murmurs of excitement from the women gathered around me clutching clothing, shoes and all manner of beauty implements, but I must admit that my heart fell. It wasn't the concept of him staring in an 'era defining movie' that gave me the shivers, but the 'I'll be going to LA' bit. When? With whom? For how long?

'I'll tell you everything later,' said Rufus with a wink. The gay hairdresser next to me giggled helplessly. Then Rufus and David, his loyal manservant, wandered off.

Now we're all here, seated at this enormous table in Rufus's formal dining room. It's all very lovely, and the old me, the me who struggled to find bus fare would have thought of this as a dream come true, but I just feel nervous. Also, I can't get the idea of LA out of my mind. What about every-thing that Elodie was saying about glamorous young actresses?

And what about Lord James Simpkins, octogenarian and the single most important person in the world of British theatre? I'm sitting next to him, and he keeps rubbing his expensively shod foot up and down my leg while his wife, Lady Simpkins, sits directly opposite her husband, chattering away to me in her unimaginably cut-glass voice, entirely unaware of all sub–table activity.

Lady Simpkins is an odd character. She hoots like an owl whenever something remotely funny happens. Actually, I take that back; she hoots like an owl – full stop. Random hoots escape from her pale, spongy face at irregular intervals regardless of what's being said or who's saying it. She has something of the woodland creature about her; she wiggles her mouth around like an inquisitive ferret and extends her neck upwards like a stoat. Add into that the hooting and it's like spending an evening in the forest.

The lady's thick, wiry hair is contained by vast quantities of hair lacquer and is fashioned into a style not unlike that sported by Princess Anne. I bet that hair hasn't moved for thirty years. When I look at her husband to see what he's making of it all, he rubs harder against my leg and is almost salivating with glee. Oh God.

Across from me is a man called Edward who, I'm working out, is a leading cosmetic surgeon. His wife, Isabella, sitting opposite him, is an anti-ageing doctor who specialises in non-surgical treatments. It seems that if you spend enough time with these two, you just won't get old. They'll iron out wrinkles, remove bags and fill out crevices until it's impossible for you to look as if you've passed your fortieth birthday (referred to here as your thirty–tenth). I look older than some of the women round the table tonight, yet I must be a good twenty years younger.

Who'd have thought age would be such an abstract concept. You'd think you just got older and looked older, but no. It's clear that no one is quite what they seem, age wise, or indeed in any way. As if to remind me of this, my balding companion with the tufts of hair shooting out of his nose shifts his foot a little higher and is now rubbing with a fury verging on the painful against a spot somewhere just below my knee. I knock his foot away sharply and attempt to pull my legs round to the other side.

On the other side of the table they are having debates about the cultural role of the media in modern Britain, and assessing the true impact of Shakespeare not just on the theatre but on mankind's very sense of himself (what does that mean?) and I'm feeling like a total idiot.

'It could be argued,' says Isabella boldly, 'that Shakespeare's contribution to the world of literature has had the impact of redefining our very understanding of ourselves as conscious beings.'

I wish that Sophie and Mandy were here so I could talk to them. It's not that I'm stupid – I did really well at school, but this sort of talk makes me want to run screaming from the room.

'His plays are certainly the only ones ever written which don't date,' says Rufus, and I feel a rush of pride. 'You feel that as an actor.'

Oh yeah, watch him go. My money's on Rufus.

'What about Oscar Wilde?' asks Jan James, a small, slim and rather mumsy–looking woman at the end of the table. She's married to Rock James, the huge rock star, but he's not here. He's on some world tour and, if the papers are right (and I happen to know now that they're not always right, so that's why I question it!), he's sleeping with half the girls in the world on the way round. The papers have been incredibly cruel, printing pictures of the young girls he's supposed to have bedded alongside pictures of Jan. She looks two decades and two kids older … because she is. But what I'm discovering tonight is that she's really sweet. She keeps looking over and mouthing, 'Are you OK?' to me and smiling warmly. Her comment about Oscar Wilde doesn't go down too well though.

'Oscar Wilde was dated before it even hit the stage. The man and his work can only be tolerated within the context of the period in which he lived. It's nonsense to understand his work in any other way. Shakespeare deals with much broader, more human issues. Wilde's overrated if you ask me.'

'Agreed, my dear. Agreed,' hoots Lady Simpkins and the couple smile warmly at one another before she turns her attentions back to the rather dashing–looking Edward.

The debate rages across the table. It turns out that Oscar Wilde is overrated; is underrated; is sometimes overrated; can be overrated, depending on your point of view. I feel like saying, 'Isn't that the point? Isn't the point that everyone has a view and no one's views are wrong because it's art, not science,' but I know that'll be wrong, so I shut up and concentrate on Edward. Now, he's an interesting man because he's fabulously handsome – a combination of Barbie's boyfriend (Ken) and the Kennedys.

He has hair that's so thick and glossy it looks almost black against his tanned skin. His eyes are the colour of hazelnuts with an intensity that borders on lunacy. His suit is immaculate, and he wears cufflinks and shoes that are so shiny, someone must have been polishing them for days. There's the perfectly ironed shirt and the thick and well–knotted tie. The man looks as if he's been cut out of a magazine. Really, he's an incredibly handsome man but – this is the thing – desperately unsexy. He's too doll–like, too perfect to be considered a handsome man. I mean, there's nothing manly about him at all. I can imagine him hanging up his shirt and making you shower before he'd touch you. I bet he's got his initials written on every towel. There's just something mind–numbingly asexual about him even though he's model good–looking and perfect in every way. Isn't that interesting? His good looks are very different from Rufus's which are far more rugged, more masculine and sooooo much more appealing. I look up at Rufus as I compare them and see him take a large gulp of wine. 'This is the point though, isn't it? The very reason that we're here and why art matters so much to us is that it provokes these differences in opinion. We all have different views – this is art, not science.'

Fuck, I should have said that.

Edward's wife Isabella applauds him (she fell out with Elodie so they can't be seated together – I hope you're keeping up here). She is as good–looking as her husband, but very, very feminine and somehow sexy at the same time. She radiates beauty and I keep feeling myself drawn to look at her. No wonder she winds Elodie up so much. She's dressed classically, with none of the flair of Elodie, but she looks divine. Her skin is plump and fresh (as well it might be given the various solutions that have undoubtedly been injected into it) and her hair runs down her back in glorious, luscious golden waves. She wears a simple cream shirt and subtle gold jewellery and she reminds me of Grace Kelly. I have to stop myself staring. She must be mid–forties but there's something so luminous and divine about her; she's very thin (I'm finding this is a common theme) and her tiny birdlike frame makes her appear slightly helpless but at the same time so cool and in control. I wish she wasn't with the rather stiff and pompous– looking Edward, but had someone warm and kind.

'Kelly, dear, do tell us how you met our lovely Rufus. Was it through the theatre?' says Lady Simpkins.

'It was; I work there,' I say, quite pleased to be able to talk about work. I do know about theatre administration even though I know nothing about Shakespeare's contribution to man's understanding of his very consciousness.

'Really. I don't recognise you. What are you in?' she asks.

'In the main office,' I say. 'Right by the windows that look out onto Richmond Green.'

'Sorry?'

'That's the office I'm in, the main one.'

'So, you're not in a play?'

'Oh no, no, sorry. I thought you asked which … it doesn't matter.'

'What do you do, Kelly?' asks Isabella kindly. I knew I'd like her.

'I'm head of theatre administration,' I say.

'Oh my,' says Lady Simpkins with a loud hoot and a rather absurd chortle, before she turns to shout over to her daughter Olivia, sitting at the far end, next to Rufus, a vision of Sloaney loveliness – resplendent in the family pearls and taffeta, exuding wealthy, youthful beauty.

The food has finished but we're all still sitting there. I'm not sure what to say to anyone. I know this is daft, and a little ungrateful, but I find myself longing for the life I've left behind. I'm looking forward to going to work, and chatting to my mates. I want to be in the office catching Maltesers in my mouth; they'd better not have been practising while I've been away.

'Kelly, can I borrow you for a moment?' Elodie taps me gently on the shoulder.

'Sure,' I say, as I follow her towards the main doors. Two smartly dressed porters I've never met before swing the door open for us to pass through. In the corridor there's a cluster of women clutching clipboards and talking intensely. As we approach, they fall silent and nod respectfully. This is so weird. Such an odd lifestyle when you have a couple of mates over for dinner and suddenly your house, your home, is full of strangers.

'You OK?' asks Elodie, when we're out of earshot.

'Sure,' I say.

'You didn't seem very comfortable in there; thought I'd better come and rescue you.'

'Thanks,' I say, amazed at her perceptiveness.

'Look - these people may seem bright and worldly but the truth is that they're simple, deluded egomaniacs. All of them. You're worth twenty of any of them. You just need to smarten up and embrace this lifestyle of Rufus's if you want him to fall in love with you, and that's going to mean getting tough, girl.'

'He's already in love with me, there's no question of that,' I say.

Elodie looks at me as if I'm stark, staring mad.

'He is,' I say rather pathetically. 'He is in love with me.'

'Yep, that's why he's going to Los Angeles without you, but by the time I've finished with you, Rufus will be begging you to marry him, and certainly begging you to go on every foreign trip with him. OK. Is that a deal?'

'It is,' I say, not quite sure what deal I've agreed to, but figuring that any help I can get is worth taking at this juncture given that I'm struggling to get through dinner, let alone the rest of my life.

'OK. When we go back in there, you take my seat and I'll take yours. That way, you'll be able to keep an eye on Olivia and make sure she doesn't flirt with Rufus too much.'

'Right,' I say. 'Thanks. But, what do you mean – flirt with Rufus?'

'Oh you know what Rufus is like,' she says. 'He's used to having women throw themselves at him. He's used to taking a different woman home every night. He can forget he's got a girlfriend if you're out of sight. Might be better if you're next to him.'

'A different woman every night? What are you talking about? That's not Rufus at all. He doesn't have different women every night.'

'Sweetheart, he's a man; a rich man; a rich, famous and incredibly beautiful man. He could have five hundred different women every hour if he wanted to.'

'I know he could,' I try. I can feel my voice rising and ringing with an unhealthy mixture of anger, frustration and confusion. 'All I'm saying is that even though he could, he doesn't.' But even as I say it, I remember what he said when we were telling each other our deepest, darkest secrets on the bench at Hampton Court Palace...he has been unfaithful.

'Your devotion is truly touching,' says Elodie. 'I think you are extremely kind and patient with him, especially given the history with those two.'

'History? I didn't know … What history? Are you saying that Olivia likes him, or something?'

'Likes him?' says Elodie, her eyes so wide they look as if they're about to burst out of her face. 'Likes him? She's totally obsessed with him. Lord Simpkins introduced them in the hope of Rufus helping Olivia to become an actress. He thought that it would assist her modelling career too, if she was seen strutting around the place with Rufus. The two of them just fell into bed together and pretty much that's their history. You need to keep your eyes on him all the time.'

'I can't keep my eyes on him all the time. It's impossible.'

'Then you'll lose him.'

'But what am I going to do when he goes to LA?'

'For the James Bond film?'

'I don't know; he didn't say which film. Something about a press trip.'

'Yeah, that's right. They're promoting Frozen Lives, then he has meetings for the new James Bond.'

How does she know so much more about what my boyfriend's up to than I do?

'Look, if you want my advice, get private detectives lined up in LA before he goes,' she insists. 'Go through his case and his pockets, obviously, arrange for bugs to be put in the hotel room and have him followed everywhere. It's the only way. Cindy Kearney's in that film, you know.'

'Is she? Excellent. I think she's great.'

'Yes, and she's also a complete maneater. She used to go out with Rufus, you know. She once joked that she and Rufus couldn't be in the same room without ending up in bed together.'

'Oh. But I trust him. Cindy can be the world's worst maneater, it doesn't mean that he has to sleep with her.'

'But it will, Kelly. Have you never met a man before? Nice necklace by the way. But I wouldn't have worn it with the dress. What happened to the one I gave you?'

'The one you gave me is upstairs. This is from Rufus. That's why I'm wearing it.'

'No, no, no, no, no,' she squeals, leaning over my shoulders and unfastening it.

'I don't want to take it off,' I implore.

'Sweetheart, you're going to have to listen to me. Wearing his necklace is like wearing his ring, with none of the security that goes with a ring. It needs to come off. Christ, you have so much to learn. Thank God you stumbled upon me.'

'But Rufus will be upset if I take it off.'

'Making Rufus upset is good. Don't be a doormat. Anyway, he'll be more upset if you don't look the part and the necklace doesn't go with the dress at all. He'll think you don't know how to dress. You don't want that, do you? Not on top of all the other problems you're facing.'

'No,' I say, unconvinced.

'Speeches. Three minutes, ladies.' One of the business-like women with clipboards appears at the bathroom door.

'Speeches? There are only a handful of people here. Why the need for speeches?

Elodie and I walk slowly back into the main ballroom and the door is, once again, swung wide open for us.

'Don't eat pudding,' she whispers as she turns to take her seat. 'You need to lose a stone if you're going to compete with all the young glamour pusses. And keep an eye on Rufus. Watch what he's doing with his hands.'

I slip quietly into the seat next to my boyfriend at the far end of the table, still reeling from Elodie's words but hoping that the amazement isn't evident on my face. I need to exude elegance from every pore, not to return to the table with the demeanour of a startled rabbit.

I smile at Rufus as warmly as I can, and see the look of confusion in his eyes. 'Why are you not over there, talking to Lord Simpkins?' he asks. 'Is something the matter?'

'No. Elodie wanted to sit next to him,' I say. I can't exactly tell him the truth, can I?

'No, Elodie wanted to stay here,' he says. 'But she said you kept signalling over to ask whether you could change seats. And where's your necklace?'

Before I can answer or explain things any more fully, I'm cut off by the sound of a gavel being banged. I look over at Rufus, hoping to catch his eye and to mouth some explanation but he's too absorbed in talking to Olivia. She seems unnecessarily close to him. Why didn't I notice this before? Her nose is practically touching his nose.

'My lords, ladies and gentlemen,' says a tall, crooked man sporting immaculate white gloves. If we were playing Cluedo, he'd be the one who did it. 'May I give you your host, Mr Rufus George.' His voice is deeper than you'd imagine it would be for such a frail man. It reminds me of Barry White.

Rufus smiles, radiating that charm and dignity that he wears so lightly for most of the time but somehow springs from him on these formal occasions, making him irresistible to the eye, impossible not to stare at. I notice that Olivia feels the same way; she's looking up at him with those saucer–like blue eyes, her head tilted to one side. I try to catch her eye but it's no use.

Rufus holds back the tails of his jacket as he rises to his feet and scans the room to make sure everyone's looking at him. He thanks everyone for coming in a way that makes you feel like he's talking straight to you.

'It's been a most incredible few months for me,' he is saying. 'Because I have met the woman of my dreams; a girl whose very presence makes the world a better place. I'm not given to making grand, romantic statements, as you all know, but that was before Kelly.'

I look up at him, and the warnings from Elodie melt away.

'Sweetheart, I love you more than I've ever loved anyone. You mean the world to me. I can't begin to explain to you how much better my life has become since you came galloping into it, knocking everything sideways, making everything better. I love you. Thank you for making me so happy.'

Everyone cheers and claps and smiles lovingly at me. Me? I clap, too, smiling through the confusion, letting the delight of his words wash over me and surround me, protecting me from the fear I felt just a few minutes previously. He loves me; that's all that matters. Elodie must be wrong; he's not going to go off with anyone else. Suddenly, the world looks bright again and people are smiling again.

'I love you too,' I mouth over to Rufus, but I can't catch his eye, and the lipstick words float in the air between us, eventually fluttering down and landing somewhere on the table, before reaching him.

Elodie comes over and kisses me on the cheek. 'That was nice, wasn't it?' she says, looking over at Rufus.

I look at her and smile. 'It was wonderful.'

'He's a very good actor, isn't he?'

CHAPTER 10: OFF TO MUM AND DAD'S

Rufus and I go to bed that night without really speaking. Not in a bad way: we haven't fallen out or anything, but everyone takes so long to leave that I drift away and into the bedroom and am half-asleep by the time he comes in. 'Thank you for what you said about me earlier. I was really touched,' I say, tucking into him as he lies down beside me.

'Good,' says Rufus. 'I want everyone to know that this is a serious relationship.'

'Me too,' I say. 'And did I tell you that Lord Simpkins was trying to play footsie with me all night?'

'Ha. Really?'

'Yes, I kept trying to shake him off.'

'Not aggressively, I hope,' he says. 'Remember how influential he is.'

'No, not aggressively.'

He seems far more concerned about my reactions to the old man's advances than the fact that the old man-made advances in the first place. Isn't that a bit odd? I've had boyfriends in the past who'd have gone and threatened

Simpkins with certain death, no matter how important he may be.

'Remember we're going down to see my parents tomorrow.'

'Oh yes. I know that was the plan, but I might have a few things to do first thing. A couple of zoom meetings with the producers in the US organised by Simpkins. It might be easier if you go ahead and spend the day with them and I'll come another time. Henry can drive you.'

'No, I don't want Henry to drive me. I want you to come and meet them. They are looking forward to seeing you.'

I feel like crying. First he stands up my friends, now he won't come and see my parents.

Rufus slides out of the sheets and wanders off towards the bathroom.

'I even got the go-ahead from Christine,' I shout after him.

'Yes, I know. I'm sorry,' he says, walking back into the room. 'Of course I'll come with you. I'm looking forward to seeing them. I'm just a little bit stressed. And I'm sorry that Simpkins was being so boorish. Next time I'll make sure you're sitting next to me.'

That's better. Happy now.

I wake up the next morning alone in the bed. There's no warm patch next to me, so Rufus must have been awake for a while.

I wander through the house to his office on the floor below and find him dressed for work, sitting with a man I vaguely recognise, and talking to a third on Zoom.

'Give me half an hour,' he mouths to me.

Oh good. I'd have hated it if he'd tried to pull out of going to Mum and Dad's again.

I head downstairs to the kitchen and make myself a cup of coffee. I'm not supposed to do this. I'm supposed to summon someone to make it for me, but I don't fancy doing that just now, so I walk into the kitchen, much to the consternation of Rose, who is hovering by the coffee pot.

'Do we have any mugs anywhere?' I say. These fancy coffee cups with their matching saucers are all very well, but they're so small and delicate, and the handle is so small that you have to pinch it rather than put your finger properly through it, and I feel as if I'm going to drop it at any moment.

Rose looks appalled but instructs Julie to fetch a mug.

'Thanks so much,' I say to Julie. 'I fancy a nice big cup of coffee.'

Julie smiles. 'I don't blame you,' she says.

Rose, meanwhile, doesn't move from her position beside me. She's hovering without speaking, but giving the air of someone who has much to say.

I make the coffee and take it through to the snug.

Rosemary immediately appears at my side. 'Rufus tends to drink his coffee in the front sitting room,' she says.

'I prefer the snug.'

Rose just stands there.

'Was there something you wanted?' I ask. I'm trying hard not to be rude, but she does have a rather dampening effect on the day when she hovers without purpose.

'Nothing at all,' she says, eventually leaving.

God, what a completely freaky woman she is.

We arrive at Mum and Dad's house in something of a state, with Rufus having nearly killed us en route. He didn't mention that he was yet to drive on the left for any period of time, having designated all previous long-distance driving to

Henry. Rufus said he was eager not to have Henry drive us on this occasion for fear that it looked too 'flash'. It seemed slightly ridiculous given that Rufus is an international film star and one of the best–looking guys on the planet. He'd look 'flash' lying in rags in the gutter, begging for food. Rufus is the very personification of 'flash'. He could no more avoid being flash than I could avoid being female: that's just what he is.

Still, I appreciated the gesture. I was glad he was worried about how he might be perceived by my parents. I loved that he cared. Just a shame that he had to demonstrate it by risking both our lives.

'Mum and Dad, this is Rufus,' I say when we arrive at the front door.

'Oooo, hello,' says Mum, patting her hair and fussing over her flowery apron. She might not know her Rufuses from her Johnnys, but she knows a pretty face when she sees one.

'Nice to meet you, son,' says Dad, patting him on the back in a manly fashion. 'Do you want to shove that car of yours up onto the drive so it doesn't get bashed into? The cars come round at a hell of a pace.'

Mum and Dad live on a crescent and most of Dad's life is spent fixating on what's going to become of the cars parked outside.

Rufus thanks Dad and heads off to 'shove' his Maserati GranCabrio onto the drive while Dad stands there in his brown cardigan, directing him into the tiniest space, with all the skill of a drunk. It is a scene which has disaster written all over it.

'Come inside, dear,' says Mum. 'We'll leave the men to it.'

I look over at Dad waving his arms wildly as if to indicate acres of space, while Rufus manoeuvres the £100k car slowly and cautiously into the three inches available. The very last thing I want to do is to 'leave the men to it'. It seems to me that 'the men' are far from capable of being left to it.

Still, I follow Mum into our small, cluttered family home. The smell of cooking leaks out from the kitchen. Mum is preparing a large Sunday roast and it smells absolutely delicious. I walk into the kitchen to find eight of our neighbours, all crammed up against the window and peering through it as my boyfriend and father bond over car manoeuvring.

'Oooo, Betty, he's better looking in the flesh, isn't he?' says Margaret, the lady who runs the coffee shop at our local church.

'He is,' says Betty with a leeriness to her voice. 'Oh yes, he definitely is.'

'Hi,' I say, and watch as the ageing ladies jump back and pretend to be admiring the petunias on the shelf by the window.

'Lovely shade of purple, Jayne,' says Betty. 'Oh, Kelly, how nice to see you.'

The others mumble their greetings, comment on how well I look, and how gorgeous my dress is. 'Must have cost a fortune!' declares Doreen. 'But I guess you can afford it.'

'Lovely to see you all too,' I reply. Then I walk into the sitting room and push the cats off the sofa so I can sit down. Mum runs in behind me.

'Sorry, love, I couldn't stop them!' she says. 'Once I told them about Rupert, they all wanted to come and see him.'

'Rufus, Mum. His name's Rufus.'

'Rufus. Yes. Funny name. He seems nice though. I'll throw this lot out when he comes in, and I can get to know him a bit better. Pretty dress. It must have cost a fortune.'

I often think that Mum and Dad's generation are obsessed with how much things cost. They mention the price of things all the time, and whether things seem cheap, expensive or reasonably priced.

'Rufus bought it for me,' I reply.

As we sit side by side in the warm sitting room, enjoying the late morning sunlight coming in through the patio windows at the back of the house, it sounds as if a small commotion is developing in the hallway. We rush out to see what's going on to find that Rufus has come into the house and Mum's friends have all gone diving out of the kitchen to say hello to him, with the result that he can't get in.

The problem is further complicated by the fact that local boys have seen the Maserati and are gathering outside to see whom it belongs to. One sight of Tarzan and the crowds are growing. Rufus needs to get in to escape the throng outside, but is prevented from doing so by the throng in the hallway. It would be safe to say that nothing like this has ever happened in Leemarr Crescent before.

Mum pushes past me and moves herself onto the stairs that run just off the hallway, next to the sitting-room door. She claps her hands loudly and everyone falls silent. 'You can all meet Rufus later,' she says. 'But right now I'd like him to be able to get into our home, so would you mind leaving. There'll be plenty of time for autographs later.'

There is mumbling and moaning from inside the house, and grunting and groaning from outside but, to be fair to the old dears, they do depart, and the youngsters outside retreat to pore over the car.

'Thanks,' says Rufus to Mum, causing her to blush hysterically and giggle like a ten-year-old.

Before long Mum and Dad are chatting away to Rufus as if they'd known him all their lives. We sit in the kitchen to eat 'because it's cosier' than their dining room, and Mum has drawn the blinds, just in case there are a few people still hanging around outside. 'Now it's really cosy!' she exclaims as we sit in half-darkness while the late September sun shines gaily outside.

'More lamb?' she asks Rufus.

'No, I'm full. Thank you very much.'

'Not dieting, are you?' she enquires. Mum doesn't think that men should be on diets. She thinks it's 'unmanly'.

'No, just very full now,' he says.

'Leave the boy alone,' Dad interjects, protectively. I love the way he does that; treating the multi–millionaire film icon as if he were a snotty–nosed teenager. He calls him 'boy' constantly and talks about the financial instability of Rufus's 'line of work'.

'Must be tough for you,' he says, on more than one occasion. Happily, Rufus has the good grace to nod and smile in the semi–darkness, and fails to mention that he earns enough to buy the country.

'Why don't we pull the blinds up, Jayne, there'll be no one there now,' says Dad, as Mum lays huge bowls of apple pie and custard down before us. 'It would be nice to enjoy the natural light.'

'Good idea,' she says, pulling the cord. We all look up, and there, in front of us, stand around 500 people, packed onto the lawns, peering right through the window and cheering madly at the rising blind as if at a rock concert.

'Rufus, Rufus, Rufus!' they chant. 'We want Rufus.' Camera flashes explode and people come running towards Mum's little kitchen from all directions.

'Jayne, let's not have the blind up after all,' says Dad, quickly and calmly. 'It's quite nice to eat without the sun bothering us.'

CHAPTER 11: OFF ON TOUR

'Do you remember that promo tour I said I was going on?' asks Rufus when we're in the car and on our way back to Richmond.

'Sort of,' I reply. To be honest, I'd kind of pushed the thought of Rufus going off to LA out of my mind.

'We're leaving on Wednesday. I'll be promoting *Frozen Lives* at the same time so will be gone for a couple of weeks. I'm not sure of the details. It might be worth you checking with Christine, or Rosemary.'

'I'll check with Christine,' I say quickly. 'I'm not a fan of Rosemary. She reminds me of Mrs de Winter in Rebecca. So creepy.'

'Don't be daft,' he says with a laugh in his voice. 'Rosemary is great. She's efficient, loyal and one of the gang.'

'Yep, I'm sure she is, and it's a gang she definitely doesn't want me to be any part of.'

'I'll call Christine now,' he says, dialling her up on his fancy dashboard.

It turns out that my boyfriend will be flying to LA on Wednesday, leaving Heathrow at 10 pm.

'Will you be travelling alone?'

'I don't get to travel anywhere on my own, sweetheart,' he says vaguely. 'There's an entourage accompanying me when I go to the toilet on these film trips.'

'Oh.'

And that's it. Later that afternoon I try several times to get him to run through who'll be there but it's impossible; he's locked in his study, reading and rereading a script, pacing round his room. The pattern continues for the rest of the week. I realise now why he's an Oscar-winning actor - he takes it REALLY seriously.

'Your name's Bond, James Bond,' I say, on one of the rare occasions when he emerges to ask Julie for a glass of water, but he's not amused. He just smiles at me indulgently and asks me why I don't go and have a chat to Rosemary and form a friendship with her (because Rosemary is the world's most frightening person, and she looks at me as if she's preparing to murder me).

To be honest, I'm looking forward to getting back to work on Monday. I've missed it; there's something I never thought I'd say...I've missed being valued for *me*, and have what *I* do praised or criticised, rather than being this odd adjunct to Rufus and everything being about him. I can't wait to see the girls and for things to feel normal again.

CHAPTER 12: BACK TO WORK

I wake up on Monday morning to Rufus brandishing a copy of the Daily Post. It's about 6.30am. I glance up and see Katie Joseph's name on the piece. Oh God. What now? On this occasion, she's written about the fact that Lord Simpkins was flirting with me at the dinner party. How the hell on God's earth does she know that?

'Did you mention it to your former flat mates?' asks Rufus.

'My former flatmates? You know their names, Rufus.'

'Did you mention it to them. This is quite serious. Lord Simpkins is an important benefactor.'

The implication is clear; he thinks I told my mates and they told the newspapers. As if Mandy and Sophie have a direct hotline to Fleet Street's leading showbiz reporters. It's bloody ridiculous.

'There's no way that Mandy or Sophie would talk to journalists,' I say. 'No way at all. They've never heard of Lord Simpkins.'

'Unless you mentioned him to them.'

'I might have, I can't remember. They wouldn't have gone to the newspapers though. That's not how they think. That's how people in your world think, not their world.'

Rufus calls his lawyer and about three of them turn up an hour later. Christine is summoned to take notes and I sit quietly while they debate a strategy. I want to go to work, but they're taking it so seriously that I feel I ought to stay exactly where I am.

I have clearly broken some unwritten, unarticulated golden rule by being in the newspaper, even though there doesn't seem to be anything I could have done to prevent it happening. They write about me whatever I do.

'How has this happened?' asks a lawyer with very little hair. I feel quite sorry for him, as he stands next to Rufus. The lawyer's thin strands of ageing hair look all the limper and more hopeless for their proximity to my boyfriend's healthy, thick, dark–brown mop.

'I don't know,' I reply with absolute honesty.

'Which of your friends know that Lord Simpkins was at the party?' asks the portly lawyer.

'Well, my two closest friends – Mandy and Sophie – but you know them, Rufus – they wouldn't have spoken to journalists. No way.'

As I'm being quizzed about something I have no understanding of, and no power to control, David pops his head round the door.

'It's Lady Simpkins on the phone,' he says.

'That's all we need,' says Rufus, looking at me like it's my fault that some mad bint with a lecherous husband has decided to call.

I don't know how this happened. I did nothing wrong and now I appear to have caused a major international scandal, embarrassed my boyfriend and disgraced the film company he's about to link up with. Not bad for a morning's work.

Rufus advises David to tell Lady Simpkins that he will call her back in an hour or so. He has never looked more furious. It does cross my mind, fleetingly, that he looked nowhere near this angry when they accused me of having a boob job yet, to my mind, that was a much more serious allegation.

I decide to get ready for work; at least I know the rules when I get to the office. I know what's expected of me, and everything is reasonable and balanced. Boring, sometimes, but boring is exactly what I'm craving right now.

I walk up to my closet: I've got loads of new clothes to wear. Elodie, bless her, gave me lots of little suits and skirts and some fabulous tops that really suit my colouring. I'm slipping into a fabulous silk kimono–style top when the inevitable call comes. 'Kelly, could Rufus see you in the drawing room,' says Rosemary. 'It's rather urgent, so do hurry.'

I trudge through the house and knock gently. It may be the house I'm living in but, not for the first time, it doesn't feel like my home.

'I have to go to work,' I say.

'That's what I wanted to say. Make sure you are driven door-to-door and don't mention any of this to anyone at work, OK? Don't leave the office at lunchtime and come straight back afterwards so no paps can get pictures of you. I'll call Seb and make sure you're properly protected while you're there.'

My heart sinks. This isn't what I want.

'Henry will drop you,' says Rufus, addressing Christine.

'No can do,' she replies, looking down at a set of notes that have been scribbled all over. You'd think she was preparing the country to go to war and managing the expectations of a nation. I feel like screaming, 'You're managing a diary, lady, not a military campaign.'

'Where's Henry?' asks Rufus, and Christine rummages through her notes.

'Driving Elodie.'

'What?'

'Elodie called and said that Kelly said it would be fine for her to have Henry for the day.'

'No, I didn't...' I try to say, but I'm cut off by an eager Rosemary who insists that's what Elodie said.

'Well, never mind about that. Who can drive Kelly?'

It turns out that David is the only man up to the task.

He drives more slowly than Henry, and it takes considerably longer to get to work than it would have if I'd walked, but I take Rufus's point. I was cross earlier when he started laying down the law about what I could and couldn't do, but I suppose if Lord Simpkins is hugely influential and this is all deeply embarrassing then I understand why the last thing he'd want is for me to be pictured out and about with the girls at lunchtime and attract more attention to the issue.

'Here we are,' says David. 'Safely at the office.'

I jump out of the car and walk into the familiar building.

'Morning, Miss Monsoon,' says Fred, the guy on the front desk. He's a bit of an odd–job man - he opens the place up, checks it's clean, opens the offices and mans the phones until the proper front–of–house woman (Barbara) arrives at midday, then he tends to work backstage, making sure the lighting and sound people have everything they need. He's never called me 'Miss Monsoon' before.

'You're a right famous celebrity now, aren't you?' he says, in that chippy Cockney accent of his. 'And look at your lovely clothes. My. You've gone all posh on us.'

I should have realised right then, in that minute, that

things had irredeemably changed in my life. But I didn't. I told him not to be so silly. 'I'm Kelly and I'll always be Kelly.'

'That's good,' he shouts after me, but I can hear the concern in his voice as keenly as I see it in his eyes. He thinks I am a different person now that he has mentally linked me with Rufus. Rufus is always treated differently from everyone else at the theatre, of course. From the moment he comes into the building to the moment he leaves; people act as if the queen were on the premises. Now I've moved in with him, I guess they consider that I'm a bit different, too, which is a shame because I'm not. I've no desire to be different. I like things the way they were; I like me and the world I've created for myself; I like my friends and I like my life. I've fallen in love with someone. Does that mean the rest of my life has to collapse and reform itself around him?

I've been in the office for about two minutes, surveying the two desks where once there were three when Sebastian comes in. 'Welcome back,' he says rather grandly. I remove my beautiful new cashmere coat and hang it on the coat stand. The brooch on the collar sparkles under the fluorescent lighting. I've been dying to show it to the girls – they're bound to want to try it on and no doubt borrow it for their next date.

'We've missed you,' says Sebastian.

'Thanks,' I say, with genuine relief and gratitude. It's nice to think that people have actually missed me rather than that they feel obliged to be polite because I'm Rufus's bird, and Rufus is very important indeed. 'I've missed this place.'

Christ, you'd think I had been away fighting a war for five years.

'Where will I sit?' I ask, realising that it's my desk that has disappeared!

'Ah yes,' says Sebastian. 'We've been thinking about that, and I spoke to Rufus this morning. We rather thought it might be a little difficult for you to sit with the other girls and be so highly visible to all who come into the theatre. Given the interest in the press, we thought it might suit everyone if you were to be given your own special office.'

Now, I'll admit, just a few months ago, the idea of my own special office, indeed my own office – whether special or not – would have been overwhelmingly exciting to me, but so much has happened, so much in my life has changed – where I live, how I live, how I'm seen, how people speak to me. I want some things just to stay the same and be part of the old 'me'. It's a small thing, but I want my desk back. I want the messy drawers and the dog–eared books and the Post-it notes everywhere reminding me to do things because I'm always forgetting. 'Can I have my desk back?' I ask.

'The office we've got earmarked for you is much nicer than the one you were in,' says Sebastian kindly. He can see the way my face has fallen.

'I appreciate the thought,' I say, not wanting to offend, 'but I'd like to sit with my friends and go back to working the way I did before.'

One of the things I love about my job is being around the buzz of theatre life and seeing the various people come and go: the set designers and costume–makers and the odd actor drifting in and out. It's not going to be anything like the same if I'm stuck upstairs in a tiny office of my own. Sebastian can see how reluctant I am, but he's stuck.

'Do me a favour, go into this new office upstairs for now, will you? I'll call Rufus and see what he thinks.'

'Rufus isn't my boss,' I say and I notice the look in Sebastian's eyes. If it weren't for the money that Rufus's presence in the play brings in, we'd all be out of a job. Rufus may not be my boss, but he's providing all of us with a living, so his needs must be met.

'You can look through the marketing leaflets,' he says, by

way of compromise. 'Make a note of anything you think needs changing.'

I walk into the office and call Rufus straight away, hanging up like a schoolgirl when Christine answers his mobile. I can't face talking to her right now. I want to talk to Rufus and explain to him why it's so important for me to have some semblance of normality back. I need him to understand why I need to be within touching distance of the real world.

While I scan through the marketing leaflets, I hear the girls arriving downstairs. The kettle goes on and small talk is exchanged: what they bought at the weekend, what they spent, who they kissed. The yearning to go and join in is almost physical. I feel a need to see them and remind myself that my old life is there, still, waiting for me to reclaim it. I grab the box of Maltesers I brought with me, and tiptoe down the stairs towards the main office; I want to burst in and surprise them with my chocolates. As I creep down the old wooden staircase, excitement rising in me, I start to tear at the plastic covering on the chocolates. I want the box open when I walk in so I can burst in through the door and start pelting them with chocolates. I tear at the cellophane with my teeth, smudging my lipstick in my efforts to get the box open. Then, at last, the plastic tears and I begin to remove it. Ha ... this is going to be fun.

'Did you see the paper today?' says Jenny. 'Kell's in there, flirting with some old guy in front of Rufus.'

I stop dead outside the room. There's a rustle of newspaper and the stifling of laughter from the girls.

'Fuck. That guy's like eighty!' says Jenny, and I can hear the distaste in her voice. This is the thing with newspapers: people read them and believe them. Jenny and Katie have known me for bloody years, but they'll believe something written in the newspaper in a heartbeat, without considering whether it might be true or not.

'Wow … look at this,' says Jenny.

'God, that's beautiful. Must have cost a bloody fortune,' I hear Katie say.

'It's Kelly's,' says Sebastian, and I realise they're talking about the coat that I've left hanging up in the office. The one I only brought in today to show them, because I knew how much they'd like to see it.

'So, she's here,' says Jenny.

'Yes. She's going to be working in her own office from now on,' I hear Sebastian say.

'Her own office?' Disgust, amazement and horror combine in Katie's voice to give it a slightly high–pitched edge. 'How can she have her own office? She's junior to us. She's admin and we're marketing and accounts.'

'We thought it was for the best,' says Sebastian and the pause that follows is all twisted up with the frustrations of the girls. Shit. I just know what's coming next and I can't blame them one bit; I know how this must seem to them.

'I guess getting your own office isn't something you work for any more. It's something you get if you shag the right person.'

Now if I were a more confident woman, I'd storm out there and challenge them. I'd explain that I had been really looking forward to coming back to work and seeing them. I'd show them the box of Maltesers in my bag.

'Come on now,' says Sebastian. 'What was I supposed to do? The press follows her everywhere. They're outside; look. She'd just be hassled all day. It would have become incredibly distracting to have her here, in full view of people walking past on the streets. She's in the upstairs office, and I've just got her going through the marketing brochures, proof-reading them.'

Oh God.

'Proofreading the marketing booklets? Why is she now qualified to proofread them?'

I know what they're not saying. I know how the sentence ends. The unsaid words are screaming at me so loudly that I can hardly bear it. 'Why's she qualified to proofread just cos she's shagging Rufus George?'

And the thing is – I don't feel comfortable about it either. I don't get off on the fact that people call me 'Miss Monsoon' and open doors for me. I don't like having to be driven to and from work and being locked away from everyone.

What's strange to me is that this is all happening now when I've actually been going out with Rufus for ages. It's because people have just been alerted to our relationship, so they're only just seeing me differently. So, it's not about who I am or what I'm capable of because I've been Rufus's girlfriend for months, it's very much about how I am perceived now that they know. This is what celebrity is all about, and I'm right in the centre of it all without requesting it, desiring it or wanting it.

I feel like a celebrity's most innocent victim. I'm well aware that if my relationship with Rufus were to finish tomorrow and I were to be hurled back down through the layers of pearls and champagne, into the world of the real people, all my privileges would disappear as fast as they arrived. I'd still have the cashmere coats and beautiful silk dresses but they would not suit me quite as well because I would be Kelly rather than Miss Monsoon.

I turn and walk back up the stairs, still holding the box of chocolates and the torn plastic covering in my hands. I don't want to go down to talk to the girls, and though they pop up to say hello later on, there's nothing like the warmth between us that there was before. So much between us has changed. So much between me and people's perception of me has changed.

In the end, I proofread the marketing leaflet with little conviction or enthusiasm. This is the job I always wanted and I guess this is the office I would have dreamed of, but I feel hollow and, above all, bored out of my mind. Googling Cindy Kearney doesn't help in the least because she's truly beautiful. She's stunning in that all-American, blonde Californian way. I think I was born heavier than she is. I can't compete with anything this woman has: her looks, her skills as an actress, her fame and her sophistication. I'm fat Kelly from Hastings. I've never felt so low. There are only two people in the world who I can talk to at a time like this: Mandy and Sophie ... my sisters-in-arms.

'I'm ugly and fat,' I wail into the phone.

'Kell, it's difficult to talk right now,' says Sophie under her breath. 'My boss is around.'

'Oh,' I say, and it feels like a personal slight.

'Sorry,' whispers Sophie. 'I'll see you on Wednesday night for Mandy's party. And ... for the record, you're neither fat nor ugly. You're going out with the world's most gorgeous man, for God's sake. Doesn't that tell you anything?'

Yep, what it tells me is that no matter who you go out with or what happens to you externally in this world, if you feel crap inside, you feel crap inside – end of story. I'm going to the Rose Garden to sit on a bench with no name and watch the butterflies play.

CHAPTER 13: PHOTO BOMBED

*R*ufus couldn't have been kinder or more understanding. When I got back from work and told him how hard I found it, he apologised madly and said of course he understood and felt bad; it was all his fault that I was going through this.

'I know you're not going to want me to say this, sweetheart,' he said. 'But I think you should give up the job; it's going to be too hard for you to carry on. Have a think about it.'

'But I like my job. It's all I've got,' I said.

'You've got me,' he insisted.

'It's all I've got left of my old life. I never see my friends and can't leave the house without a driver. I just want some of my life back. Can't I be me, but with you?

'Of course you can.'

'Then I need to keep my job.'

It's Wednesday evening and we're in the car on the way to Heathrow Airport for Rufus to catch a flight to LA. The car glides through the traffic, with Henry at the wheel.

'I understand what you're saying, but there's more to you

than the job. You need time to settle into this new life. I talked to Sebastian today,' he says. 'I suggested that you take a month off to have a think about things and get settled in. Just say if you'd rather not, but I think there'll be a lot of adjusting for you to do, and it might make things easier all round. What do you think?'

I feel like everything's slipping away from me, that's what I think. My flat, my friends, my old life and now my job. There'll be nothing left of me; I'll just be a female-shaped extension to him.

'I'll try to think of some more sensible solutions to this conundrum in the long term,' he says. 'But for now, with me going away and everything, wouldn't it be better for you to have a break from the theatre and get settled in and adjusted to your new life?'

All I really want is for Rufus to give me a hug, of course, but he's a man, so he has to come up with some practical answers to pull me back from the emotional pit I'm staggering into.

'Don't look so sad,' he says. 'I hate having to leave you so soon after you've moved in. This promotional tour has come at the worst time imaginable. Will you be alright? Make yourself at home in the house; invite friends over, redecorate … anything. OK?'

He does seem genuinely concerned about whether I'll be OK, which is touching. Not half as touching as it would have been if he'd asked me to go to bloody LA with him, of course, but touching all the same.

'I might do something in the snug,' I warn him. 'I'd love to fill it with flowers and plants and make it come to life.'

'Be my guest,' he says with a smile. 'I guess the whole place does rather lack a woman's touch.' He gives me the almightiest squeeze then. 'You'll be all right, won't you? I do worry about you.'

'I'll be OK,' I say, and I will because I've got loads planned. Tonight is Mandy's thirtieth birthday and she's having a huge party at The Sun – this pub in Richmond that we often go to. We know loads of people in there, and now I'm living in Richmond it's about five minutes away from my house.

I haven't really talked to them properly since I left the flat, and the issue with the phone line being recorded hasn't helped things. We've had odd snatched conversations and loads of texting, but nothing like it used to be. It's funny, but I've never had to try that hard with my friends before.

Every morning I'd wake up and Mandy and Sophie would be there. I'd hear about the great things and hear about the bad things. I was there to offer support when the call came through that Mandy's mum had died. I also remember sharing in Sophie's joy when she got a call to say that she'd got a new job.

Then I'd go into the office and sit down next to Katie and Jenny, and we'd chat about life. If Mandy or Sophie were having problems in their love lives, and none of us could work out what to do, I'd solicit the help of Katie and Jenny, and they'd offer their advice, which I'd then share with the girls. Jenny and Katie did the same things with their flat-mates and between the load of us we had a kind of network that buzzed and fizzled with advice and feedback. We've helped each other so much over the years.

Rufus slips his arm around me and I nestle up to his broad chest, feeling his heartbeat through the soft cashmere of his jumper. There we remain, silent, warm and happy, while Henry hurls the car through the traffic and out towards the airport.

It's hard saying goodbye to Rufus, and it's not made any easier by the fact that I have to be escorted out by security because of the photographers at the airport trying to get to Rufus. Henry gives me a warm, welcoming smile and opens the door. I've slipped on my sunglasses to hide the fact that I've been crying, but the tell-tale signs are there: the gentle snivelling as I slide into the back seat and the tracks left in my freshly applied make–up.

'Where to?' he asks, smiling warmly at me.

'The Sun, in Richmond please,' I sniff.

'He'll be back in no time, you know,' says Henry.

I'm silent because I know he's right, but if I speak, I'll burst into tears.

'Use this time to really settle in properly,' he suggests.

I just nod.

'I think Rufus's mum's coming over next week, isn't she?'

'Is she?'

'She usually comes for the Interior Design Awards. She's a sponsor of them. I'm sure Rose said it was next week. I'm surprised she didn't mention it. Rose should be letting you know what's going on. Make sure you speak to her.'

'Will his mum be staying in the house?' I ask.

'Sweetheart, she'll be taking over the house.'

I laugh in a 'this is not very funny' sort of way and catch Henry's eye in the mirror. Gentle classical music wafts through the car and I sit back and concentrate on the night ahead. Back with my old mates, in The Sun. Perfect.

We turn off the motorway and head towards Richmond as my phone bleeps. It's Sophie. 'Am sooo pleased u r cming 2nite. Mandi's been talking bout u all nite; she'll die of happiness wen sees u lol :).'

The idea of Mandy's face lighting up when I arrive fills me with a delirious satisfaction. Off come the sunglasses and out comes the make–up bag. As the car rolls into Richmond, not a trace of my former, tearful condition remains. I want to make this the best night of Mandy's life; I want to burst in there and give her the best birthday ever, with the three of us reunited and drinking all together once again. Bring on the Purple Nasties.

We're just minutes away from the pub when I spritz on a little perfume, check my hair in a small hand mirror and add a dash of lip gloss. I notice that Henry has slowed the car down to such a degree that we're crawling along. 'It's not quite here,' I say. 'Just about a hundred yards further on and we'll be there.'

'Yes, I know. I'm just a bit. Um...'

'What is it?' I ask.

'Don't worry,' he says. 'I just want to check something first.'

We arrive outside the pub.

'Don't get out of the car just at the moment,' he says. There's a steeliness to Henry's voice that I've never heard before. 'Just wait here a minute, love.'

It feels like I haven't been here for ages. There was a time when I'd meet the girls here most nights...a little drink on the way home was always a nice way to end the working day.

'Right,' says Henry. 'Behind us there are two cars with photographers in. I know the registration plates. If you go into the party, they will follow you and try to get pictures of you and your friends.'

'Sod it, I'm going in anyway. Why should I let some horrible photographers ruin my chance to say happy thirtieth birthday to one of my best mates?' I say, moving to open the door. I've got a great present for her and can't wait to catch up with all her gossip.

'Rufus wouldn't like it, you know, if there were pictures of you all over the papers,' says Henry. 'Sorry, ma'am, I don't want to speak out of turn, but I know how these photographers can be, and they really will look for the worst photographs possible. They'll end up ruining your friend's party.'

I don't want anything to ruin Mandy's party, but I do want to go in there and have a drink. I've been looking forward to this.

'The photographers are getting out of the car. Can you wind your window up, ma'am? We really should get out of here.'

I think of Mandy's sweet face and of her family all gathered round her and realise Henry's right; I can't plough in there tonight with the world's press on my tail, and ruin her evening. I'll get to make it up to her really soon by taking her somewhere special.

'Drive on,' I say to Henry, and he speeds off like Lewis Hamilton.

'Sorry, I can't do tonight,' I text Sophie, not revealing why because the truth sounds so absurd. 'But will defo b there for lunch on Sat. Kxx'

CHAPTER 14: ELODIE IS IN THE HOUSE

'You'll get used to it, honestly, don't worry,' says Elodie. 'You get to the stage when you worry if the papers don't follow you everywhere. I miss the mad press attention that I used to get when Jon was alive and we were hosting the show together; God it was exciting.'

'But I missed my friend's party.'

'I know, but that's life.'

'How will I ever get to go out and have any fun, ever again?'

'You're really not going to complain about having every woman's dream come true, are you? I'd die to have what you have: this house, the world's attention, not to mention Rufus-bloody-George.'

I look over at her strangely but she doesn't notice. She's far too busy wandering through my dressing room and tossing aside some of my favourite items of clothing with gay abandon. She thinks I need lots of new clothes ('need' you notice, not 'want' – in this new life of mine, designer clothes are needed, not wanted). In the process she's unburdening me of 'old' stuff (I thought it was new stuff until she got going, now I realise that anything that's been on the catwalks is deemed to be already 'old'). What we're after, I've been told, is the designer collections that are fresh off the sewing machines and unseen by anyone but the sharpest fashionistas in the world. I'm lying on the chaise longue trying not to think about the stuff she's rejecting. I get quite attached to things; I'm one of life's hoarders.

More than anything, though, I'm thinking about how I should be out with Mandy and Sophie and I'm really cross that I'm not.

'Did the photographers get pictures of you earlier?' she asks, as she examines the buttons on my cream blouse.

'No, I don't think so. I didn't get out of the car at the pub. I don't know why they're interested in me anyway. I'm not the film star; he is. I'm just Kelly from Twickenham who met this guy and fell in love with him. What's so bloody interesting about that? I'm exactly the same person I was six months ago, and no one wanted pictures of me then.'

'D'er,' says Elodie, dropping the shirt and walking over to me. 'That's exactly why they want pictures of you – because you're a normal girl who's going out with a big star; you're living the dream. You're hot stuff right now. Designers are going to want to dress you, stylists will want to advise you, TV producers will want you on their shows and – yes – photographers will want pictures of you. Everyone likes the new big thing and that's you.'

I know the papers are interested in me because I've had about twenty–five interviews requested through Rufus's agents. They want me to do everything from photo shoots to lunch with the editor. I can't think of anything worse, so I just say no. I appreciate that makes them want me all the more, and that's why the house has a cluster of photographers permanently at the gate, but nothing will make me pose in lingerie for men's magazine or have lunch with a journalist who wants to know all about Rufus's home life.

'When will they give up?'

'There will be lots of times when they aren't there,' she replies. 'We'll go into Richmond shopping soon – perhaps this weekend - and we'll be able to go round and happily shop without there being a problem. It's only if someone knows you're going to be somewhere, or if someone tips them off. Then you'll have problems. Normal life will never be quite 'normal' but that's the fun of it all, isn't it?'

'Not my idea of fun. I miss my friends.'

'I'll be your friend,' she says. 'Try this on.'

She hands me a black sheath dress. It looks simple and elegant but, if I'm honest, it doesn't feel that different from the sort of thing that I'd pick up in Dorothy Perkins for £15. The only thing with this dress is that it has a price tag of £2,500 on it.

'Shit!!!' I exclaim on seeing the ludicrous cost of the thing.

'I didn't pay; don't worry,' she says.

'I know but, my God, who'd pay that for a plain black dress?'

'Lots of people, my dear,' she says. 'Don't look so surprised. Rufus will want you to have the best. You're moving into a new world now. The better dressed you are and the more sophisticated and polished you look, the quicker you'll ease your way into it. Let's find the diva in you.'

'Oh, OK,' I mumble. I love her for coming round as soon as I told her the photographs had prevented me from going to Mandy's party. I am also truly grateful for all the new clothes she's adding into the wardrobe. She's very kind when she wants to be. I'm growing to like her, but she's so different from me. It's like we belong to different worlds.

I slip into the black dress and Elodie pulls a slight face as she runs her hands over my curves. 'Shame you're quite so curvy,' she says. 'Dresses don't look good on lumps and bumps. Mmmm ... I'll have to think about that. We need to disguise you a little. Now, what else is in here?'

The phone rings as she rummages through my wardrobe and I reach over to take it. 'Leave it,' says Elodie, but it's too late, I've picked up the mobile and Jan James is chatting away into my ear.

'Hi. I was just calling to see how you are. I know Rufus left today, didn't he? Are you alright?' she asks.

'I'm fine,' I say, thrilled that she's taken the trouble to call. With all the stuff about Rock in the paper recently, anyone could have forgiven her for not even remembering that Rufus was going away.

'Look – I won't keep you. I just wondered whether you fancied coming round tomorrow night for a few drinks: a girlie champagne evening.'

'I'd love to,' I say. I feel a renewed confidence about these sorts of things now that I'm friends with Elodie. A champagne evening with someone as famous as Rock James's wife would have terrified me just a week ago. I wouldn't have had a clue what to wear, but knowing that Elodie will sort all that out for me has given me renewed hope. 'Thanks very much for inviting me.'

Jan tells me to be at her place for around 9 pm. 'You'll meet Zadine at the drinks party,' she promises. 'She's just lovely. You'll adore her.'

'Zadine? As in Joe Collins' girlfriend?'

'Yes, do you know her?'

'No,' I admit. But I feel as if I've known her intimately for years. She's the one who's on every reality TV show; she's the most unbelievable woman – a walking, talking Barbie doll. I feel myself overcome with desire to call Mandy and Sophie and tell them that I'm going to be meeting Zadine.

'Who was that?' asks Elodie with unnecessary aggression when I put down the phone.

'Jan.'

'What did she want?'

'Just to invite me for drinks at her place tomorrow.'

'What time?'

'She said around 9 pm.'

'I'll come here for 9.30 pm, then we'll go,' says Elodie. 'Best not to arrive on time: very unsophisticated.'

I don't like to say that it sounded like a very informal get–together or that I'm not entirely sure whether Elodie's invited, so I just smile and we're soon back to discussing clothes.

'Let's work out what you should wear then, shall we?' says Elodie taking my phone off me, switching it off and dropping it into her pocket. 'I'll book you some beauty treatments tomorrow so you're looking your best.'

'It's only going to be women there,' I say. 'I think it's just a casual evening, no pressure.'

'Exactly,' says Elodie, her palms lifted to the ceiling imploringly. 'That's why looking good is so important. They're trying to catch you out, sartorially. It's a good job I'm here. Now, do you have any wine?'

Rufus has more wine than the average off–licence. He has a cellar, no less, as well as a fabulous wine rack in the kitchen, made out of slate.

'Sure,' I say, leaving the room to get her a drink. I wouldn't mind a glass myself, to be honest.

'Sancerre OK?' I ask, returning with two glasses that Pamela suggested would be just right. I know nothing about wine at all.

'Lovely. Now … clothes for tomorrow,' she says, pulling out a few items and then pushing them back in again.

'I'll bring something for you to wear,' she says. 'There's nothing in there that's suitable.'

With that, she throws her wine down her throat and stands up dramatically. 'Elodie is going,' she says.

'Ooooo ... Do you have my phone?' I ask, running after her. 'You took it off me earlier.'

'Yes,' she says, handing me the phone from her bag with a big smile. 'Here it is.'

I notice that the phone is back on again, but I was sure she switched it off.

CHAPTER 15: DRINKS WITH THE GIRLS

J am ready for the drinks evening, resplendent in the finest red dress that money can buy. The long scarlet gown falls to the floor making me look statuesque and regal. My face glows so much with all the lotions, potions and oils that have been rubbed into it and plastered onto it that I fear I might spontaneously combust. Blimey. I never knew so many beauty treatments existed and all delivered to me in the comfort of my own home. I called Rufus from one treatment and was explaining what they were doing to me. He was in hysterics and told me to make sure I enjoyed myself and that he missed me desperately and couldn't wait to see me again. It's funny, but when I speak to him, I feel totally relaxed and happy; it's only when Elodie talks about what he might be up to that I start to panic. I even asked him why he needed so many assistants with him.

'Because this is Hollywood, babes,' he said with resignation. 'And they seem to think that your talent is somehow reflected in the size of your entourage. It's nonsense. I miss you, Kelly. I miss you more than I've ever missed anyone or anything in my life before.' He's employing that deep, resonant voice that he normally reserves for the screen and bedtime.

It's 9.45 pm by the time Elodie makes her appearance, and I'm starting to feel a bit awkward about this 'turn up there late' theory of hers. If someone invites you to drinks at 9 pm, surely you turn up at 9 pm.

'You are delightful,' says Elodie, when I express my concerns. 'But so naïve.'

Elodie has arrived with her huge bag of tricks. 'But I don't need it today,' I say confidently. 'Look, I'm wearing the dress you brought round.' I twirl so she can see the full extent of the transformation. It's pathetic how desperate I am for her approval.

'You know,' she says with a smile. 'You're right. You've learnt well. You look beautiful. Let's go.'

As we sit in the car, I can't help but think about how weird all this is. My real friends haven't called at all, and Elodie is being so friendly that it's verging on overbearing. I wish I could have got hold of the girls today. I glance at my phone but there are definitely no missed calls. No one since Jan rang to invite me to the party yesterday.

We walk into the James' family home, and as soon as Jan answers the door, I realise this is all wrong. She takes in my ultra–glamorous appearance and super sexy designer gown and smiles. 'You've been somewhere else first?' she asks. She's wearing jeans and a white shirt. Designer jeans, of course, and the shirt looks like it was made from angels' wings, but she's not wearing a dress that would be better suited to the red carpet, nor does she have the crown jewels hanging from her ear lobes. God I feel a fool.

'I think I'm a little overdressed,' I say, rather unnecessarily, but Jan's not paying too much attention. She's rather distracted by the sight of Elodie in the doorway.

'Oh, it's you,' she says, her words twisted with bitterness. 'What made you think you were invited?'

'I'm sorry,' I say, interrupting. 'She came with me. I didn't realise it would be a problem.'

'Of course not,' says Jan through gritted teeth.

'Look … Elodie's come too. How nice,' says Jan, addressing the collection of people gathered in the sitting room. Elodie blows an air–kiss out to the guests and the air seems to freeze as she does.

'I'm sorry we're so late,' I say as Elodie glides into the James's sitting room, whispering, 'Stop apologising, Kelly,' as she passes me. She instructs some poor minion to bring her the very best champagne which, judging by the sour look on her face, angers Jan even more. I'm torn between feeling embarrassed about Elodie's domineering nature and incredibly impressed at how confident she is when she's clearly not welcome here at all.

'Meet Zadine,' says Jan, taking my arm and directing me gently towards a small blonde woman with quite alarmingly large breasts (and I speak as one who knows about these things).

The lady herself steps forward and puts out a small, slim hand. She has sparkling blue eyes, honey–coloured hair streaming across the smallest shoulders and bandages around her head.

'Did you hurt yourself?' I ask.

She smiles and her entire face lights up. She's nothing like I thought she'd be. She's like a little girl, smiling sweetly and explaining that she had 'some work done'. Jan takes me aside later and, along with Isabella, explains that no one has ever seen Zadine in the flesh without bandages of some sort on.

'It's an addiction,' says Isabella, giving me a big hug when she realises how concerned I look. 'She's the most adorable creature but desperately insecure. When she's not on television on some sort of terrible game show, she's booking up with Edward to have operations to help her look better in time for the next terrible game show. In between all this, she works tirelessly in the hope of impressing her husband who's six years younger than she, and is rumoured to be sleeping with every young model, male and female, in the business.

'Anyway, how are you?' Isabella asks. 'Are you coping OK without Rufus? I called a few times this morning but couldn't get hold of you. I just wondered if you fancied going for a coffee, or having lunch some time?'

'I'd love to,' I say. 'Are you around tomorrow? We could meet up for coffee in the afternoon?'

'That would be great,' says Isabella. 'I'll mention it to Jan, shall I?'

'Yes do,' I say, delighted.

'What's the gossip?' Elodie appears and stands unnecessarily close. She's clutching the bottle of Cristal champagne, and tips it to fill my glass to the top, then refills her own. 'This is what life's about,' she is saying in a slurred and affected voice. 'It's all about the quality of the drink. Cheers!'

I excuse myself and head off into a corner of the white–walled room where I pull out my phone. Still no missed calls. I don't understand.

'Don't call them,' says Elodie, appearing at my side. 'Leave it for tonight; they're probably out anyway. We'll make a plan tomorrow if you're worried about those friends of yours.'

And the thing is, even though she's starting to get on my nerves now, with the way she's always telling me what to do (or 'helping' as she would call it), and the way I seem to have become her special little project, I still put the phone away. She's so extraordinarily persuasive. She also has this aura around her that leads you to assume she's right.

I sit down next to Zadine, and she and I chat in whispers, so that Elodie doesn't hear from her position by the mirror where she's simultaneously checking her hair and quaffing large quantities of Cristal. Zadine's dressed all in pink. She looks like a little marshmallow. Her tiny frame is swamped by a pale– pink sweatshirt, and pink denim hot pants worn with cowboy boots.

I tell her about Mandy and Sophie, and how I fear that I let them down. 'They're my best friends in the whole world and we swore that when I moved out and moved into Rufus's house, we'd stay the closest of friends but that hasn't happened. It's all been so much harder than I thought it would be, and I just haven't seen them and I can't ring them while they're at work and I can't get through to them on the home phone. I feel awful. Seeing you has really brought back how much fun we used to have together in that flat because we'd always watch the reality programmes that you were in. We always voted for you; you know.'

'Did you?' she asks, and the thing is – we did!

'Then let me call them!' she says. 'I'll tell them that you're really sorry and you love them and can't wait to see them. It'll be funnier if I do it; it'll take the edge off things and save you having to make an embarrassing call. Go on; let me.'

'That would be so cool,' I exclaim, giving her Sophie's number.

'Shit. Answerphone!' she declares. 'I'll leave a message, shall I? What are the girls called again? Hang on. I'm through … Hi, this is Zadine Collins,' she says, her voice rising to the girly squeal her TV fans have come to associate with her. 'Just wanted to say that I'm here drinking with your beautiful friend. We have the finest champagne in the world and she looks gorgeous. Bet you wish you were here!'

She puts down the phone and gives me a little hug. I try to picture the girls when they pick up that message. They will laugh their socks off, squealing with delight. I can't wait to see them. I have so much to tell them about.

'We should go,' says Elodie, appearing at my side.

It seems we've only been there five minutes. 'We have some fabulous parties to go to tonight ... We can't hang around.'

'Oh.' Do we? I thought this was the only place we were going.

'I'm introducing you to everyone who's glamorous and important in London tonight. Let's go.'

We kiss everyone goodnight and Zadine says, 'I hope your friends like my message,' with such kindness that I could hug her. 'Come to mine next Friday night. Everyone welcome!' she declares. She glances at Elodie and glances away. Elodie's clearly not welcome but I know in advance that that won't stop her.

CHAPTER 16: SHOPPING, GAMBLING AND AN UNCOMFORTABLE MEETING

*t's Saturday and we're back at the wardrobe ... again. Now I love clothes, like most girls, but this utter obsession with them is something entirely new. I don't mean to sound ungrateful, and I think Elodie's amazing when it comes to styling, but I just don't feel that I need a 'glove draw' or someone to come in and organise my jewellery collection. I want to go and sit in the Rose Garden and dream about Rufus but I can't. There's no escape from the dreaded mistress of the wardrobe. She says we have to address the issue of my 'severe clothing deficit' as a matter of absolute urgency, as if we're talking about child poverty or a threat to national security.

'Did you never go out before?' asks Elodie, pulling out my lovely little white dress (one of my very best). 'I mean, this is stuff you would not want to be seen wearing in public; let's be honest. Perhaps you were burgled and all your nice clothes were stolen.'

'I do have nice things, and I love that dress,' I say. I can feel tears burning in the backs of my eyes. Why does everything have to be so brutal? She takes clothes so seriously. I guess that's her job, but honestly, they're just clothes. If I happen to like different ones to her, why does that matter?

She's fiddling with that gorgeous necklace of hers as she speaks, clinking the two large diamond–covered stars together. There's always trouble when she's wearing that; it's like her war paint.

'Listen, you wanna sexy white dress, babe, you'll have the sexiest white dress that money can buy, but it'll be one made of the finest materials that will hug you and flatter you. No more Topshop shit.'

'There's nothing wrong with Topshop,' I say. I'm slightly reluctant to take on Elodie when it comes to matters of a sartorial nature, but some of the best–dressed people wear Topshop clothes and some of their stuff 's quite cutting edge.

'All I'm saying is that you can do better, and I will help you do better,' says Elodie, sinking onto the chaise longue next to the vast wardrobe. 'In fact, I will teach you everything today.' She looks up suddenly and I expect a light bulb to appear above her head. 'Let's go shopping now.'

The prospect of getting out of the house is very appealing, but I made half a plan to meet Jan and Isabella for coffee. Perhaps if I text them, and suggest meeting later, say 6 pm, at mine, then I can do the shopping trip and an enjoyable girly chat after. Ideal!

'OK,' I say. 'I'll just get my coat.'

'You'll do more than get your coat. You need to dress to shop. If you want the assistants to take you seriously, you need to be properly attired; you need to be better dressed than they could ever be, only then will you be taken seriously.'

Oh Lord. This is hard work. She spends an hour dressing me up and making me look like a film star before I'm allowed to leave home. She slips large black sunglasses onto the end of my nose, in case the paparazzi are out in force, and we're off. 'Head up, shoulders back,' she orders as we march out to the car. She'll be making me salute her next.

I have to say that shopping with Elodie is a mind-blowing experience. When we walk in through the doors of shops she is greeted as if she were Princess Diana risen for one last trip to the boutiques of West London.

'Wow. It's you. Come in.'

They treat me like I'm a supermodel, too, telling me how beautiful I am, rushing around to get me a seat and showing me all the latest clothes. Elodie is desperately rude to them, but it seems the ruder she is, the more these women dote on her and seem to want to help her. 'Diva rules' as Elodie calls it.

'Have you not been shopping at all since you moved in?' asks Elodie.

'Yes,' I say. 'I went out and bought loads of plants and flowers to put into the snug.'

'No, not that – clothes shopping.'

'Oh, no. I haven't had the time yet,' I explain.

'There is always want to the time for clothes shopping,' she insists, shaking her head at me in a mocking, but quite friendly, fashion. 'And see how we're doing it with no press attention. We made a spur of the moment decision to come out, so no one knows where we are; no one was able to ring the paps.'

I must admit that last night I was really going off Elodie. This morning, though, I'm seeing her through different eyes as we wind our way through the streets of Richmond, tearing past the shops I'd normally go into, and heading straight for the ludicrously expensive ones. I buy a terrifying amount of stuff egged on by Elodie at every turn, of course, and thus I blame her entirely for my excesses. The clothes are all given to me at half price or less. Despite the hefty reductions bestowed on us, I still manage to spend more money on clothes than I have in my life before. I hand over my credit card sheepishly, convinced that it will be rejected every time.

'What will Rufus say?' I ask Elodie. 'Won't he be cross?'

'You can't spend enough to make him cross,' she says. 'He'll make more every time he smiles in this new film than you could spend in a lifetime. Lady, you're going out with one of the richest men in the film world; enjoy it, for God's sake.'

She has a point. I decide to enjoy it. When I get home, I'll go through the bags and take back any clothes that are too expensive. I don't want Rufus to think I'm taking advantage of him. I'd hate it so much if he thought that.

'OK, I've got an idea,' says Elodie, looking at me quizzically. 'What are you like at gambling?'

'Gambling? I've never been gambling in my life before.'

'Well then, today's your lucky day. I'm going to introduce you to the best sort of fun you can have with your clothes on. Follow me.'

Elodie leads me up Richmond Hill a little way, towards a small lane on the left. I've been here before; there's a bar at the end called The Anglers where we went with Sebastian for a drink when he first joined the theatre. I'd never noticed before that, halfway down the lane, there's a discrete black door with a large brass knocker. Elodie knocks it twice, and a man in a tuxedo answers and greets her warmly. I'm desperately nervous. What am I doing here?

'Elodie, I don't think this is my thing,' I say. 'It's the middle of the day and I'm not a gambler.'

'Coat over there,' she responds, indicating the cloakroom.

'I don't want to stay.'

'You'll love it,' she insists. 'I promise you. It's fantastic fun. You're going to totally adore it. No question. Coat over there and follow me.'

To be fair to Elodie, we do have a fantastic time, tearing

126

through the place, clutching handfuls of brightly coloured chips as we bet on a random collection of games. I fall hopelessly in love with the roulette wheel, while Elodie is far more taken with poker.

'Try it, you'll love it,' she insists, but it seems all too hard–core for me. You have to actually think about it and, if I'm going to have to think about things, I'd rather save myself for work or reading newspapers. Instead, I settle myself in at roulette, avoiding the eyes of the men who circle round me, looking me up and down and trying to engage me in conversation.

'A drink, perhaps, pretty lady?' asks one man. He's twice my age, with that pitted skin that comes from spending too much time indoors and not enough time in the fresh air. I hold up my hand in a rather juvenile fashion as if to say 'talk to the hand'. It's a gesture he seems familiar with, as he nods and backs away. I look up and see Elodie looking over at me. 'OK?' she mouths, thoughtfully. 'Fine,' I reply, feeling an unexpected warmth that she's looking out for me. Things happen from time to time to remind me that she's actually a very good person, even though there are occasions when she's mortifyingly embarrassing.

I've decided to throw myself wholly behind the number 29 on the roulette wheel, because it's come to represent so much to Rufus and me. It's the date that we met – 29th April… it has to bring me luck, surely.

I stick just one chip on the first time, prompting the croupier to give me a rather patronising smile. I decide that if I am to disabuse him of the notion that I don't have a clue what I'm doing, I'll have to play big–time. I've got £200 of chips in my hand. (Elodie has £2000 but she's way out of my league; I feel bad enough spending a tenth of that!) I push all the chips along the green carpet–style covering, towards the number 29.

The croupier nods and hurls the ball into the wheel so it clatters around, spinning, ducking and diving its way through the numbers. There are two people gambling alongside me. One is a woman who I would guess to be in her mid–forties. She looks like a housewife who's escaped from the kitchen for the day, but plays like a pro. She's full of confidence, speaking to the croupier in language he understands, chatting about 'the rake' and 'comps'. There's a man the other side of me who's much older, painfully thin and looks as if he doesn't go for too long without a cigarette between his fingers. His hands are stained yellow and they shake and quiver as he leans over to place his bet. No one has bet as much as I have.

'Go on number 29,' I say, as the ball dances across the wheel. 'Go on.'

'It's not horse racing, sweetheart.' Elodie has appeared at my side, and is watching in amazement at the fact that I've thrown all my chips on one throw, literally.

'I never had you down as a gambler,' she says, hugging me affectionately. 'Turns out you're a natural.'

The ball slows down. 'Go on, go on.' Eventually it stops, nestling in the number 29 position.

'Yeeeeeessss,' I shriek, throwing my arms up into the air like a goal–scoring footballer, and running around the room in jubilation. Elodie is jumping up and down and squealing, while I clap my hands and join her – the two of us bounding on our invisible trampoline while everyone else looks on coldly, emotionless and miserable.

'That was such enormous fun,' I say to Elodie, as we emerge from the casino like burrowing creatures coming up for light. 'I don't remember it being this bright outside when we went in,' I say, while Elodie smiles to herself.

'Why are you grinning so much?' I ask. The woman lost

most of the £2000 she gambled; it seems to me that she has precious little to grin about.

'I'm smiling because I think you're fab,' she says. 'You know that, don't you?'

I look at her, filled with delight that she likes me. I hope she tells Rufus that she thinks I'm fab. I'm almost tempted to suggest it to her but fear that might change her view of me entirely.

'Come on,' she says. 'We absolutely have to get you this season's 'must have' handbag.'

I'm dragged, screaming and kicking, into Matches (OK, maybe not screaming and kicking, but certainly protesting mildly), where we're treated to the best kind of service that money can buy. I now have the latest handbag from the Chloe range, eight dresses, three pairs of trousers, countless tops and a collection of shoes that would not disgrace Imelda Marcos, but it's clearly not enough.

'Outerwear,' she instructs, as we walk down the concrete steps outside Matches and descend onto the pavement below. 'But first, we need to stop shopping for a while and talk.'

'Really? Stop shopping? That sounds most unlike you...'

'There's something I've been meaning to say,' she utters, ominously.

'I'm going to be frank. There's no way to dress this up. It's something I have to tell you for your own good.'

Inside I'm thinking, 'Nooooo ...' because we all know that when Elodie is frank, she might as well just belt you with a really big stick ... She's brutal!

'Sure. Be frank,' I say confidently, then I feel like putting on a helmet and jumping in an armoured tank.

'When we were at the dinner at Rufus's house, one of the girls said that you had a face like Baywatch and a body like

Crimewatch. Don't take it the wrong way, but that's what they said. I think they're right.'

Don't take it the wrong way? What's the right way to take it?

'It's just that you are really quite fat,' she continues.

'Oh.' The thing is, I thought I'd lost weight. I thought I was looking slimmer and better than ever. 'I'm a size 12,' I say with real pride.

'Size 12!' she exclaims, her eyes wider than any eyes have a right to go. 'My God, it's so much worse than I thought! Are you really a size 12? I thought we'd been buying you size 10 dresses in the shops; that was embarrassing enough. Size 12! Zut alors! That's terrible. You have to let me help you or you'll never win Rufus back.'

Win him back? From where?

'I don't need to win him back,' I protest. 'He's mine, thank you very much.'

'Sweetheart. He's in LA with his ex–girlfriend and a gaggle of skinny beauties. He didn't invite you on the trip. I hate to be brutal but it's not looking good. If you were skinnier, I'd rate your chances of keeping him more highly.'

'No. You're wrong,' I protest. 'Rufus likes me curvy. He's always saying how much he loves my breasts and hips and how much he dislikes the Hollywood skinny types.'

'Does he?' says Elodie. 'Interesting. He's trying to keep you fat, is he?'

'What? What do you mean 'trying to keep me fat'?'

'Well, so that no one else wants you; let's be honest when you're this fat, you're unlikely to run off with anyone else, are you?'

'I'm not fat. Lots of men like me.'

'I know they like you … because you are sweet and kind. You are my lovely little fat friend and the men who like you were probably brought up by very severe nannies then sent to boarding school at the age of six. They yearn for someone sweet and matronly. But, hey, don't worry. I can help.'

She can help? What sort of help is she going to be?

'How?' I ask, and I notice that I'm sucking in my stomach and clenching my buttocks so tightly it's starting to hurt. 'Should I start going to the gym or Weight– Watchers or something.'

'Nothing of the kind,' says Elodie with a warm though slightly mischievous smile. 'Come on, let's go for coffee.'

We walk down the road, away from the shops and into a small lane leading down to Richmond Green where I order a latte and am reprimanded. My order is corrected immediately to a strong black coffee. 'Decaffeinated,' I request, but – again – I'm wrong, it turns out. Dining out with Elodie is a little like being in court with a really pernickety judge. 'Overruled' she shouts in her severe voice.

'The caffeine is good because it gets the heart going and pumps the blood round your body faster,' she explains. It sounds like a state of affairs that any sane person would avoid.

'And that's good?' I question.

'If you're trying to burn as much excess fat as you are,' she says, prodding my fleshy hips rather vigorously, 'every little thing helps.'

Right, that's me told.

'I haven't got that much to lose. I wouldn't want to be too skinny,' I protest.

'There's no such thing as too skinny,' she drawls.

'Some bigger women are really attractive,' I say. 'Take Nigella Lawson. Men love her.'

Elodie looks as if she's about to be violently sick all over the table, she's turned a kind of puce colour and has her hand over her mouth to stop her from gagging.

'Don't fall into that trap,' she says sternly. 'Don't start

thinking that you can get away with fatness any more than you can get away with large boils on your face. You can't, sweetheart. Men say they like fat women so that the fat women they are married to feel better about themselves and allow them to have sex. They don't really like them; how could they?'

And, you know, even though I'm fairly sure that if you asked 150 million men whether they'd rather spend the night with Nigella Lawson or Elodie, they'd all scream, 'Nigella,' I still don't argue back. Elodie's terrier–like determination leaves me thrashing in her wake. I'd rather acquiesce than fight.

As she talks, Elodie lifts her immaculate black Chanel handbag onto the table between us and fishes inside. The gold chain rattles as she pulls out a small bottle of what look like prescription pills and pushes them towards me. 'Take one a day, every morning, with a large glass of water, keep drinking water all day and you'll find that your appetite dramatically reduces and the weight falls off.'

'Really? That's amazing. Are they legal?'

'Yes, of course they're legal. This is what everyone in Hollywood does. It's dieting the easy way.'

'Thanks,' I say. 'But shouldn't I get them prescribed to me by my own doctor? I can't take your pills.'

'Darling, you can't get them over here yet. Take mine and I'll get some more shipped over.'

'Why can't you get them over here? Are they dangerous?'

'Not at all,' says Elodie, with a smile. 'You know America is always way ahead of Europe when it comes to medication. Everyone I know is taking them.' She lowers her voice and whispers a jaw–dropping list of superstar names. 'And Cindy Kearney has been taking them for years. How do you think she got that perfume campaign? They're quite safe. The only side effect is that they keep you awake at night sometimes, but that's OK, as long as you're not eating. You burn off more calories when you're awake than when you're asleep so it's best not to sleep too much in any case.'

Right. It would be good to lose a few pounds. It sounds like this would be a simple way to do it. The thought of going to the gym, and finding pictures of myself in Lycra all over the papers, fills me with horror.

I take one of the tablets out of the bottle and swallow it with a large gulp of coffee. It tastes OK. Well, it tastes of nothing, to be honest, which is all you ask of a pill really, isn't it?

By the time we leave the coffee shop, I'm feeling great, bursting with optimism. We walk past a skinny girl in great, skin-tight jeans and I think, Yeah! That'll be me in a few weeks.

'Thanks, Elodie,' I say giving her an entirely unwelcome hug. She has just been kind to me, in her own way, so I reckon a hug is called for. But as soon as I make contact with her, she recoils; clearly hugging is not something she's comfortable with. I wonder why ... I don't know all that much about her. She seems to have no friends, certainly no boyfriend, and she never mentions family of any kind. The only hint she ever gives to a softer side is when she talks about Jon. Not for the first time, I find myself wondering who this woman is ... where did she come from?

'Kelly?' says a familiar voice, breaking through my thoughts.

I disentangle myself from Elodie's embrace and find myself face to face with Mandy and Sophie.

'Hi,' I say, jumping with joy; I'm so pleased to see them. They look scruffier than I remember, wearing cheap-looking coats and with Mandy's hair flying in the wind. It's great to see them though, really great. Just odd that they look so different from Elodie.

'You look unbelievable,' says Mandy. 'Like a film star.'

I lean over and kiss Mandy on the cheek but notice that Sophie is scowling at me. When I move in her direction, she jerks her head back as if I'm going to hit her. Elodie tuts beside me.

'What's the matter?' I ask, thinking that Sophie would be as delighted as me by this unexpected reunion, and would be dying to ask about Zadine. 'Did you get the message last night?'

'Yes, yes, we're very impressed,' says Sophie. 'Although I'd be more impressed if you'd made it for Mandy's birthday drinks.'

'Yes, sorry. There was nothing I could do about that.'

'And why didn't you return my calls. I must have rung about twenty times yesterday!' says Sophie. 'You don't take my calls anymore.'

'That's rubbish. Of course I'd take your calls. What are you talking about?'

'I guess you're much too important for us now. I guess you're too busy for us.'

'That's completely untrue,' I say. 'I think about you girls all the time. I'm sorry about the birthday party but Rufus's flight was delayed so I ended up being stuck at the airport all evening.' I'm lying because the truth sounds so wholly ridiculous.

Mandy starts telling me how much it doesn't matter and that she totally understands. Sophie, on the other hand, has a look on her face that spells absolute anger and fury at me. 'What's the matter?' I ask. 'Why do you look so cross? There wasn't a lot that I could do.'

'Don't worry at all,' chips in Mandy. 'I wasn't expecting you but it's really nice that you tried to come. You look gorgeous by the way, have you lost weight? You look really slim.'

'Really slim?' says Elodie under her breath but perfectly audible to everyone within a mile radius. 'As if.' She spits these last words out as if they were rancid mussels.

This is not going too well.

'This is Elodie,' I say, as my new friend puts out a small, slim hand wrapped in a black, silk glove. Mandy puts out her hand; it looks twice the size and is all wrapped up in a big, puffy cream mitten in that material they make skiing gloves from. Elodie looks like she can't work out whether to shake it or club it to death. Sophie looks Elodie up and down, taking in the sheer black maxi dress, black cropped leather jacket and jet–black sunglasses. She keeps her hands stuffed deep into the pockets of her pale–blue anorak.

'I saw you, Kelly. I saw you arrive in that great big, black car, with the flash driver at the wheel. I saw you slow right down and look through the windows at us, then change your mind and drive right off. I saw, Kelly. Don't pretend you were at the airport. I guess we're just not good enough for you now, are we?'

'No,' I say, appalled at the conclusion she's leapt to and alarmed at how badly this is all going.

'We're not good enough for you?' says Mandy, clutching her face between her hands. 'Is that what you think?'

'No!' I say. 'No, no, no. Absolutely not. Of course you're good enough for me. You always have been and always will be.'

Elodie is mumbling away to herself in French by the side of me, like some terrible comic character from 'Allo 'Allo. I can only imagine what she's saying.

'Why lie then?' says Sophie.

'Lie about what?' I'm feeling all flustered and worried now … which doesn't seem fair considering all I've done is avoid dragging the world's press along to wreck their party. I acted out of concern for them; of course I wanted to go to the party, but to do so would have been unfair on Mandy and rather selfish of me.

'You just said that you were stuck at Heathrow all night but I saw you outside the pub. Why didn't you come in?'

'I thought you wouldn't understand if I told you the truth, but the reality is that my limo was followed by paparazzi.'

'And the last thing in the world that you needed was to be pictured next to us, I guess. That would do your image amongst your new posh friends no good at all, would it?'

'No, listen …' I try, but Sophie is determined to be heard.

'You don't care about us at all. You didn't come to the party; you won't take our calls. Katie and Jenny say you insisted on having your own office then as soon as one was arranged for you, you flounced out and never came back. We talked to them and they were calling you too yesterday and you never returned their calls, then last night we get a message from your new famous friend telling us how wonderful life is for you now.'

'Let it go, ugly,' Elodie screams at Sophie, wading in and placing herself rather alarmingly between me and Sophie and Mandy. She is pouting at them and staring with her heavily made–up catlike eyes. Because she's so thin, though, and Mandy is, er … .well, wider, she doesn't provide much of a physical barrier at all.

'It's OK, Elodie,' I say. 'These are the girls I used to live with. They're my best friends in the whole world. Every-thing's fine There's just a misunderstanding.'

'The ones in bad clothes you told me about.'

'I didn't say they wore bad…' but my protestations are drowned out by a furious-looking Sophie.

'Bad clothes? Is that what Kelly said to you? That we have 'bad clothes'? The reason I don't have loads of new clothes is because I spent my money on a lovely present for Mandy, and the reason I'm not clutching dozens of carrier bags like you two is because I've not spent my lunch hour shopping, I've spent it in Pizza Express, waiting for Kelly.'

Oh shit. Lunch. Fuck … I forgot that we were all supposed to go for lunch today?

'Oh God, I'm really sorry, Sophie,' I say, now feeling about an inch high. 'I completely forgot. We were at this casino and the time just flew by, and I …'

'Casino?' says Mandy, looking all worried. 'Why were you in a casino?'

'God, you've changed,' says Sophie angrily. 'You'd rather ponce around clothes shopping than see us? You know, when we didn't hear anything from you, I really thought you were going to turn up for lunch today with balloons and a present for Mandy to make it all right again, but you couldn't even do that, could you?'

'I'm sorry. It's just hard getting used to this new life.'

'It must be hell,' says Sophie, guiding a tearful Mandy away from us. 'I feel devastated for you.'

'I feel awful,' I tell Elodie as soon as they have gone.

'I know. I would too if I had friends like that.'

'No, I feel awful because they are my friends.'

'That's what I'm saying,' she says. 'It's embarrassing. We are agreed. But I know what will make everything perfect again.'

'What?' My heart lifts. I'm hoping she's going to suggest something magical to get my relationship with the girls back on track again. I'm hoping she can think of a great plan for me to sort out this mess that's been caused.

'Shoes,' she says. 'If you feel awful, you have to buy shoes. It's the only way.'

'Yeah, but shoes aren't going to change the fact that I've let down two of my best mates, are they?'

Darling. You are in a different world now. Those two are from your past. Come with me … into the future. I need to introduce you to some of my best friends. She strides off with her arm through mine, down one of the many lovely little roads that run off Richmond Green.

'Here … look … these little darlings are called Louboutins … they will become your best friends too,' says Elodie.

'Is this your answer? Shoe shopping?' I say.

'The answer to everything.'

'I'll be back in a minute,' I say, and I go tearing out of the shop, back down the lane and up the road in search of Sophie and Mandy. They are nowhere to be seen. I call Sophie's phone but there's no response. In the end, I stand in the street shouting their names, hoping they're in a shop and will come out when they hear my call.

'Come on,' says Elodie, turning up by my side. 'One of the rules of a happy life is always to buy shoes when you are in distress.' She leads me back towards the shop and sits me down, then she slips her feet into shiny black numbers with these odd-looking studs up the heel. 'Shoe shopping is a calming experience,' she says. 'Good to comfort you and help you relax.'

'I usually find that thickly buttered toast, a large mug of tea and a Twix sorts me out,' I say. I'm texting Sophie as I speak, urging her to call me.

'Stop teasing me,' says Elodie with lightness to her voice. 'You're being silly now.'

No, I'm not.

It's 5 pm by the time we get back to the house, laden with bags, and feeling exhausted. My head's spinning and my feet hurt. The more time that goes on without Mandy and Sophie calling, the more worried I become. I've phoned Sophie a total of 14 times. I'm not sure what else to do. I really don't want to lose their friendship. The thought of it is giving me a large lump somewhere between my throat and my stomach. It's like that horrible feeling you have when someone you really like cheats on you or dumps you. You feel like the pain has formed into a bundle of hurt inside of you. It's like you can feel it, sitting inside your body, like a real thing. That's how I feel now.

'Wine?' asks Elodie. She looks as if she's settling herself in for the night.

'I won't. Thanks,' I say. 'I've got the most terrible headache.'

I've no idea whether Jan and Isabella will be coming round at 6pm, as I suggested in my text, because they didn't reply to it, but just in case they do, I don't want Elodie here.

'Listen, I'm exhausted,' I try. 'I think I'm going to have a bath and get an early night. Do you mind?'

'Oh. Is it something I did?'

'No, no. Of course not. I've had a lovely day, but I'm dead on my feet now.'

'Well I've got like a ton of parties to go to anyway, so I'll leave you to it. Call me if you get lonely and need company, and thanks for being such a great friend today.'

'No problem,' I say with a smile. 'It is I who should be thanking you.'

Elodie leaves and I feel instantly guilty. I should have told her that Isabella and Jan might be popping round, and I should have asked her if she wanted to stay. The problem is that she's so unpopular. If they arrive and see that she is here, they'll stay five minutes and leave, and I'm keen to get to know some of the other women, not just Elodie.

It's bang on 6 pm when I hear that someone has arrived at the gates.

'Jan and Isabella,' says Pamela enthusiastically. 'They're such lovely people. I'm glad you're getting friendly with them instead of … Well, I'm just glad you have new friends.'

'Come in,' I say, ushering them into the sitting room, then quickly changing my mind. While Elodie's always keen for us to sit in a rather formal fashion, I'm much happier in the snug at the back of the house.

'Shall we go through to the snug?' I say. The two women look at me blankly. I don't suppose they've even seen the room.

'Come on, I'll show you.'

I lead them to the back of the house and swing open the door to the snug. They both gasp appreciatively. 'It's beautiful,' they say. 'My God. It's a lovely girly oasis.' It does look good now I've finished messing with it. I have filled it with plants and flowers, and put little sparkly fairy lights up around the edge. In the evening it looks almost magical and, in the daytime, when the winter sun shines through the glass it's like being outdoors. The rest of Rufus's house is so formal and kind of masculine that I wanted somewhere that would be fun for me to hang out with my friends. I imagined bringing Mandy and Sophie here and the three of us lying around, getting drunk and gossiping under the twinkling lights and the soft smell of flowers. After today, that seems incredibly unlikely.

As my new friends settle themselves down, I head into the kitchen to find David and ask him which sort of wine I should offer them. I feel a responsibility to get this right.

'Were you thinking of white or red?'

Bollocks. I don't know. I always drink white but isn't red supposed to be better? I just have no bloody idea about this.

'Hang on,' I say to David and I walk back to the snug.

'I have a confession,' I announce. 'I know nothing about wine. All I ever drink with my friends is the cheapest wine available … and I usually add lemonade to it. Last night Zadine asked me what wine I wanted and I nearly died. I'd love to bring some nice wine but David asked me whether I wanted red or white and I fell at the first hurdle ... I didn't know what to say. I don't know which is better.'

'You big fool,' says Jan, standing up. 'The best wine is the wine you prefer. It doesn't matter about cost or what's 'trendy'. You just need to find out what wine you like and that is, officially, the best wine. I think we should do some wine-tasting. Don't you? That way, you can work out what you like.'

'Oh yes,' I say, overcome with delight.

'Lovely idea,' says Isabella, standing up gracefully, and stroking her cream wraparound dress across her knees. The woman is flawless, honestly; I don't think I've ever seen anyone look more effortlessly glamorous.

Jan is in the kitchen, telling David what our plans are.

'Brilliant idea,' says Pamela from the other side of the kitchen, heading for the elaborate French–looking dresser in the dining room where Rufus keeps the glasses. 'You can tell me what wine I should be drinking too. I normally serve what I'm told to serve without having a clue what it all tastes like!'

'Then you must come and join us,' I instruct. 'And bring Julie too.'

'No. I couldn't,' says Pamela, wiping her hands on her apron. 'Look at the state of me.'

'Yes, you could. I want you to come. I insist you come.'

So, three becomes five.

'This is a Chablis,' says Jan, sipping gently and allowing the taste to wash around her mouth. 'See what you think.'

'It's a lovely wine,' says Isabella with confidence. They seem to take tiny sips, while Julie, Pamela and I knock the whole lot back every time.

'You're supposed to spit the wine out when you're tast-ing,' says Jan. 'But that's so inelegant that we've decided against it.'

'And it's more fun zis way,' says Isabella, with a distinctive slur. 'Now … what next?'

It's nearly midnight. Five women, about forty glasses, nine half–empty wine bottles and the sound of hysterical laughter permeate the house.

'And finally, the tenth wine. This is Sancerre,' says Jan, passing around glasses. 'I think you might like this one.'

'I ly them all,' I say, with an almighty hiccup. 'All bloody loverly if you ass me.'

Pamela is asleep in the corner and snoring rather loudly, while Julie is trying to cope with a fit of the giggles. I'm just deliriously and hopelessly drunk and loving every minute of it. I now know that my favourite wines are Pouilly Fumé in white and Châteauneuf–du–Pape in red. Will I remember them in the morning? Hell, no. Jan assures me that she'll write it all down for me, and even keep the labels so I remember what I liked.

'Howdyastaysosobernsensible?' asks Isabella, one leg falling off the other as she attempts to recross her legs the other way but fails miserably. 'How do you, Jan? Stay sooo sensible?'

'I don't swallow,' she replies.

'Don't swallow?' says Isabella, almost tumbling off her chair. 'Don't swallow?'

It's too much for the three of us to bear. We practically fall backwards off our seats, laughing hysterically until tears pour down our faces. Then Jan laughs too; more, I suspect, out of amusement at the state we're in than anything else, but once she starts, she can't stop. 'Not that sort of 'don't swallow',' she says. 'I meant I'm taking tiny tastes, barely enough to swallow.' But we're laughing so much that we can't hear her.

'Oh, sod it,' she says, reaching for one of the half–empty

bottles and taking a large slug from it. 'I might as well get pissed too.'

CHAPTER 17: ZADINE COLLINS

*T*here are 10 days remaining before Rufus returns from Los Angeles and I have to be honest with you; I'm starting to lose the plot. I talk to him a couple of times a day but it doesn't help to quell the growing feeling inside that he's with someone else. These actresses he hangs around are so incredibly gorgeous and skinny. So skinny! I realize now, after spending so much time with Elodie that men really like thin women. That's what I need to be. I'm taking the pills that Elodie gave me, and eating very little, but they also stop me from sleeping properly which is so hard to cope with and they make me feel like I'm on the verge of tears constantly. I feel nauseous and irritable all the time.

The papers are full to brimming with pictures of Rufus on various LA beaches with attractive girls swooning around him. I spend most of the time on Mail Online, obsessively looking at them, to reassure myself that he's not up to no good. Every time I see the pictures, I ring Rufus and get cross with him for no good reason.

'It's my job,' he says, but that depresses me further because I don't have a job thanks to him. I'm tired and hungry, and trapped in this terrible vortex of misery that's sucking the life out of me.

'And don't ever think that Cindy Kearney is someone I'm likely to run off with, she's a friend.'

A friend? I think to myself: *that must be nice. I used to have friends*. What's making matters worse is that no one ever phones me. I mean, not ever! I have been ringing Sophie and Mandy like mad. With them making no effort to communicate with me, it means we just don't talk anymore. Despite sending texts and leaving messages, nothing comes back. I can't believe they're willing to cast years of friendship aside so easily.

The only thing I've done since Rufus's departure that has made me smile, is to go back to the Rose Garden. I sat there among the wintry remains of the summer blooms and it was like Rufus was with me; it was pure magic sitting on our bench and remembering that day. I even chatted to Frank the gardener. He told me about the amount of work that goes into keeping the place looking so wonderful. I felt so much better about the world by the time I left.

As long as the press don't manage to discover my secret floral hideaway, I'll feel safe there. I hope they never, ever find out. I certainly won't be mentioning it in public, and I know Rufus won't, so hopefully our secret place will remain just that for a while longer.

There's a sharp knock at the door to pull me out of my thoughts and the sight of Elodie peeping round it.

'Oh, hi, Elodie. I wasn't expecting you.'

'Kelly darling,' she says. 'I couldn't sleep last night. I kept thinking of your footwear crisis. I think it would be a good idea if we reviewed your shoe situation and ordered some more in from designers as soon as possible. It's just not right at the moment; not right at all.'

Oh God. I can't do this anymore. It's stultifying; all this

talk about what goes with what and how 'anyone who's anyone' is wearing boyfriend–style blazers. I don't even know what those are and – you know what? – I don't care. 'Why don't we go out and have fun instead!' I suggest boldly. 'Or we could go and stuff ourselves in Pizza Express and collapse on the sofa and watch a movie afterwards.'

What's the point in being rich and having loads of free time if you spend it all in such a boring fashion? I'd rather have less money and less free time, but at least be having fun with the little I have.

By the time we get to Zadine's house, I've calmed down a little, but I still feel teary. Elodie storms up to the door of the modern house and rings the doorbell furiously. The Spice Girls song '2 Become 1' bursts out: a rather nasty tinkly-plinkly doorbell version of it, which is more offensive than the real thing.

'Christ,' says Elodie under her breath. 'What on earth are we doing in this place? I mean – Zadine Collins? Why would I – Elodie Elloissie – come to a party organised by Zadine Collins? Christ, if ever there was a woman untouched by charm and uncluttered by talent or style it was Zadine bloody Collins …'

'Zadine! Darling! So wonderful to see you. How are you? You look wonderful. Fabulous.'

'My God!' exclaims Zadine, looking past the fawning Elodie and staring straight at me. I think she's going to get cross with me for bringing Elodie, but she seems to have hardly noticed her. 'You've lost sooo much weight! How are you doing it? Jan and Issy said you were looking thinner but I wasn't expecting you to look so thin. Make sure you don't overdo it; you don't want to lose all those lovely feminine curves of yours.'

In the room there is the usual collection of the rich and well-connected London-types, including an older–looking couple watching from the corner of the room, holding their champagne glasses gingerly by the long stems and glancing with alarm at events taking place before them. I vaguely recognise the woman. She must be an actress; she has that impossibly well–groomed look that so many of these ageing stars have. She looks a little like Jane Fonda; a tiny creature with the smallest wrists and the slimmest ankles I've ever seen. Gosh, I bet she was a stunner when she was younger.

Elodie walks over to them and they embrace her passionately, kissing her cheek, remarking on her incredibly high shoes, and examining the necklace round her neck. I can imagine the conversation now.

'Oh but, Elodie, you always look so perfect. Your jewellery is divine.' People have a habit of noticing, remarking on and admiring Elodie without seeming to actually like her that much. You get the feeling that they'd be first in the queue to tell her she looks wonderful, but last in the queue to hold the sick bowl if she was unwell. Not like Mandy and Sophie. Oh God, I miss Mandy and Sophie.

CHAPTER 18: THE TRUTH ABOUT ELODIE

꧁

*J*ust one more day before Rufus returns and I CAN'T WAIT. My God, I'm just yearning to hold him and kiss him and get him away from that horrible bitch from hell Kearney. If I see another picture in the paper of her smooching up to him with her pretty little heart–shaped face aglow and her blonde hair rippling over the shoulders of her painfully thin body, I think I'll scream. I know I'm irrational because of the diet pills, but they are working brilliantly. Did I tell you that? There was even something else about me in the paper this morning, saying that I had lost loads of weight because I was pining for Rufus. Not strictly true, but I'd rather they wrote that than revealed that I've been taking these drugs. If mum read that I'd been taking them, she'd have a fit.

I just wish that I could sleep; I don't sleep at night any more, I just pace around and go onto Google and terrify myself half to death as I see pictures of Cindy Kearney.

But he's back tomorrow, and everything will be back to normal. In future, I will go with him on these trips. I'm not staying here, with no job, and no one but Elodie for company, with Rosemary stalking around the place all the time - I go with him, or I move out, back to my flat.

My feelings towards Elodie have definitely ebbed and flowed, these past couple of weeks, in direct proportion to her crassness and thoughtlessness. Some days I think she's really sweet and helpful and I don't know how I'd cope in this strange new world without her. On other days I could strangle her. She seems so callous, so cruel and hurtful. I know I'm feeling particularly vulnerable because of the diet pills, which have left me feeling depressed and tired, but she's still way out of line sometimes.

'I'm coming off these pills,' I tell her. 'They're turning me into a monster. I can't keep taking them and feeling this horrible.'

'You can,' she insists. 'You just have to get through the difficulty of the first few weeks and you'll get used to them, and they'll get used to you.' Elodie insists that if I persevere for another couple of weeks, I'll have dropped two stone in total by Christmas and that way I'll be able to guarantee that Rufus will forget all about the charms of Cindy and return to me.

'What do you mean 'return'?' I ask.

'Well, she's attractive. He's away for weeks. With the best will in the world, it does rather seem as if he's up to no good out there. I mean – what sort of evidence are you after, woman? Would you like a video of them having sex? Is that what you need?'

'No,' I say. 'Of course not. But there isn't any evidence at all.'

'That's because men are very good at hiding evidence, which, in itself, proves that they are having affairs. Have you been through all his things?'

'Been through his things? No. Of course I haven't been through his things.'

'No?' Elodie takes a step back in amazement and does nothing to hide her incomprehension. 'What sort of woman doesn't go through her husband's things when he's away with his hot, young and glamorous ex–girlfriend?'

'He's not my husband,' I retort rather pedantically. My heart is racing, my head is throbbing and I feel like shit. Frankly, pedantic is about as good as it's going to get with me at the moment.

'No, my love, and he never will be your husband unless you get a grip.' She illustrates this last point by gripping her tiny hands into tense bundles, squeezing them so tightly that all the sinews in her hands stand out; even the sinews in her scrawny neck have jumped to attention, making it look gnarled and knotted like the trunk of a tree. She looks old, and I feel myself strangely and rather uncharitably pleased by this.

'Get a grip, ma petite fleur,' she continues, her eyes narrowing and her eyebrows struggling to raise themselves against the barrage of Botox in her forehead. 'A woman must do due diligence before committing to a man. Taking a husband is like buying a house or a business. You have to know what you're buying into. You have to be sure you're getting your money's worth. While he's away you have a perfect opportunity to pry; don't lose this valuable chance. He would be disappointed in you if he didn't think you were taking this relationship seriously. Now, I'm going out for a while to get my skin plumped so it looks its best for Friday night's party. I may be some time.'

Elodie disappears, clip–clopping dramatically down the wooden corridor. I see her stop and speak to Rosemary. Those two get on extraordinarily well. Then off she goes again - lip-clopping towards the front door. She probably thinks she sounds like Marlene Dietrich; a fusion of drama and style wrapped up in tiny footsteps. The truth, though, is that she sounds more like a show horse. Once the sound of hooves has faded into the distance, I turn immediately to the room in front of me. Is she right? I suppose there would be no harm in looking through his things, if only to reassure myself that, as I suspect, he's not doing anything wrong.

OK, let's try to be logical about this. Logic's not my strongpoint, to be fair, but I do need a little bit of it now. If I were a handsome Hollywood film star with things to hide from my depressed, overweight, unadventurous girlfriend, where would I hide them? With a speed that would impress Usain Bolt, I'm straight onto the obvious places: the bedside cabinet, beneath the bed, in his sock drawer, in his cufflink drawer, his handkerchief drawer (yep, I know, a drawer – but he does have a lot of cufflinks and hankies, so he has to keep them somewhere). Nothing. Not even a slight hint that anything untoward has ever been there. In the boxer shorts drawer, there are boxer shorts and in the tie drawer there is nothing but neatly rolled–up ties.

In his office everything is so organised I'm worried about even standing there for fear of marking the walnut wood floor. I'm worried that my breath will mess up the carefully ordered air. Really, I've never known anything like this. I know he has tons of help, and that there are people racing around after him to tidy up with every step he takes, but still … to be this tidy … it's kind of weird. Well, to me it is. There's not a thing out of place. It looks like no one's ever been in here. It's like some upper-class gentleman's club in Mayfair that is no longer frequented but is still cleaned every day by diligent staff.

To be honest, I don't know where to start when it comes

to searching through his stuff. The idea that there'll be anything secreted away is quite absurd. Everything's so perfectly filed and organised. Honestly. How would he have something incriminating in here? The chances of finding a used condom in his scripts drawer, or a pair of lacy knickers in his file of rejected Broadway offers are about as likely as me finding out that my mother is actually Posh Spice.

Also, I'm aware that there are CCTV cameras throughout the house. I'm hoping that Sam, the guy who heads up our security, will just think I've mislaid something and am searching for it, but I hope he doesn't work out that I'm a paranoid girlfriend looking for evidence of infidelity. What if I'm the latest in a long line of girlfriends who have behaved like this? Shit. The thought of Sam and the security guards all sitting around the TV screen saying, 'There she goes ... just like all the others ...' makes me feel quite queasy.

I'm swaying between a reluctance to behave badly and a determination to uncover the truth. If Rufus is being straight, then he has nothing to fear from my search through his office; if he's not being straight then he deserves every-thing he gets.

I open the main drawer of his desk (walnut ... everything in this room is walnut with a green leather desk pad and green leather cushion on the chair). In the drawer there's mainly stationery and a couple of personal notes that are bank related or film related or business related or agent related or... Oh, what's this? There's a small internal drawer at the back of the main drawer which doesn't open ... that must be where he keeps all sorts of incriminating things that he doesn't want me to see. Shit. Where can the key be? I'm going through every drawer in a mad hurry now – not searching for photos or letters as I was previously, but for a key to let myself into this drawer that I'm convinced must contain something incriminating, derogatory or downright mean.

Why would someone have a drawer within a drawer that's locked and no sign of a key anywhere? If that's not dodgy then I don't know what is. Clearly there are things in the drawer that he doesn't want me to see ... why else would it be all locked up like this? Has he taken the key with him? I have to get into that drawer. A hammer? If I could splinter the front of the drawer and stick my fingers inside, at least I'd know what was in there. Then if I could feel something that concerned me unduly, I could take the whole drawer out. If not, it would be easy enough to get someone to repair some splintered wood.

I reach up and open the glass case on the wall, which contains many of Rufus's awards and gifts. Most of the very expensive things are kept in a big vault under the house that no one in the world knows about. (When I moved in, he asked me whether I had anything very expensive that I wanted to put in there for safe-keeping ... er ... no! The only valuables in my possession are my lovely jewellery box and the things that Rufus buys me, and there's no way I want those hidden away. I want them with me so I can see them, touch them and enjoy them.).

Rufus is the same. There are things locked away in the safe, but he also keeps some things in the cabinet that he likes to look at. One of those things is a big, chunky dagger, covered in jewels. It's magnificent. Apparently, it was presented to Rufus by the Prime Minister of India and two Bollywood stars, when he went there with the United Nations food programme. They gave it to him to celebrate his Oscar for The Jewelled Dagger.

I pick it up, feeling the weight between my fingers, and admire its shape and style. Then I begin smashing into the little drawer. I smash some more until the front of the drawer is reduced to splinters of wood. There's nothing in there. Shit. I drop the dagger onto the floor with a dramatic flourish.

'Kelly?'

I spin round like a woman possessed to see Rose standing there.

'What is it?' I spit out. I don't mean to sound so venomous but I'm embarrassed. I had no idea she was watching me.

'What are you doing?' she asks.

'Would you leave and close the door, please.'

Rosemary shakes her head and closes the door. I hear her walk away, then I hear another set of footsteps. Oh Christ, is this Elodie back now?

There's a knock at the door.

'Not now, Elodie.'

'It's Julie,' says a gentle voice. 'I want to talk to you.'

Julie's lovely, but this is not a great time.

'Can we talk later?'

'Sure, but there's something I wanted to mention - about Elodie. I mean, it's none of my business and I'm guessing now's not a good time but I've been wanting to talk to you over the last couple of days, but this is the first chance I've had.'

'What is it?' I ask impatiently, opening the door, with the dagger still in my hand. It feels like everything's falling apart around me. I'm not really in the mood for guessing games with this woman, however much I like her.

'It's just that a lot of letters have come for you. They go to Rose, then Elodie takes them all. A letter came this morning marked 'URGENT – please, please give this to Kelly Monsoon'. I pulled it out of the pile to make sure that it went straight to you, but when Elodie left, she took it with her, as she always takes all your letters.'

'Why does she take my letters?'

'I don't know. She told us that all your post was being dealt with by her people.'

'Oh.' The truth is that I didn't know that I'd even had any letters. Why would Elodie have taken everything? 'Thanks,' I say, managing to force out a smile as Julie backs out of the room. 'I really appreciate it.'

CHAPTER 19: COLIN THE CARPENTER

'*E*lodie. It's me, Kelly. Where are you?'

I'm ringing her from the mainline because my mobile seems worse than useless. Hopefully Rufus will be able to sort out when he's back, but I've now accepted that it's dead. There have been no calls going out, and none coming in for ages.

I need to ask her about these bloody letters. How can she have taken them? Did Rufus ask her to? It's all insane. I need so many answers to so many things, and she appears to be at the root of everything I need answers to.

'Can you come round?' I ask. 'I really need to talk to you.'

'I'll be there before you can say 'Gucci',' she says. 'Once I've dealt with some essentials, I'll be with you.' The essentials, it turns out, take quite a long time. By the time she arrives, I'm frantic.

'I took your letters so we could check there was nothing rude or offensive in them,' she says. 'You're on the verge of being famous. There are nutters out there. Of course I sent your letters to be opened independently. Rufus would never forgive me if I didn't.'

'So, where are they now?'

'They're being catalogued, but don't worry I'll drop them all in tomorrow morning for you to have. They're just letters, Kelly. Don't get so het up. Now, show me the desk.'

I take Elodie into Rufus's office.

'You smashed it up with this?' says Elodie, quizzically, pointing to the hefty, heavily bejewelled dagger that's lying on Rufus's chair. She notices the blood on the top of the blade.

'Ooooo ... blood.'

'Yes,' I say. 'I had to give it quite a whack. My hand slipped and I cut my fingers.'

'This is the award he received from India.'

'I know.'

'It's priceless,' she continues.

'I realise that.'

'It shouldn't even be in here. It should be in the safe under the house.'

How the hell does she know there's a safe under the house? Rufus said that no one knew about that.

'I wasn't thinking and I grabbed it and used it to ram open the drawer,' I try to explain.

'Well, was that wise?'

Der! Wise ... fucking wise? No of course it wasn't wise.

'It doesn't matter,' she says dismissively. 'Tell me what was in there?' Her limited interest in my welfare is now overruled by her fascination with what secrets I may have uncovered.

'There was nothing in there,' I say almost apologetically.

'Men are always cheating on women. They are: that's what they do. The fact that you can't prove it is your fault. There are things to find, Kelly; why haven't you found them?'

'Elodie,' I say, my exasperation showing through. I can be as paranoid as the next woman but, for Christ's sake, this is getting ridiculous. 'Let's just stop this now. I know there's nothing to worry about. Everything's fine. I just need to get on with my life and stop worrying. I need to stop taking these pills and get myself thinking rationally for a change.'

'Stop the diet pills? Are you insane?' she cries. 'Are you?' She grabs me by the shoulders and shakes me. 'You have to keep taking the pills. You have to. Don't let me down. Don't make me look a fool.'

What's wrong with her? It's like she's taken leave of her senses.

'It's time for you to go,' I try.

'You called me and I came,'

How I wish the girls were here now. They'd be encouraging me, reassuring me, helping me and distracting me. They'd have troubles of their own that they wanted to share. I'd help them and our friendship would build on our sharing and helping. God, but life's so different with these women I've met through Rufus, or certainly with Elodie it is.

'Fine,' she says. 'I'm going. You are no friend. Stay fat if that's what you want. Look frumpy. I can do nothing else.'

Elodie storms out, slamming doors and barging past the staff in the corridors. As the front door shuts behind her I collapse into Rufus's armchair and utter an almighty sigh of relief. Outside I hear running across the gravel and see Rosemary running out to her.

I pick up the phone straight away and call Sophie's mobile but it's no good. There's no answer. There never is. It doesn't even go to her answerphone, it just rings and rings. I feel tears start to run down my face. I'm not normally so pathetic but right now I feel awful. These pills. My God, they're horrible.

OK, sharpen up, Kelly. I go onto Rufus's computer and call up the name of a local carpenter, hitting the 'contact us now' button and summoning him to the house as soon as possible.

It's clearly wholly inappropriate to invite a bloody carpenter whom I know nothing about into the private home of one of the world's richest and most famous actors. But the fact that I have a desk smashed to pieces and in desperate need of fixing before Rufus comes back tomorrow night has assumed a far greater importance in my mind than home security.

It turns out the carpenter can't come till the following morning ... the day of Rufus's return.

'If I pay you double, can you come first thing?' I ask, plaintively.

'Not till I've finished a job in Putney.'

It's midday, after another sleepless night, and the carpenter has just turned up. He's quite handsome actually, in a rugged and dishevelled sort of way – just the type I'd have gone for before Rufus came wafting into my life. He's in the office, having taken in the undeniable magnificence of the place while trying to look cool, calm and relaxed, as if he really hasn't noticed its splendour. He's clearly awe–struck. I guess I forget just how lucky I am to live in a place like this. I tend to think of it as a prison these days; what with the paparazzi keeping me locked inside, and my friends no longer wanting to see me, and me not being able to hold down the most basic of jobs (I'm not bitter at all; hell no, not bitter in the least).

'I had a bit of an accident with this ...' I tell the carpenter. His name's Colin. Colin the Carpenter. That's nice. I always have a particular fondness for people whose names and job titles combine to make them sound like characters from Noddy.

I indicate the desk drawer and Colin peers inside.

'It looks OK to me,' he says.

'No, inside the drawer,' I explain. 'There's a little drawer in the main one that's all splintered. You'll have to look right inside the drawer to see it.'

He peers in and sees the damage. 'No problem,' he says. 'I'll have it fixed in no time.'

Thank God.

'It needs to look the same,' I plead. 'You know, as if no damage has been done.'

'I'll do my best,' he says, looking up at me. He sees my worried face. 'Is everything OK?' he asks, warmly. 'You seem agitated.'

'No, I'm fine. As long as I can get this drawer mended, everything will be fine.'

'Good,' he says. 'Only I wondered, because of the woman waiting in the car outside. She looked angry.'

'What woman?'

The carpenter has pulled the drawer out and is matching slivers of wood to it as we speak.

'She's outside. Just sitting there. Take a look.'

I peer through the window, and see Elodie in the back of the car, with Henry at the wheel. She's staring ahead, motionless, and he's looking down at the steering wheel as if he doesn't know quite what to do. What the hell does she want now?

'It's nothing,' I tell my carpenter friend. He's pulled out the drawer completely and is fashioning a new one out of matching wood.

'I'll call you when I've finished,' he says. 'There's no need for you to sit here if you don't want to.'

I hear the doorbell ringing in the distance and know that it will be Elodie. Perhaps she saw me looking at her through the window? Perhaps she's decided to return my letters to me?

The carpenter is sanding, sawing and slicing through wood and looks for all the world like a decent, honourable man – grafting away before us. I'm sure he's perfectly trust-worthy, so I leave him to it as I head off to answer the door.

'Just call me if you need me,' I say.

I hear the shuffle of Pamela's sensible working shoes as the housekeeper heads for the door. I know that if she answers, Elodie will barge past her and be in the house before I can stop her.

'I'll get it,' I say, skipping down the stairs, past Pam, as if I have not a care in the world. I swing open the door and come face to face with Elodie.

'You are still taking the diet pills, aren't you?' she says, looking me up and down once again. The deeply shameful thing is that I am still taking them. I'm kind of hell–bent on losing weight because somewhere deep within me I'm convinced that this will make me more attractive to Rufus. I know that this is just nonsense I've absorbed from Elodie, and the reality is that Rufus has told me time and again that he likes me curvy, but it's difficult to shift thoughts like that from your mind once they're lodged there, especially when you're in the sort of vulnerable position that I was in when I first came staggering and stumbling into this celebrity world. I also think there's a part of me that wants Elodie's approval, which angers me. Why do I want her bloody approval? I don't need her approval.

'You can't come in. I'm busy,' I say. Then I add: 'Sorry,' because I hate having rows like this.

'What do you mean, I can't come in?' she says. 'I have your letters. Your precious letters that you were so desperate for. Anyway, it's not your house. I'll come in if I want to come in. It's Rufus's house and I'm always welcome here. Rosemary will let me in. You're the outsider here, you're the one who doesn't fit in, not me.'

'What? This is my home, Elodie.'

I say goodbye and shut the door. I don't need any more

abuse from anyone, certainly not from Elodie. I don't think I've ever done anything quite as bold in my whole life before, as shutting the door in someone's face. I'm standing there in a state of semi shock when there's an almighty clattering on the door: fists banging, a voice shouting and even kicking. I hear the staff behind me rush to see what's going on, and I realise I can't leave her out there. I open the door and Elodie reaches in and grabs my hair, dragging me outside by it, pulling me so fast that I trip over the step and fall to my knees on the gravel.

'You bitch!' she cries, kicking me in the side of my thigh. 'You absolute evil bitch.'

'Get off me, get off me.'

I look up, and Henry is attempting to pull Elodie away as she continues to lash out at me and at the ageing driver.

'You have Rufus. I hate you. Why is he going out with you? You have no style, no panache. You're not thin. Just leave him. Let me have him. It would make my mother so happy' she cries.

'Stop it,' I say to her, as I hold my hair protectively against any further assaults.

'I lost Jon, and now I've lost Rufus,' she wails. 'I've tried to be your friend.'

'And I have been your friend,' I retort. 'But you're not treating me like good friends treat one another.'

'Oh what? Like these friends?' cries Elodie, tipping a pile of letters onto the gravel. All of them are penned in the familiar writing of Sophie and Mandy.

'Where have these come from?' I ask.

'Letters come every day,' she responds dismissively, with a shrug of her skinny, little shoulders. 'Every day these girls are writing or turning up at the gates and demanding to be let in to see you. Always calling, writing and turning up. Do they not realise you've moved on?'

Oh shit. All this time I thought the girls had forgotten about me and weren't bothered about staying in touch, and they were trying to reach me.

As I scramble around on the ground for the letters, Henry bundles Elodie into the car. She looks back at me, tears staining her face, her hair flying everywhere. She looks scared and vulnerable and for the first time I notice that she's actually very pretty beneath her armour.

'You've got everything I want,' she shouts, as Henry starts up the engine. 'I wish someone loved me. I wish Jon were here. He died two years ago today. Two years ...' She screams through the open window as the car sets off on its way, 'I wish Jon were here.'

Pamela comes running out across the gravel and helps me to my feet.

'Are you OK?' she asks kindly. 'You aren't hurt, are you? Here, let me help you. Gosh after all you've done for that woman, she does this to you. You were so kind to her when everyone else refused to talk to her. Honestly.'

She helps me inside as the carpenter comes jogging down the stairs.

'Everything all right?' he asks. 'I heard the fight.'

'Yes, fine,' I say. I've now got Colin the carpenter, Pamela and two of the security guys who have arrived on the scene to check everything's OK, standing round me.

'I'm fine, honestly. Just fine,' I keep reiterating.

'Where's she gone now?' the security guards ask, adding: 'Shall we go after her?'

'Everything's fine,' I reiterate. I don't want to make a big fuss out of this, and sending the security guards after her or phoning the police, as Pamela suggests, won't help at all. In my mind I keep seeing Elodie's desperately sad and lonely face, the smudged make-up and the cries for help. I know that I don't want Elodie here anymore and, once Henry gets back, I'll tell him that he mustn't drive her around from now on. It's not that I wish her any harm but I think she needs more help than I can give her. Professional help, perhaps? Once things have calmed down, and I get the opportunity to talk to her rationally, I'll try to persuade her to talk to someone who can help.

'Right then, I'm done,' says the carpenter. I've been so busy watching the space from which the car departed five minutes ago that I'd forgotten he was there at all.

'Sorry. I was miles away,' I say.

'I just wanted to say that it's all fixed. No one will ever know it's been touched. Would you like to come and check?'

You know I really can't be arsed. I'm just sick of all this now. I can see Pamela looking at me quizzically.

'Don't worry, I'm sure it's perfect,' I tell him, and I smile at Pamela to tell her that everything's OK.

'Just one thing. This was inside it …' he says, and he hands me a small key and a bracelet with two large diamond covered stars on it. The bracelet is made of thick platinum but it's tiny; it would only fit round the smallest of wrists. There's no doubt that this bracelet was made to match Elodie's necklace. Fucking hell.

'Shall I invoice you for the work?' says the carpenter.

'Yes,' I mutter, as we shake hands. In my left hand I'm holding the bracelet and the small key.

'It's like paradise here,' says the carpenter as he steps out of the front door.

'Sure is,' I say, but, you know, I'm not so sure.

CHAPTER 20: LETTERS FROM THE GIRLS

✤

I feel like an absolute shit. It's official. The letters from the girls are unbelievably warm and loving. I've spent hours just reading and rereading them, bursting into tears time and again as I'm reminded of what utterly fantastic friends I have. Christ. They say that they understand how busy I must be, but that they really hope we can all stay mates because they miss me so much. Bloody hell. If only they knew how much I'd missed them these past few weeks; I've been craving their company every day.

I desperately want to talk to them, but I still can't get hold of them. Sophie's mobile is never on, the home phone line just rings out, and I know they're both off work this afternoon because it's Thursday, so there's no point in leaving messages there.

As I pace around the sitting room, thinking about what to do next, there's a loud bang outside forcing my knees to buckle beneath me in fear. I peer out of the window to see what the sound is. Thank God. It's just Henry, back from dropping Elodie off. I smile at him, grinning from ear to ear and forcing him to look at me quizzically.

'Thank God it's you,' I explain. 'I thought it might be Elodie, back to beat me up.'

'No, she won't be back,' he reassures me, explaining that he took her to the Royal Institute of Fashion. I know Elodie loves that place. It's where she first bumped into Jon many years ago, and where she goes to seek solace and to feel close to him whenever she's feeling low.

With a bit of luck, she'll calm down after a few hours in there, and leave me alone.

'She seemed more relaxed when we got there,' confirms Henry. 'It's like she was almost in a trance when she drifted out of the car and into the building.'

'Well, thanks for taking her, Henry.'

'You might be the only person in the world who ever says thank you to the staff here you know. We've all become very fond of you.'

'Thanks, Henry, that means a lot to me,' I say. Then I give him the news that I notice is very gratefully received; he won't be driving Elodie around anymore. 'I need you to do me a favour though,' I say, and he smiles and cocks his hat.

'That's what I'm here for, ma'am.'

'I need to go back to my old flat in Twickenham to see the girls. Do you remember where the flat is?'

'Of course I do.'

It's funny when we stop outside the old flat. Life's changed so much since I was last here. I'm all dressed up in a gorgeous ruby red dress, fabulous gold earrings and bangles. I need to be dressed up so Henry can take me straight to the airport to meet Rufus afterwards, but I'm worried that the way I'm dressed is almost a barrier, a hurdle between my old life and my new one. I hope the girls don't think I've dressed up on purpose, just to make them look bad by comparison.

Henry pulls up outside and I ask him whether he'll come and collect me around 7.30 pm to take me to the airport.

'So, you won't need me before then?' he asks.

'Nope.'

'And Elodie can't use me.'

'Nope.'

'And Rufus is abroad.'

'He is,' I say.

'How nice,' says Henry with a grin. 'Then I'll go and spend a few hours on my allotment.'

I must remember to introduce Henry to Frank from Hampton Court. They'd get on very well ... both loonies when it comes to gardening

I walk purposefully towards the door, pleased that I've allowed Rufus's faithful driver the time to tend to his cabbages. It's 4.30pm. The girls have definitely had enough time to get home from work, and surely it's too early for them to be in the pub. There's every chance that they'll be in. I'm nervous as hell.

Henry drives off as I stand at the door. I ring the bell. No response. What now? I don't like standing here on the street in case I get papped. I know that's unlikely...it's not been half as bad recently, since the photographers have realised that Rufus is out of the country so they won't manage to get a snap of us together.

I wander around with my head down, hoping to go unnoticed but aware that I really stand out in my bright red dress. I go for a wander into a couple of the pubs they might have popped into, but there's no sign of them, so I go to a small café and get myself a coffee and settle into a corner table to drink it.

'Kelly?' I look up to see Dave, the guy from Pilates, standing there.

'Oh. Hi. How are you?'

'I'm fine. You look amazing. Absolutely unbelievable. Like a movie star.'

'Thanks.'

'You haven't been at Pilates recently.'

'No, I've been busy. Look, excuse me. I have to go.'

I don't want to make small talk at the moment, so I head back onto the street and cross over to the flat and knock on the door again. There's no answer. Dave has followed me, so I keep walking, and when a black cab pulls up, I flag it down. There's only one place I can think of going.

'Hampton Court Palace, please,' I say, and leave Dave standing on the pavement as we pull away.

I only spend about 10 minutes at the palace before heading back, but it's enough to make me feel fresher, happier and more relaxed. This time when I ring the bell, Mandy opens the door. She grins madly when she sees me.

I take one look at her and burst into tears.

'I'm sorry, I'm sorry, I'm sorry,' I wail. 'I've been so horrible but I didn't mean to be, I couldn't get hold of you, and life's been so difficult and please, please, Mandy, please tell me we're still friends.'

'Of course,' she says, hugging me. 'Come in.'

I explain that I came earlier but there was no one in, so I went for a coffee and bumped into Dave, then headed to the Palace.

'Why didn't you call us? We'd have come back sooner.'

'I tried. Like I always try. I ring you all the time on Sophie's mobile but I never get through.'

'How weird. Are you ringing the new number?'

'What new number?'

'Sophie's got a new number,' says Mandy. 'I phoned to tell you. Elodie answered your phone, as she always does, and she said she'd pass on the message. Soph's with Tandem mobile now and she's saved a fortune.'

'Oh good,' I say vaguely. So Elodie never passed the message on. She knew how eager I was to talk to the girls.

She knew I was calling them, yet all the time she must have known that I was calling them on the wrong number. What a horrible thing to do.

'You don't look very happy,' says Mandy, and I suddenly feel more lost and confused than I ever have in my life before. I look at Mandy's warm and tender face and break down into fits of tears until I find myself sobbing into her large chest. 'I can't cope. I feel like I'm going mad. I don't know what's right and what's wrong and who's decent and who's not. And the bracelet and Elodie and I never knew you'd changed your number and I never got any of the letters and I didn't know you'd been around to see me. I feel so scared and so alone.'

'Calm down, calm down,' Mandy is saying, stroking my hair as I let the tears pour down my heavily made–up face and all over the front of her dress.

'Come in the sitting room,' she instructs, and I follow her up the flight of stairs to our little flat on the first floor. I walk into the familiar room with its cheap and tatty furniture, and all the while I'm sobbing my heart out.

'What on earth is the matter?' asks Sophie, jumping up from her cross–legged position on the floor where she's been examining bills and jotting figures onto Post–it notes. It's an activity I remember all too well. The money coming in is never enough to satisfy the demands, so we'd work out how we could shuffle money around and invariably work out that we had about £5 between us to pay the rent, the bills and all food. We'd sit a while and wonder whether there were any part–time jobs that we could get to ease the burden, contem-plate the idea of getting jobs behind the bar in the evenings then decide to worry about it some other time. Those times seem so long ago. The problems then seemed insurmount-able, but they seem tiny compared the problems I'm facing now.

169

'I can't cope,' I manage to mumble to Sophie, once she's coaxed me into a sitting position. 'I can't. I don't want to go on leading a life like this. I don't understand the rules; I don't know how to behave. It turns out I don't know anything at all. Nothing that's any use to me, in any case.'

'Leave him and come back here then,' says Sophie in that incredibly down–to–earth, cut–to–the–chase way of hers. 'Just pack your things and come home. You don't have to wear all these posh clothes or have all these absurdly over-dressed friends to be happy; they're certainly not making you happy, are they?'

'No, I guess not.'

'Are these new friends of yours making you happy?'

'No.'

'So, leave.'

'But I love Rufus.'

'Well, then, carry on being the girl who Rufus fell in love with but from back here, in your own world. Everything will be OK then. Surely.'

I'm staring at Sophie because what she's saying makes perfect sense, but I'd feel a failure if I moved out, and Rufus would hate it.

'I can't do that,' I say. 'None of this is Rufus's fault; I've just got myself into a total state since he's been away. I feel these astronomical pressures on me because of the lifestyle and the things people say and think. I don't want Rufus to be rich and famous. I want him to be a completely normal bloke from down *The Sun* so he's not surrounded by weird control-ling women, and so we can pop out for a drink like normal people do, without the world's press coming too.'

'Then you need to talk it all through with Rufus.'

'But he can't stop being an actor because I'm insecure about it all.'

'Well, he might be able to reassure you; perhaps in future he'll think about taking you with him when he goes away.'

'I think it's deeper than that. I think I'm just not cut out for this,' I say. 'I need Rufus to stop being a film star and then the two of us can run away together and live in a forest or something where no one will bother us, the papers will leave us alone, and no one will care where I got my clothes from or which parties I want to go to. I love Rufus; I just can't handle all the crap that goes with being with him. It's horrible.'

'What crap is this then?'

Oh God, here we go. I know that if they're going to help me, I have to be honest with them, and tell them how horrible it all feels sometimes … so I do. I explain all about the terrible drinks parties where Elodie makes me get all dressed up and everyone's bitchy about her. I try to explain the unbelievably obsessive need to be slim and how everyone seems to judge everyone else on the way they look and what they're wearing. I explain again about the paparazzi. 'I know it sounds like I'm being silly, but I promise you until you've been through it, you have no idea how absolutely terrifying it is to have the papers reporting on your every move, especially family and personal stuff from your ex–boyfriends and making digs at you, and writing about things they shouldn't know about, so you've no idea who's spoken to them and you're terrified about what will appear next and who you can talk to and trust and … I don't know – it ends up just completely undermining you. I have to be honest there were times when I wondered whether you would end up selling stories. It seemed like everyone else did. And Rose the housekeeper is just horrible. She doesn't like me at all.'

'Not everyone,' says Sophie miserably. 'We'd never do that to you. You've got lots of friends, Kelly. Lots of people think the world of you and would never turn on you. Stop focusing on those that have.'

She's right, but it's hard to get a perspective on the world when you're bloody cooped up in a massive house looking at the outside world through the eyes of the press. 'It's just that I never go out now unless it's to a pre–arranged night with the people on the Hill,' I try to explain to her. 'I feel I can sort of trust them because they understand what it's like being in this little glass–walled world, but it is hard being at home all the time; it makes me more and more depressed. Especially with the diet pills. It's horrible.'

Sophie and Mandy are staring at me with their eyes so wide open they look like a couple of frogs in the early stages of going through a lawn mower.

'Diet pills?' Sophie eventually asks. 'What bloody diet pills?'

I reach into my bag and pull out the small bottle of Vanitas.

Sophie and Mandy both mutter the name as if it means something to them.

'I've read about those,' says Sophie. 'They're bloody lethal. Bloody hell. There was a big thing in the Mail about people getting addicted to them and people have died taking them. You know they're illegal in this country because of the trouble they cause, don't you?'

'Are they?'

'God, Kell, where did you get them from?' asks Mandy, full of concern.

'Elodie gave them to me.'

'What a fucking witch,' says Sophie. 'Does she know how dangerous they are?'

'I don't know, but they are helping me to lose weight.'

'You don't need to lose weight,' they both say.

'Kelly, you look worse now than before you started taking them; can't you see that? You look tired and pale and, yes, about a stone lighter and dressed in a load of fancy clothes.

That red dress really suits you, but you're not the pretty, vibrant young thing that you were when you left this flat.'

Sophie takes the diet pills and walks out of the room.

'Where are you going?' I call after her. Then I hear the toilet flush and I know what she's done.

If I'm honest, I feel a pang of relief. I'm sure I would have just kept taking those pills yet I know this feeling of helplessness brought on by lack of sleep and the depressive qualities of the pills is bringing me down.

'You know you're going to have to talk to Rufus about all this, don't you?'

'Mmm,' I say, without real conviction.

'You are, Kelly. You can't bottle everything up.'

'I don't bottle things up. I told Elodie how I feel about things.'

'Great, cos she's really going to help you … the crazy lady.'

'She's OK,' I say, not entirely convincingly. 'Well, maybe a little mad, but I'm sure her heart's in the right place.'

'Yeah, in her expensive Gucci wallet,' snorts Sophie.

'To be honest, Kell, she does sound pretty crazy when she answers the phone, and refuses to allow us to talk to you. And the mad housekeeper wouldn't let us into the house when we came to visit, you know,' Mandy chips in.

'I didn't know about any of that until today,' I say. 'I didn't know you'd been sending letters or anything. I'm sorry, Mand. I thought the two of you were pissed off with me and weren't answering my calls.'

'I told you she wouldn't know anything about it,' says Mandy, loyally, looking over at Sophie.

'We've been calling non-stop,' says Sophie. 'But, like we said, Elodie answers and says you're not available. We assumed you didn't want to talk to us. We thought you were too busy with your flash new friends.'

'Why didn't you just ring the mobile?'

'That's what we were ringing,' says Sophie. 'It's the only number we've got. You said you'd text us your home number but it never came through. We must have rung that mobile about 550 million times. When you missed our lunch then bumped into us in Richmond and we had that horrible argument, I was ringing you constantly the next day.'

'I don't understand. Try it now.'

Sophie dials my number and hands me her mobile. The phone rings and goes to Elodie's answerphone. What?

I look up at the girls. They are looking as confused as I feel.

'Elodie, it's Kelly here,' I say. 'Can you give me a call back straight away? I'm completely bloody confused about this … why are all my calls diverting to your phone? Why are you doing this? These are my friends. You've stopped them from calling me even though you knew I was desperate to talk to them. Fucking hell, Elodie, this is just ridiculous. I'm really pissed off.'

The doorbell rings in the distance, somewhere beyond the anger releasing itself from its pent–up position in every fibre of my body. Mandy opens the door and I hear galloping up the stairs. 'We really should be heading towards the airport in about fifteen minutes. I'll be waiting in the car for you.'

'Thanks.'

Henry walks downstairs and I sit back down on the sofa.

'There's something else,' I say cautiously.

'Oh God,' says Sophie, with prescience. 'What on earth's coming now?'

'Well, I went through all of Rufus's drawers and cupboards and boxes and files and personal stuff to check if there were any signs he was having an affair. You know – doing due diligence.'

'Doing what?'

'Due diligence.'

'Isn't that what you do if you're going to buy a company or something?'

'Yes, but it's essential for a girl to do it if she's about to commit herself to a guy. The truth is that you have to be sure what you're getting yourself into.'

'Fuck me, Kelly. What have you turned into?'

'Elodie said that it's …'

'Elodie? There's a surprise.'

I accept that Elodie's name does crop up a great deal in connection to everything bad that's been happening in my life.

'Anyway, what did you find when you were doing this 'due diligence'?'

I pull out the beautiful bracelet.

'Shit! That must have cost a fortune!'

The girls start ahhing and cooing over the dazzling diamond stars.

'Amazing!' they are saying, while stroking it as if it were a fluffy new-born kitten.

'He probably bought it for you,' says Mandy. 'He probably hid it away and was planning to give it to you when he gets back tonight.'

'But it matches a necklace that Elodie wears all the time. I can't help it – I'm convinced he's bought it for her.'

'No way!' they both howl. 'Why would he be interested in that harridan?'

'Look,' says Sophie, taking my hands, 'there's one thing I'm absolutely sure of: he loves you. I'm convinced of that.'

'So, why's he being so secretive about the fact that he's starring in a new film alongside his glamorous ex– girl-friend? When I ask him on the phone, he says that she's not his ex.'

'Who? Elodie?'

'No Cindy Kearney, the girl he's starring alongside in the film.'

'She's not his ex-girlfriend. We Googled her straight away, didn't we, Mand? We wanted to know all about her.'

'Yes, she is. They were madly in love and they just kept it from the press because they didn't want the press to intrude on their love story.'

'Who said this?'

'Elod ...'

'Fucking hell, Kelly. Elodie is a nightmare. Why couldn't you see that? I think she wanted you to feel horrible and vulnerable. She tried to weaken you as much as possible.'

'Yep, so I'm starting to realise,' I say. I don't know why I didn't google the woman's background to find out for myself. I was so fixated on googling pictures of the two of them together that I never thought of that.

The rain pounds away at the window as my two friends dispense sharp splinters of wit to burst the bubble of gloom and depression settling around me. I know it's time to go to the airport and I know that Henry is too polite to keep knocking, so he'll be sitting downstairs, getting all worried about whether we'll be on time. I reach over for my bag and hug the girls goodbye, promising them that I'll call my phone operator and get my mobile calls and texts sent to the right phone. I take Sophie's new number and promise I'll text to say that Rufus is safely home.

'Can I leave you some money to help out for a while?' I ask. 'Pleeeaassse. I remember how tough it always was, and I've got loads of money now. Please let me help.'

'No, Kell. We're fine,' says Sophie, but I look down at the Post-it notes, then up into her face. 'This is me you're talking to.'

I leave them £200 plus an extra £20 and ask them whether they'll go out and buy me the beautiful dove- grey dress that they bought me as a leaving present with the £20. I really loved that dress but Elodie threw it away. It's time for me to start doing and wearing what I want to instead of pandering to the increasingly bizarre wishes of a mad French fashion stylist with trouble seeping out of every perfect pore.

It's lovely and warm and snug in the car, and Henry's his usual doting self, checking whether the temperature's right, whether I want the radio on or whether I'd prefer a CD. 'Can we talk instead?' I ask him, and I can see the raise of his eyebrows. It might be the most peculiar request ever made of him.

'Do you know Elodie very well?' I venture, and I see the eyebrows rise again. I haven't known Henry long, but I think I have the answer to any question I might ever ask about Elodie, wrapped up right there in those eyebrows, lifting up towards his hairline.

'I wouldn't say I know her well,' he says.

'Would you say that Rufus knows her well?' I try.

'No,' he says, without hesitation. 'I wouldn't think so.'

Henry's too bloody discreet for words. Perfect quality in a member of staff, of course, but makes him utterly useless for gossiping with. Instead of grilling the old man any further, I suggest some music, and call the phone company to find out how on earth I rejig the phone setup so that my phone calls come to me instead of drifting off to a phone manned by a crazy fashionista. Turns out it's remarkably easy to do, which is alarming. You just press a series of buttons on someone's phone and all their calls come to you. Bloody hell. Who knew?

'Can I interrupt?' asks Henry, suddenly, cutting through the gentle sound of violins wafting through the car.

'Sure.'

'If you want to know anything about Elodie, try Dr Bronks–Harrison. I think she knows her well.'

'Thanks,' I say, and since Henry never says anything without considering the consequences and ramifications, and utters nothing without first debating the appropriateness of speaking out, I realise that Isabella must know plenty about Elodie and have a view that I should probably hear. Certainly, it would be worth me calling to find out.

'Hi, Isabella, it's Kelly Monsoon,' I say sheepishly. I'm not very good on the phone and I hate the idea of disturbing her when she's probably just got back from work. 'Are you OK to talk? I mean, I'm not interrupting anything, am I?'

'Don't be silly; it's lovely to hear from you,' says Isabella. 'Isn't Rufus back tonight?'

'Yes. I'm just on my way to the airport now,' I say. 'Can I ask you something?'

'Go ahead.'

'What do you think of Elodie?'

'Aaahhhhh,' says Isabella. 'I think it's obvious to everyone what I think of Elodie. I think she's bad news. I think she's bitter and twisted and there are times when I want to kill her. What do you think of her?'

'I thought she was a friend, but I'm feeling used,' I say. It's a relief to talk to someone like Isabella about it. 'I've just found out she's been alienating all my friends and making me rely on her more and more. And you know you asked me how I'd lost so much weight so quickly? Well, you were right; I have been taking diet pills. Elodie gave them to me and told me they were harmless, but they've been making me feel just awful. Really awful.'

I burst into tears as I'm talking to her; I can't help it. I feel all this emotion come tumbling out again.

'OK. Don't take any more of those pills, and don't see Elodie again.'

'I won't,' I say. 'My friends took the pills off me and threw them down the toilet, so I can't take any more of them, and

Elodie and I had a row and I threw her out of the house, so I won't be seeing her again. Sorry, I shouldn't be saying anything but ...'

'Of course you should be saying something. I'm very glad you called. I feel terrible that you didn't tell me sooner as perhaps I could have helped. I should have come round to check you were all right, but you seemed to be out and about going to parties all the time with Elodie. When I saw you at our little 'wine-tasting' you were on great form, and when you didn't return my calls afterwards, I assumed that you were busy.'

'No, that was Elodie. She had my phone calls diverted to her phone so I never knew people were calling me. I would definitely have called you back. I always call people back.'

'I can't believe she did that. What an absolute bitch. Have you managed to talk to Rufus about all this while he's been away?'

'I've spoken to Rufus,' I say. 'But I haven't told him about Elodie diverting my calls because I've only just found out. Something's just occurred to me. He was texting me every day from LA, but I never received the texts. I thought it was something to do with texts not coming through properly from LA, but that's it, isn't it? It was Elodie's fault; that's why they didn't come through. Christ.'

'How have you managed to talk to him at all, if all your calls are diverted to Elodie's phone?'

'He always calls on the home phone,' I explain. 'He thinks it's safer not to use mobiles unless it's absolutely urgent. Apparently, a tabloid journalist once managed to listen in on his mobile and he's never trusted them all that much since.'

'Sounds like he's right,' says Isabella. 'I wish I'd called you at home.'

'Why would Elodie do this?' I ask in dismay. 'Why would she want me to feel so bad?'

'Because she's a very sad woman who's desperate because her career is on the slide and she's got nothing else in her life except for the distorted memory of Jon - a boyfriend who died years ago. Her ex made her, and she knows it. She'll never get back the life she had with him, and she takes it out on everyone she meets who's in any way happy. Also - she probably fancies Rufus a bit. At least, her mum always thought they ought to be together.'

'Her mum? She never spoke about her family to me. I assumed that her parents had died or something.'

'Her mum works in the house. Rose. Rather sinister-looking woman.'

'Oh My God. Rose? Rose has been horrible to me from the start. I didn't realise that was her mum. Bloody hell.'

'She never tells anyone, but she came in for surgery and we needed to know for personal reasons so she told us. I'm not sure that Rufus even knows. They seem to have an odd relationship.'

'Christ, yes. That's so strange.'

'Besides her mum she has no close friends ... except you and Rufus and I think he just tolerates her because he's too kind not to.'

'Yes,' I say weakly.

'Look, I better go, but text me to say that Rufus is back safely,' she says. 'And make sure you tell him everything, or I'll be round to tell him myself.'

'OK?' asks Henry.

'Fine,' I reply, thinking that everyone seems to have worked out that Elodie is a witch except for me. 'I've been a complete bloody fool. I could kill her. Sorry, Henry, but I could.'

'No problem, ma'am,' he says and we roll on through the traffic, heading for Heathrow.

CHAPTER 21: RUFUS RETURNS

*H*ow my moods seem to swing these days. A few hours ago I was in tears - terrified that I was going mad, worried about my friendships and smashing into Rufus's desk to check he wasn't cheating on me. Now I'm wrapped up in his arms and have never felt happier.

'So, what was it like when I was away. Did you have a good time?' he asks. I hadn't wanted to burden him with the problems I'd faced in his absence as soon as he touched down on British soil, so have told him nothing of the fight with Elodie or the issue with her taking my letters, and the bizarreness of my phone redirecting to hers. He has to know though.

'It was horrible,' I say.

'Oh, I thought you'd have the girls round to the house and be partying non-stop.'

'No, nothing like that. It was quite a depressing time. Elodie kept hinting that you were off with all these other women, and I just became paranoid about it all. I'm sorry, Rufus. I know Elodie is a friend of yours, but we really fell out. She gave me these diet pills because she said you wouldn't love me if I didn't lose weight, and even though I know that's not true, I still took them and they made me feel horrible. Anyway, I ended up having a huge row with her and throwing her out of the house. I haven't seen her since, but I worked out that she diverted all my mobile phone calls and texts to her phone. It's been horrible. I mean – she was nice to me sometimes and took me shopping and everything, but then I ended up feeling guilty about spending your money, so I took most of the clothes back and that made her cross.'

'OK,' he says gently, stroking my hair and pulling me close to him. 'Tell me all about it, but promise me you'll never worry about spending money. We have lots of it, and I want you to enjoy it. In fact, I'm going to put some into an account for you tomorrow, for you to spend however you want. Now, tell me everything ...'

It's 3 am in the morning before we stop talking. Rufus listens to everything I say. He really listens, and for the first time I think he properly understands how different our lives were, and how difficult this has been. I keep bursting into tears and I know I'm still on an emotional roller coaster thanks to the drugs. They've been thrown away, but I imagine they'll be in my system for a while yet.

'Can we go to the Rose Garden tomorrow?' I ask Rufus. 'I went a lot while you were away and I love it.'

'You haven't told anyone that's where we love to go have you?'

'No of course not.'

'We'll go tomorrow, angel, but let's try to keep it a complete secret.;

'OK,'I say.

Then he does something really strange. He gets out of bed and stands on the carpet next to me in all his naked glory. Even after months of being with him, the sheer bloody beauty of his body drives me nuts sometimes. As I'm staring at his thighs rather unashamedly, he drops onto his knees next to the bed, his eyes not leaving mine.

'It's been a difficult few weeks for you, hasn't it?'

'Yes. It hasn't been too much fun.'

'I hate the fact that you've been so miserable. I love you,' he says.

'I love you too.'

'How can I prove to you how much I love you?'

'You don't have to prove anything,' I say.

But he seems determined to try. He looks into my eyes. 'Kelly, I love you. I'll always love you. Please will you marry me? I want you to be my wife. I want us to grow old and grey together. I want us to have children and grandchildren. Please say yes.'

'YES!' I squeal. It comes out more loudly than I'd intended, and Rufus jumps a little, if I'm honest.

'I will,' I say once more, just in case there was someone in west London who didn't hear me the first time. Then I throw myself into his arms. 'Of course I will.'

'Then you'll need this,' he says, and he opens his hand to reveal the most beautiful and enormous diamond ring I've ever seen. 'I was going to continue the theme and get you a ring with three diamonds in a row on it, but I fell in love with this one, with twenty on it,' he says.

'I've never seen anything so beautiful,' I tell him as I study the ring sitting elegantly on my finger. 'It's amazing.'

'You are amazing,' he says. 'You're super–amazing.'

'I have to tell the girls,' I say. 'They'll kill me if I don't tell them straight away. You have to let me call them.'

'But it's 3 am.'

'I'll text them then.'

'Go on then,' says Rufus indulgently. 'But then you switch your phone off. Deal?'

'Deal,' I say. 'As long as you switch yours off.'

CHAPTER 22: THE END OF ELODIE

I wake the next morning to the feel and smell of Rufus right beside me. We've been cuddled up together all night ... me and my husband–to–be. Aaaaahhhh ... my husband–to–be ... how mad does that sound? How could I ever have doubted Rufus? After he dropped off to sleep last night, I found myself thinking through everything and wondering why on earth I'd spent the time away from him so convinced he was up to no good and out to hurt me. It was Elodie of course. Every word spoken, every dark thought in my head – they were all planted there by her. I blame myself for trusting her but I'd felt so awful and isolated and bloody lost. She exploited me.

Rufus stirs next to me but doesn't wake; he just snuggles up a bit closer and pulls me to him until I can feel his chest hair tickling my nose and find myself twitching like a bunny rabbit. God, this is fabulous.

What I like most of all, and truly the only thing I'm really enjoying about not working, is that we get up when we are ready to get up, without that horrible alarm clock thing. I also love the fact that it's so warm in the house, not like in my old flat where I'd leap out of bed and run to the bathroom, hoping not to catch pneumonia on the way, then hurl myself into the shower which was always too cold, trying to wash quickly and without breathing in. Somehow the cold lost its awful impact if you held your breath. I sometimes think that the ultimate measure of how much my life has changed, and how far up the social scale I've clambered since meeting Rufus, is illustrated no more dazzlingly than in the comparative warmths of the homes.

'Mmmm,' Rufus sighs as he runs his hands down my back and kisses me on my forehead. 'Come here, Mrs George.'

'Ooooo ... OK,' I say, kissing him back. 'Mrs George huh? And what if I decide to keep my own name? Will the wedding be off?'

'Keep your own name?' he says in mock horror. 'Well, if you're going to do that, then I guess I'd better change mine. I'll have to be called Rufus Monsoon; how do you think that would go down with the world's greatest film directors?'

He tickles me while he's joking about our names until I can't stand it anymore and I'm choking and crying with laughter. 'Stop,' I cry. 'OK, OK, I'll change my name to bloody Kelly George, just please stop the tickling.'

We laugh and joke about the name possibilities. 'Kelly Monsoon George? Kelly George Monsoon? Kelly Rufus George Monsoon?'

'Have you told your mum?' asks Rufus, and I realise I haven't. I didn't want to call at 3 am when I texted the girls, mum would worry if her phone made a noise and woke her up and 3am, and she's not much of a texter.

She's a mum so she has a mobile phone that is never switched on, always needs charging, and certainly won't reduce itself to doing anything as technical as texting. I don't know why she has it.

I reach over and switch on my newly fixed phone to find

about twenty missed calls. 'Bloody hell,' I say, turning to Rufus. 'I've got missed calls from just about everyone I've ever met!' There are messages waiting on the phone too, but I decide to leave them until I've spoken to Mum. She answers immediately.

'I knew it would be you,' she says. 'I've heard, I can't believe it. Are you OK?'

'Yes, never better,' I say. 'How on earth did you hear?'

'It's been on the news all morning.'

Oh God. How on earth have the news channels found out already? Is this room being bugged or something? No wonder everyone's been trying to get hold of me. I turn to Rufus and shrug my shoulders, raising my eyebrows somewhere up into my hairline.

'So, what do you think then, mum? It's good news, isn't it?'

Rufus shakes his head. He's clearly as baffled as I am by how she could possibly know already.

'It's not good news at all,' says mum. 'I thought she was a friend.'

'What do you mean. I'm confused. What friend? The man I'm in love with has proposed.'

'Proposed?' says Mum. 'What do you mean? Why does no one tell me anything?'

'That's what I'm ringing to tell you; Rufus proposed last night. So, it wasn't on the news?'

'No. Why would it be on the news?'

'Oh, it doesn't matter, Mum. Look, I just wanted to let you know that I'm getting married ... to Rufus ... how cool is that?'

'That's brilliant, love,' she says. 'I think we all need a bit of good news at the moment, don't we?'

'Yes,' I say rather vaguely. I'm not sure why particularly at the moment. Good news is worth having any time, isn't it?

'Now then,' Mum says, and I can hear her scrabbling around. 'OK. Things to do ... shall I book the church, or will you? That community centre gets booked up. Marian's daughter was trying to hold her reception there but had no luck at all. I'll get on to them straight away. What date did you want to do, love? Try and avoid the end of April and the beginning of May because your father likes to help out with the gardening down on the seafront then and he'd hate to miss it.'

'Mum, Mum,' I try to interrupt. The idea of the world's press descending on the Hastings Community Centre, and the most famous people on the planet flying in from New York for it, leaves me trembling.

'We haven't set a date yet, and I don't know where it's going to be. As soon as I know, I'll let you know.'

'Winter or summer?'

'Sorry?'

'The wedding: winter or summer? I need to get my hats out and work out which one's going to work. I can't wear brown in summer or pale pink in winter can I, silly?'

'Um. Summer,' I say.

'Oh,' says Mum. 'I look much better in autumnal shades. I'm a bit old for pastels.'

'OK, winter,' I say.

'Great. Right. Well I'll go down to the community centre just in case and see what the bookings are like for winter.'

'OK, Mum.'

As I put the phone down to my mother, and begin to regale Rufus with the mad conversation I've just endured, there's a gentle tap on the door.

'What is it?' asks Rufus. 'Mrs George and I are busy.'

'Terribly sorry to interrupt, sir.' David's distinctive old voice comes floating under the bedroom door. It has an almost ghostly feel to it. 'There are some people at the door. They've come to see Ms Monsoon.'

'There's no Ms Monsoon here,' says Rufus, laughing as he half smothers me with the pillow. 'She's changed her name. Tell them to go away.'

'I really am sorry to interrupt, sir,' says David, coughing gently as if to illustrate how terribly inconvenient he is finding all of this. 'Only it's the police.'

'For me?'

'Don't worry,' says Rufus, smiling and giving me a hug. 'You haven't got drugs in your handbag, have you?'

'Of course not.'

'Good. Neither have I, so we have nothing to worry about.'

'Elodie gave me those drugs before though, to help me lose weight. It couldn't be those, could it?'

'No. Don't be daft,' he says. 'It'll be something to do with security. We have to deal with the local police a fair bit.'

'Oh,' I say. 'But why would they want to see me?'

'Let's go find out,' says Rufus, kissing me on the forehead and leaping out of bed.

It turns out it isn't someone checking on our security downstairs, but two stern–looking police officers, pacing up and down the sitting room floor as if they were keeping guard outside a prison cell; neither is wearing a uniform. They both look solemn.

'Is there something wrong?' Rufus asks.

'Perhaps you should take a seat, sir,' says the officer.

'I'm fine,' Rufus replies, but I find myself sinking into the sofa all the same. This is about the diet pills; I just know it. What if Mandy and Sophie get in trouble because they were the ones who flushed them down the loo? Harbouring illegal drugs? Shit. I look up and see that one of the men is watching me constantly. He's very tall; a big chap with flinty blue eyes that seem to rip right through me as he stares. He doesn't stop looking at me. There's a smirk playing on his lips. He knows all about the drugs. Perhaps they had sniffer dogs at the drains outside the girls' flat? Shit.

'We're wondering whether you know anything about Elodie Elloissie,' says the smaller man, while the big guy keeps staring straight at me. I don't think he's blinked since I walked into the room.

'I know her,' I say.

'I know you do,' he replies. 'But did you know that she was found dead this morning? We believe she was murdered.'

EXCLUSIVE

By Katie Joseph Daily Post Showbiz Correspondent

ONE of the world's leading fashion stylists was found dead in the early hours of this morning.

Elodie Elloissie, 37, a Parisienne who has lived in London for most of her life is believed to have been stabbed. Her body was found by a cleaner arriving for work at the Royal Institute of Fashion in Richmond, south–west London.

Elloissie's name became synonymous with red– carpet dressing for the rich and famous when she linked up with the late fashion designer, Jon Boycott, ten years ago. They became lovers and together they designed for and styled photo shoots and magazine covers as well as working with a range of wealthy individuals and most of Hollywood's elite over a decade in the public eye.

Yesterday her styling came to an end, though, when her body was found slumped in the vestibule at the bottom of the white marble steps of the Royal Institute of Fashion. She had been stabbed through the heart. A police spokesman at Scotland Yard said that there would be a further statement today. It is expected that they will announce the launch of a murder inquiry.

The news has left residents of luxurious Richmond Hill reeling. Elodie Elloissie was a popular and sociable member of the wealthy clique and worked with some of the world's leading celebrities.

CHAPTER 23: MURDER ENQUIRY

*E*lodie dead? Dead? Stabbed through the heart? It's the most horrific thing I've ever heard. Rufus is striding around the room in a state of complete shock, while I am slumped in the chair, fighting to stop the tears and guilt. I keep thinking of that sad face looking back at me as Henry drove her away, the previously unseen vulnerability. Little did I know that I'd never see her again; that someone was waiting to stab her and end her life.

I have so many questions, and the police have so many for me.

'We think you were one of the last people to see her alive. What time was it when Elodie left that morning?

'Midday?' I say, but Christ, it's hard to remember. 'It might be worth checking with Henry.'

'How long had Elodie been here that morning?'

'What was her mood like?'

'Did she seem worried or agitated?'

I answer them all as accurately as I can, but the truth is that she was very agitated and very angry when she left and we had the most enormous row.

'Who do you think did it?' I ask, interrupting the barrage of questions being directed at me.

'We don't know yet. We're hoping that by talking to her friends and family we'll be able to build up a better picture of her life and particularly her movements yesterday. Hopefully, before too long, we'll be able to work out who had a grudge against her. Do you know of anyone who had a grudge against her?'

Most people she knew had a grudge against the woman, but I can't tell them that. I look up, see the big cop staring and look back down again. 'No,' I mutter.

'Sorry?' says the big guy. 'Didn't quite catch that.'

'No, I don't.'

'Did you have a grudge against her?' he asks.

'No,' I say, looking down at my hands. 'Of course not.'

He scribbles away in his notebook. His name is Detective Inspector Barnes; the other guy is Detective Constable Swann.

'Just a few more questions,' says the constable. It's mainly the Swann guy who questions me. The big guy just seems to stare at me and butt in every so often, wanting more information, more detail and more explanation. I know they're talking to everyone and just trying to find out what Elodie's movements were yesterday, but every time I can't answer a question properly or I stutter or stammer, I see the Barnes guy staring right through me and I feel instantly guilty.

'What time did you say she left here?' asks the big guy.

'Around 11 am, at a guess.'

'Around 11 o'clock, or exactly 11 o'clock?' he says.

Didn't I just say 'at a guess'? 'Around 11 am,' I repeat.

'How sure are you? How do you know it was 11 o'clock? You said 12 o'clock a minute ago. Was it dark or light? Did anyone else see her go? Where was she going? How did she travel there? What was the weather like?'

Once they've started, the questions come raining down on me. They get me to run through everything I did that day – from the moment I got up until I went to bed. As soon as I say something like 'then I had breakfast' they want to know what I had for breakfast and whether I washed up, and was I listening to the radio at the time? Aaaaahhhh …

The whole thing is rather complicated by the fact that I don't want to mention that I found out Elodie had been hiding my letters and that's why I called her back from her shopping trip because it seems so incredibly disrespectful to Elodie's memory.

Rufus is sitting right next to me so I can't mention the arrival of the carpenter and the fact that he saw her sitting outside in the car, and how we ended up having an argument. Rufus would go mad if he knew about that. I don't suppose it matters if I don't mention the broken drawer; it's an irrelevance. These guys aren't interested in whether I broke the drawer or not, they just want to know who killed Elodie.

'I can't remember where she said she was going, but it was Henry who took her so he'll know. You could ask him.'

'We will. You didn't mention the weather.'

'It was cold but it wasn't raining, I don't think.'

'You don't think?'

'I don't think it was raining. I don't really remember.'

'Are these questions annoying you?' asks Barnes.

'A little,' I admit. 'I just don't remember exactly what I was doing at specific times. No one looks at the clock all the time, do they?'

'But you understand that we're trying to establish specific time points in order to find Elodie's killer? You understand that, don't you? We're here to find out who killed your friend. She was your friend, wasn't she?'

'Yes.'

'Where were you at 5.30 pm yesterday?'

'I was at my friends' flat; the place where I used to live. In Twickenham.'

'Where in Twickenham?'

I give them the address, then they want a description of it, and a description of the route we took to get there. Before long they'll want compass bearings and the precise location marked out on an Ordinance Survey map. And - Oh God - I keep thinking of Elodie. Who would kill her? I mean - really? - however much of a pain she was at times - no one would actually want to kill her, surely?

'What time did you arrive there? And did you go straight in?'

'I arrived at 4.30pm and I went straight in.'

Well, I didn't go in then – I went to the Rose Garden first - but it's too complicated to say otherwise because then they'll ask me fifty million questions about what I was up to, and what I was up to is, frankly, none of their business and doesn't relate in any way to the crime they're supposed to be trying to solve so will only waste their time.

'And what did you do after that?'

'I went to the airport to meet Rufus.'

'What time?'

'At about 7 pm.'

'In a black cab?'

'No, Henry drove me.'

'And Henry drove you to your friends' flat in Twickenham.'

'Yes.'

'Now, is there anything else that you haven't told us, or anything that you think you should add before we take a statement?'

'A statement?' says Rufus. 'Why does she have to make a statement? Is she a suspect?'

'In a case like this, everyone's a suspect,' says the smaller guy. 'We need to take a statement from all witnesses at this stage in the investigation.'

'This is a murder inquiry sir,' says the big guy. 'Do you have a problem with Kelly giving a statement?'

'No,' says Rufus, standing up. 'The problem I have is with your attitude.' Then he turns to me. 'Wait here. Don't say or do anything. I'm calling my lawyers.'

Rufus comes back about five minutes later and says I'm to do nothing until a lawyer arrives. By now I'm feeling quite scared. If Rufus is insisting on his lawyer being involved, then he must think this is serious. Surely they can't think that I did it. I wish the whole bloody carpenter thing hadn't happened on the same day. I just don't want to talk about that in front of Rufus.

We're all sitting there in frosty silence when the doorbell rings and a team of four lawyers walks in. Rufus greets them and takes them off to the snug from where I can hear muffled voices. They walk back in looking quite at ease.

'It's just routine,' says Detective Swann, looking at Rufus and the two lawyers standing next to him. 'But we really do need to take a statement.'

The lawyers both nod, and my boyfriend nods. He then looks at me and I nod. I then repeat everything I said previously and sign a form. I'm sure I should be telling them about the carpenter, but how can I? I'll lose Rufus for ever if I do, and I'll end up having to tell them the carpenter's name and he'll be called in for questioning, and he'll mention the row, and that won't reflect well on

Elodie and it'll all become an impossibly complicated mess and I'll have let everyone down and yet it won't contribute in any way, shape or form to the investigation into Elodie's murder.

CHAPTER 24: IN THE NEWS

$\mathscr{B}$

'*K*atie Pound is in Richmond for London Today. What's the latest, Katie?'

Thanks, Bob. You join us live on Richmond Hill where residents this lunchtime are waking up to the news that one of their most glamorous neighbours was murdered yesterday afternoon. That's right, murdered. Police announced at a press conference this morning that they were launching an investigation after Elodie Elloissie, stylist to the stars, was found stabbed to death yesterday.

Now I should emphasise, for those who do not know this area of south-west London, that nothing like this has ever happened here before. If you look behind me, you'll be able to see the amazing houses where the likes of Mick Jagger, Rock James and Rufus George live; in these massive gated homes protected by security guards, fences and alarms. I can't go up the road to show you where Elodie lived, but if you look past the police cordon on the left, you'll see two officers guarding a door. That was Elodie's home until brutal, bloody murder cut her life short.

Now police estimate the time of death as being around 5.30 pm yesterday. They have CCTV footage of the stylist entering the Royal Institute of Fashion earlier in the day, and it is their belief that someone was lying in wait for her, clutching a knife and preparing to do the dreaded deed. Then she lay alone and dying before being found by a cleaner arriving for her morning shift some twelve hours later.

It's a terrible story and, ironically, a story not unlike the script of a Hollywood movie, the like of which so many of those who live in this part of London have starred in during their careers. If anyone saw anything that could help police, please call Detective Inspector Martyn Barnes from Scotland Yard on 08567898989; he's the man who's heading up this inquiry. I spoke to him a little earlier to find out some more about this incredible breaking news story ...'

'They're loving this,' Rufus says, as we lie on the sofa, wrapped round each other, neither of us quite able to take in the events of the morning so far. Suddenly the fact that we got engaged last night seems like a lifetime away. 'It's a media dream to have a story like this, isn't it? Glamour and murder. Perfect!'

'I'm sure they think I did it,' I say, quite out of the blue. I don't know whether I do think that, but I'm sure I must be in the frame, and the way that detective guy was looking at me ...

'No one thinks you did anything,' says Rufus, turning to face me. 'You're not capable of harming a fly, let alone killing another human being. You had a row with her. Everyone falls out with Elodie eventually. It doesn't mean you killed her. Christ, if everyone who'd ever fallen out with Elodie was in the frame for her murder, most of the women in West London would be banged up by now.'

'Very true,' I say, snuggling up closer to him. Thank God for Rufus and his common sense approach to life. 'I can't believe what happened to her, though. Have you spoken to Rosemary at all?'

'Rosemary?'

'She's Elodie's mother.'

'Really??'

'Yes. I found out from Isabella.'

'My God. I had no idea. I'd better call her. How incredibly odd for neither of them to mention it. Elodie suggested getting Rosemary in here, but I didn't realise they were related. That's crazy. And so awful for Rose. Right, let me go and call her.'

'I'm joined by Katie Joseph, showbiz correspondent of the Daily Post. Katie, you've been reporting on the inhabitants of the Hill for the past year. How do you think they'll take this news today?'

'I think they'll all be wondering who's next. Is this a serial killer? Is this a guy who's targeting the famous and wealthy?'

'A serial killer? Is there any evidence of that yet?'

'Not publicly, but my sources in the police are suggesting that this is likely to be someone who'll strike again very soon, and the conversations I've had with the Hill's most famous residents indicate that they are very, very scared here right now. The murderer is being dubbed the Hill Murderer. Like the terrible Moors Murderer of twenty years ago.'

Rufus walks back into the room behind me, as I watch the story developing momentum on television. He hasn't been able reach Rose, so joins me on the sofa.

'Do you think that's true, Rufus?'

'No way. That journalist would love nothing more than for there to be a serial killer buzzing around the place. It would keep her in stories for the rest of time. You know who she is, don't you?'

I look back at the screen where the attractive woman, madly overdressed and made–up like a clown, is continuing to talk with apparent knowledge about things she knows nothing about. 'Yep,' I say. 'That's the woman who said I'd had a boob job.'

'So, do you think she knows what she's talking about?'

'Nope.'

CHAPTER 25: ARRESTED

*I*t's 3 pm and I'm sitting here alone on the sofa with my knees tucked up under my chin, crying silently. How awful for Elodie to have been killed like that. Rufus has been trying to get hold of Rose, and has been talking to the staff about what's happened. I'm in a bit of a daze. Pamela popped in to see me and gave me a huge hug. I told her I felt guilty about throwing Elodie out, but the woman was so complicated, with such an unpleasant streak to her, that I felt I had no choice. But there was another side to her as well; a genuinely kind, warm and friendly side to her that emerged on occasions, when she thought people weren't watching.

There's a light drizzle outside as darkness begins its descent. I've switched off the television because I can't bear to hear any more murder speculation. It's alarming how the journalists will talk about Elodie and speculate about what happened to her as if she's not a real person at all. She took me under her wing and looked after me in my early days on the Hill. Now she's become an inanimate object at the centre of fevered speculation. People are building careers and establishing their credibility on the back of her still warm corpse. It's horrible.

I can't escape it though. The television is off but I can hear the radio in the kitchen which keeps going back to the 'scene of this fascinating news story'. There are apparently millions of people walking around the place 'intrigued by this story'. Good for them. I hope it's brightening up their dull lives. The trouble is, when someone who spent the previous three weeks popping by to see you is found stabbed to death, it doesn't feel like a 'fascinating' news story, it feels like a complete bloody tragedy.

'We go to the centre of Richmond now, where Sylvia Gilbert is waiting to give us the latest on this incredible story,' says the man on the radio.

When security calls to say there are two men waiting at the gate, I know straight away who it is. I know the police will want to talk to me again because I was rubbish the first time. I'd just heard about the murder and couldn't think straight.

'Take them to the sitting room,' I say to David, wanting to stay in the warmth of the snug forever.

'Are you OK?' he asks, looking at me with concern in those clear eyes of his. He may be old and craggy but his eyes remain as bright and alert as ever.

'Yes,' I say, wiping away my tears. 'If you show them in, I'll be there right away.'

I walk quietly to the sitting room, and peer through a gap in the door. The men are in there, ruddy-cheeked and looking even more stern than they did last time, if that's possible. The smaller of the two men wipes a tear from his eye. I'd like to think it's because he feels bad about interrupting me again, but I know it's got more to do with the cold stinging his eyes and nose as he walked from the car to the house.

David offers them seats and warm drinks, but when I walk into the room, I notice that neither of them is sitting. They stand in their heavy overcoats, both of them with their hands behind their backs, Prince Charles style, looking round the room. When I walk in, they walk up to me. The smaller of the men looks straight into my eyes.

'You know how serious this is, don't you?' he asks.

'Yes,' I reply.

'You must be aware that we have talked to lots of people about the time that Elodie was murdered. Is there anything you told us in your statement that you would like to change, now you've had time to think about what happened on the day of Elodie's murder?'

'No,' I say, feeling myself tremble inside.

'It's our belief that you lied to us, Kelly,' says the detective. 'Do you realise how serious that is?'

'Yes.'

'We do not think that you were in your friends' flat at the time of the murder. We think you went to Richmond and murdered Elodie Elloissie after arguing with her publicly earlier in the day, and fighting with her on the gravel outside.'

Shit. Who told them that? It must have been Henry or Pamela. Or the carpenter. Shit, no. Please tell me they don't know anything about the carpenter.

'I didn't kill her,' I say. 'I didn't.'

The bigger of the two men steps forward.

'Kelly Monsoon, I am arresting you for the murder of Elodie Elloissie. You do not have to say anything, but it may harm your defence if you do not mention when questioned something you later rely on in court. Anything you do say maybe given in evidence. Is that clear?'

CHAPTER 26: TO THE POLICE STATION

*'B*reaking news ...'

'OK, thanks, Bob. You come back to us as we've just had confirmation from the police that they have arrested someone in connection with the murder yesterday of Elodie Elloissie. A police statement issued just minutes ago says they have arrested a 28–year–old female who has been taken to Richmond station for questioning.

That woman is believed to be Kelly Monsoon, the girlfriend of Hollywood film star Rufus George, and a close friend of Elloissie. I repeat, we believe that Kelly Monsoon, girlfriend of Rufus George has been arrested and taken to Richmond police station to answer questions in connection with the brutal murder yesterday of glamorous fashion designer Elodie Elloissie. More on that breaking news story as soon as we have it.'

.   .   .

The dull grey skies hang over us; rain pours down, pelting onto the car as it makes its short journey from Richmond Hill to Richmond police station, bumper to bumper all the way. Flashes burst through the sky as eager photographers try to capture pictures of me: the world-famous murder suspect cowering behind blacked–out windows. Much of the town centre area has been cordoned off since the discovery of Elodie's body. No one's allowed through until forensic examinations have been conducted across every inch of the place. It means that traffic is backed up and stationary all the way. Even with the police outriders, it's taking forever to drive down the hill to the station.

It's silent in the car; the men attempt no small talk, and I'm too thrown and confused by developments to attempt to talk to them. I'm almost light-headed. I don't feel like screaming and shouting and banging my hands against the window like you imagine you'd feel in this situation; I just feel shocked and confused. Genuinely dizzy and amazed at the way things have developed. The small guy drives on through the rain while I sit in the back with Detective Barnes. He has his legs apart and his hands on his knees; confident and happy that he's getting another crime wrapped up. I'm sitting, cowering in the corner, as foetal–like as it's possible to get in the back of a police car. I'm leaning into the door with my eyes closed, hoping, every time I open them, that this horrible nightmare has ended and I'm back in bed with Rufus, planning our wedding … a wedding that I now fear will never happen.

I can see the dancing, flickering lights from the police motorbikes refracting in the raindrops falling all around us. It seems like there's so much noise and excitement out there. It contrasts staggeringly with the silence and heaviness in the car.

When we left the house, they had to throw a coat over my

head to protect me from the flashbulbs and the intrusive lenses trained on me at every turn. I felt like a serial killer. Perhaps they think I am.

'OK,' Detective Barnes had said, throwing the blanket over me. 'This photograph is the most wanted in the world, by anyone, right now. Let's make sure they don't get it, shall we?' He smiled at me then: a drop of tenderness in an ocean of pain and humiliation.

I'm at the centre of a worldwide storm but like everyone who's ever been at the centre of a worldwide storm before me, it's really nothing. There are police outriders, paparazzi chasing us, and non–stop communication on the radio with the custody sergeant but the truth is that I'm just a girl in a car driving through Richmond in the pouring rain with two men beside me. The two men think I murdered someone. I'm telling them I didn't. All the rest of it is just noise.

I'm sitting directly behind the passenger seat. As soon as I was instructed to sit here, I knew why. Oh yes – turns out those nights watching true crime programmes with the girls in the flat late at night weren't a waste of time after all. Who'd have guessed? I happen to know from my extensive viewing that they never sit violent criminals behind the driver in case the person bashes the driver over the head and tries to escape. That's me. I'm the violent criminal. I've been arrested for murder.

What about Mum and Dad? I hope they're not being pestered by the press. Though the likelihood that they're not being pestered is so tiny that it's not worth considering.

'I'm worried about my mum and dad,' I say to Detective Barnes next to me, and I really hope he doesn't say, 'Well you should have thought of that before committing murder, shouldn't you?'

'We're keeping the press away from them,' he says.

'Thank you,' I say, and I look at him properly for the first time. The blue eyes aren't quite as steely anymore; it's almost like he feels sorry for me. I put my head back against the window, close my eyes and try to stop my heart pounding up into the back of my throat. It's going to be OK; it's going to be OK. David promised to get hold of Rufus immediately and send him straight to Richmond police station with his legal team. It's going to be OK.

The windscreen wipers move quickly as the rain lashes down more heavily. It's dark and dismal in every way possible. The car eases towards the sealed–off area of the high street; the police cordon is lifted by a jovial, pink– cheeked policeman resplendent in his hat and fluorescent waterproof jacket.

The car swings into the back of the police station, through throngs of photographers being held back by dozens of uniformed officers. I feel scared then. Yep, for all my philosophising I now feel terrified out of my mind.

Thanks, Bob, yes – we can confirm that Kelly Monsoon left her home on Richmond Hill in an unmarked police car, heading for Richmond police station around ten minutes ago. She was accompanied by two detectives, and uniformed officers surrounded the entrance to the police station to make sure no photographers could get near. The car had previously foiled the photographers' attempts to get close by picking up Kelly inside the large security gates outside the mansion she shares with movie star Rufus George. There were blacked–out windows on the car and it went through the cordoned–off area, past the Royal Institute of Fashion, scene of the murder for which Monsoon, girlfriend of Rufus George, now finds herself arrested. Back to you, Bob.'

'Thanks, Jennie. But can we confirm; do we know for sure that

it is Kelly Monsoon in the car? Have police confirmed that they have arrested her?'

'Well, Bob, no. Police have said simply that it was a 28-year-old woman. We know that a car used by detectives was at Rufus George's fabulous Richmond mansion earlier today, and we know that car headed for Richmond police station, going through police cordons on the way. All the rumours here indicate that it is Kelly who's being driven to the station as we speak.'

'Well, what next, then, for the girl who had everything? Kelly Monsoon seemed to be living the dream when she met hunky film star Rufus George and was swept off to a world of money and fame. Today though, her dream lies in tatters as she stands accused of brutal murder. I'm joined by former Detective Chief Superintendent Mike Dover. Morning to you, sir. Could you tell us a little bit about what Kelly will be going through, and what awaits her when she gets to the police station?'

'Of course. Good afternoon, Bob. Well, when she gets to the police station, the first thing that will happen will be fingerprints, photographs and DNA samples will be taken, then there'll be a full body search. It's unusual for someone who's committed a murder not to have some marks on their body. In particular, they'll check her hands, looking for hilt wounds. If the victim was stabbed, as has been widely reported, then it's likely the perpetrator of the crime would have cut him or herself between the thumb and index finger – the area we call 'the hilt' during the attack. Unless, of course ...'

'Sorry, I'll have to stop you there, former Detective Chief Superintendent, because we're now going back over to Jennie in Richmond where I believe the car containing Miss Monsoon has arrived at Richmond police station. Is that right, Jennie?'

'Yes, Bob. That's right. The car, which we believe contains Kelly Monsoon, has now arrived at Richmond police station. Back to you, Bob.'

'Thanks, Jennie. Well, amazing breaking news there, brought to you live as it happens, twenty–four hours a day, here on Sky. So, former Detective Chief Superintendent, anything else you can tell us about what the future holds for Kelly?'

'Well, she'll be interviewed in detail and will be asked to run through everything she's said previously. The initial interviews are likely to be conducted by specialist police interviewing unit Tier Three. She'll be videoed, and then she's likely to be put in a cell overnight and interviewed again in the morning when police will challenge her on aspects on the story that they do not believe.'

'So, you're saying that Kelly Monsoon's story is not believed? Has she been deliberately lying to police?'

'We don't know that, Bob, but clearly they have reason to be suspicious or they wouldn't have arrested her. It's my view that they'll tackle these issues once she's spent a night in the cell.'

'And will she be locked up with other murderers?'

'She'll be in her own cell. They may well transfer her to Scotland Yard in the morning. Can I just remind viewers that Kelly is not a 'murderer'? She's innocent until proven guilty.'

'Are we becoming too soft on criminals? After all, this woman has committed a serious offence.'

'We don't know that yet, Bob, she's innocent until proven guilty.'

'We'll be back, after these adverts.'

A shock wave of exhaustion and displacement hits me like a thunderclap. What am I doing here? How has this happened?

'Let's just run through the whole day again, shall we?' asks the policeman. 'Everything you say is being taped and videoed.'

Arriving at the cells was the most terrifying experience of my life. We drove through a large, dark-blue, prison-like gate of metal bars, and into a small courtyard where I was taken out of the car and led into the building.

'This is the custody suite, and this is the custody officer,' they said, introducing me to a small, round blonde woman who took my details and said she needed to take fingerprints, a photo and DNA samples. Next, they strip- searched me. The lady who did it was very gentle and respectful but a strip–search is a strip–search. It was humiliating, embarrassing and horrid.

The lawyers came and kept demanding to know what evidence the police have. They asked whether the police have a warrant for my arrest and talked about 'PACE' and my rights, and all these other things I've only ever heard about on the news. They wanted know whether the police found any marks on me. The only mark I have is a bruise on my right thigh. Since I got that in a fight with Elodie, that hasn't helped my case too much.

The worst thing about all this is that Rufus isn't here. He hasn't called or made contact at all.

'Will Rufus come?' I keep asking.

'No,' they keep saying.

I know I've let him down, and I know I've embarrassed him, but surely he can see that I need him now more than I've ever needed anyone in my life before.

'Your parents are desperately worried about you,' my solicitor told me. She meant well. She wanted to remind me that there are lots of people out there who care about me deeply, but all her kind words did was ram another stab of guilt straight into my heart.

'Why have they arrested me?' I ask. 'I mean – I know they've arrested me because they think I killed Elodie, but why do they think that?'

'They think you lied to them, Kelly. The police check and double–check every statement made and if you tell them things that later turn out not to be true, it does alert all their suspicions. They want to talk to you about your alibi for the time of the murder, what happened between you and Elodie on the day of the murder, and some things that they allege you said to other people, about wanting to kill Elodie.'

Now I'm in a heavily lit interview room with fluorescent lighting that could brighten Wembley. The room's completely plain, and decorated in a cream colour. There's nothing here to distract me or provoke me. I guess that's the point of it.

I tell the police everything I can remember. Rufus isn't here, so I tell them all about the carpenter and I explain that I didn't want to mention what I did in front of my boyfriend, in case he got really cross. They shake their heads as if I'm the most stupid person ever to walk the earth … which I guess I might be, all things considered.

'This is a different story to the one you told us yesterday,' says Detective Inspector Barnes.

The lawyer in the room with me is called Sue Lawrence and apparently she's the best criminal lawyer in the world. She's also gorgeous. I don't think the detectives could quite believe their luck when she walked in. She sat down and crossed her legs over and I thought poor Detective Barnes might go tumbling off his chair. It's not so much that her skirt is short; it's just that her legs are incredibly long, slim, and shapely. I'm so glad she's on my side.

'I'd like a word with my client, please,' she says, with a batting of her eyelashes and a smile playing on her glossy lips.

Away from the guys she asks me why I didn't tell them about the carpenter yesterday.

'I was just so embarrassed in front of Rufus,' I repeat. 'I'm not normally the jealous type but I went all through his stuff while he was in LA, checking to see whether there were any clues that he was having an affair or anything and, when I couldn't get into one drawer, I smashed my way in. I had to get a carpenter to repair it. I never told Rufus. It's got nothing to do with Elodie's murder or anything.'

'You don't know that. Your job is just to tell the truth and they'll work out what's relevant. If you don't tell them the complete truth at all times, you'll get yourself in more trouble,' she says with great pomposity. I don't feel like I'm in any position to complain though. This woman, right now, appears to be the only person in my corner. To be frank, the only person who gives a shit.

'Was there anything in the drawer?' she asks.

'A bracelet which matches the necklace that Elodie always wears.'

'Say that again.'

'In the drawer that I broke into there was a bracelet which I think belongs to Elodie. It was hidden right at the back. I don't know why and I haven't had chance to discuss it with Rufus. It's pretty fucking scary though, and I'd rather not be discussing it with the police.'

'So, you think that Elodie was having an affair with Rufus?' My lawyer looks absolutely horrified. Really, she looks quite scared.

'Yes,' I say, which just compounds everything. Her pretty petal–like face looks as if it's about to completely crumble away. 'I mean no. I mean I don't know. It's just all weird. Why would her bracelet be in there if they weren't? But then he came back from LA and proposed to me and he seems to love me. I don't know.'

'You know it was her bracelet, do you?'

'No, I don't know anything. It matched her necklace exactly, though. What are the chances of it not being her bracelet, really?'

'Who have you mentioned this to?' she asks.

'My flatmates,' I say. 'Mandy and Sophie.'

'Fuck.'

So, well done to Miss UK on her charity work there. Now, back to our main story of the day. Police have confirmed that the woman arrested in connection with the murder of Elodie Elloissie is Kelly Monsoon, the girlfriend of film star Rufus George. More on that story as and when we get it and in a change to the TV listings, tonight's Panorama programme will now feature famous female killers.

Newsnight also has a change of subject. Jeremy Paxman will be hosting a panel discussion called: 'Why do women kill?' and will be talking to friends and colleagues of Kelly Monsoon, including Lord and Lady Simpkins, the theatre impresarios who became close friends with the woman now accused of brutal murder. For now, though, it's over to the regional news teams to find out what's happening in your area.'

I'm back in with the police, and the questioning is relentless.

'So what time did the carpenter arrive?' they ask … again …

'It was around midday.'

'And Elodie was outside at the time.'

'Yes.'

'How did you know she was outside?'

'The carpenter told me someone was there so I went to the window and looked out.'

'Did she see you looking?'

'No. I don't think so.'

'How did Elodie get through the security gates to be sitting within sight of the window?'

'She's known to security and Henry was driving her. He's

Rufus's driver. He would have been allowed straight through.'

'Why was Henry driving her? How often does Henry drive her? Did you not say earlier that you asked Henry not to drive her? Do she and Henry get on? Have you ever seen them arguing? Does Henry seem like a man who is capable of murder?'

The questions keep coming; some things I'm asked to repeat and other things I'm asked for the first time. Now I've decided to just tell them everything that happened, I'm much happier. I'm not very good at lying. I was only doing it to protect Rufus. There are some little secrets we have that I just don't like to reveal, and some things I did (like smashing up the desk) that I don't want to have written about in the papers when they're nothing to do with Elodie's murder, and will just be embarrassing for Rufus.

'And you're sure that you went from your home in Richmond to visit your friends in Twickenham?'

'Yes.'

'And Henry drove you all the way there?'

'Yes.'

'What happened then?'

'I knocked on the door but no one was in so I hung around until they got back.'

'You told us yesterday that you went straight in.'

'Yes, I know. I got confused by everything.'

'We came back and asked you again, and you still insisted on the same story.'

'Yes, as I said – I was very confused by everything.'

'You lied to us. You told us you had an alibi and you don't.'

I sit there silently, not knowing what to say.

'Where did you 'hang around'?'

'Just in Twickenham.'

'Where in Twickenham?'

'I don't know, just around the coffee shops and stuff.'
'Which coffee shop?'
'Julie's.'
'So, you're saying that between the hours of 4.30 pm and 6 pm you were sitting in Julie's Coffee shop in Twickenham.'
'Yes.'
'On your own?'
'Yes.'
'So, you have no alibi for the time when Elodie was murdered?'
'No. I just sat and had coffee.'
'What sort of coffee?'
'Skinny cappuccino.'
'Where is the coffee shop?'
'It's on the High Street.'
'Where on the High Street? Describe how you got there from the flat.'
'I walked to the traffic lights and turned right into the High Street and there it was, on the right.'
'And you walked in and sat down.'
'Yes, I did.' For God's sake, what does he think I did? Disco–danced across the tables?

'Welcome to London Tonight where we are asking the question: what happens when best friends turn on one another? Every-one's seen the wall–to–wall coverage of the Elodie Elloissie murder case today, and the fact that Kelly Monsoon, Elodie's best friend, has been arrested for her murder. Could you murder your best friend? Do you ever feel like murdering her? What happens when best friends turn on one another? Can best friends get so close that love turns to hate? Why do women have best friends and what happens when it all goes wrong?'

CHAPTER 27: INTEROGATION

*T*he cell is not as horrific as I feared it might be; It's got pale–pink walls because the colour is supposed to make people feel calmer and I'm in an all–female section. Apparently, there are ten cells for women and forty-two for men. I haven't seen anyone else though. There's a plastic mattress in the far corner of the room in the kind of royal blue favoured by the makers of school uniforms. The colour reminds me of gym knickers.

The bed lies beneath a long, thin window too high for me to look through, but big enough to cast natural light in. There's fluorescent lighting everywhere. That's the thing I noticed most when I walked in here. Light floods the long cream corridor, forcing brightness into every hidden corner of the cell. The place has the feel of a hospital ward. It reminds me of where Dad went for an operation years ago. All very clean and sterile, but characterless. Desperately soulless.

There's a stainless–steel toilet in the corner of my room and the door is the same deep blue as the barred gate that we came in through on our way into the courtyard. The huge, metal cell door is the worst thing about the place; it's big and sturdy and when it clanks shut with that horrible metal slam, I feel myself shiver all over. It has a kind of heavy metal cat flap through which they look every hour to make sure I'm OK.

The police come to the cell in the morning to wake me and feed me, but I'm already wide awake, as I guess they knew I would be. I don't suppose that many people locked up for murder sleep soundly on their first night behind bars. I'm not hungry either; strangely I seem to have lost my appetite. It's like Elodie's controlling me from beyond the grave.

It's 7am when I'm taken to wash and prepare myself for the rather gruelling day ahead. The grimy sinks and plastic mirrors mark a bitter contrast between my life before the death of Elodie and life afterwards.

I'm taken back up to the interview room when I've finished washing, and instructed to sit face to face with my detective friends. This time there's a real frostiness in the air. If I thought the guys were miserable yesterday, I was mistaken. Today there's real grade–one freeze going on. The two detectives are pacing the room when I walk in. My solicitor sits quietly in the corner.

'Would you like to tell us again what you did on the afternoon of Thursday 3 December?'

Again, I explain about the visit to Starbucks.

'We have been through CCTV footage taken at Starbucks on that day and you were seen going in there, having a quick coffee and then leaving after 10 minutes. Don't you think that's a bit strange?'

My solicitor touches my knee and tells me not to say anything.

'So, you don't think it's strange then?'

'I just get confused.'

'Let me help you,' says Detective Barnes, leaning in so

close to me that I think his nose is going to touch mine. 'I think you're lying to us. I don't think you went to a coffee shop so much as popped in there to secure a receipt that would act as an alibi. You then went to confront Elodie about the fact that you had found jewellery that you think belonged to her in your fiancé's drawer. We know you're capable of aggression because of the way you smashed up that desk and fought with Elodie on the driveway to your home, resulting in the large bruises now present on your right thigh.

'We know very well that you're capable of lying because you've been doing that to us since we first came to talk to you about the crime. We know you and Elodie had a huge fight and we know that you told several people that you were having real problems with Elodie. Henry, Mr George's driver, admits that during a conversation you told him you hated Elodie and 'I could kill her'. We have a message on Elodie's phone in which you are hurling accusations at her and expressing deep dislike for her.

'We know that you did not stay in Twickenham because we have CCTV from outside Suga Daddy's nightclub of you getting into a black cab. You weren't in a coffee shop for more than 10 minutes, Kelly. You took that cab to Richmond didn't you, Kelly? When you were in Richmond you murdered Elodie Elloissie. Come on, Kelly. We know. You murdered her.'

'I'd like a word with my client NOW,' screams Sue Lawrence.

'I bet you would,' says Barnes. 'I bet you fucking would.'

Sue Lawrence is looking at me as one might look at a naughty child who has just spray-painted the Mona Lisa orange. She's annunciating every word as if talking to a three-year-old. 'You must tell the absolute truth,' she says. 'The absolute truth. No lies. Do. You. Understand? Do you?'

'Yes, I understand, and of course I know I have to tell the truth,' I say, rather too dismissively.

'No. No, Kelly you don't seem to 'know' anything of the sort.' She's raising her voice again now. 'You don't seem to understand that if you tell one more little lie for whatever reason, you will be charged with murder and there is every chance that you will go to prison for a very long time. Now, I don't believe you murdered Elodie, and I suspect that these policemen don't think you murdered Elodie, but, if you keep lying, you will end up in jail. I don't know how to make this clear for you, Kelly.'

'It is clear,' I say. 'I understand. It's just that there are things that I don't think should be said.'

'You need to stop deciding what should and shouldn't be said, and start answering the questions honestly.'

'But Rufus always said that anything I say will, at some stage, find its way into the papers. And we have this special place at Hampton Court Palace that means the world to us. If I say I went there, our place will be ruined.'

'Kelly, you need to forget about all that. If you don't stop lying to the police, the fact that you are in the papers and you don't have a special place will be the very least of your concerns. I don't care how petty some of the questions seem, answer them honestly. If you're worried, don't say anything at all, just don't lie. Whatever you do, don't lie.'

'OK,' I say, suitably chastised. It's not like I'm lying to cover up anything terrible. I just don't see why the public has to hear how awful Elodie could be when the woman's body is lying on a slab, and I don't want to ruin our favourite place by telling everyone that's where I was.

'Surely to God they don't honestly believe I murdered her. They can't have any possible evidence because I didn't murder her. Don't they need some actual evidence rather than just pinning it on me.'

'Of course they need evidence,' she says, and there is a lot of work going on behind the scenes here to remind them of that. They can't charge you without evidence, but they can scare you into confessing.'

'But I'm nothing to confess. I didn't do it, they have no evidence that I did it, and if I mention all the details of what I did that day, I'll have a huge falling out with Rufus and our special place will be ruined forever.'

'Hello, welcome to Breakfast Chat with me, Lucy Loveshaw. Well, there's only one thing being talked about at the moment and that's the shock news that Kelly Monsoon, the pretty young girl who stole the heart of film star

Rufus George, has been arrested for the murder of top fashion stylist and her best friend, Elodie Elloissie. The story is causing excitement across the nation because it's so unusual ... most killers are men.

So today we ask: Why do women kill?

I'm joined in the studio by a panel of experts including our very own Breakfast Chat agony aunt Gillian O'Connor. Next to Gill is Mandy Mitchell, whose mother was jailed for murder, Lady Helen Simpkins, one of the few people who spotted Kelly's potential as a murderer before the gruesome act, and Petra Moon from Women Against Violence. Gillian, let's start with you. This was a particularly brutal murder, wasn't it? Has it surprised you to hear that a woman would murder another woman in this way, and what do you believe is the motivation behind it?'

'So now you're saying that you didn't go to a coffee shop in Twickenham? Sorry if we're being a bit slow keeping up with all of this, but your story is changing a lot.'

'No,' I say, sobbing uncontrollably. 'I'm saying that I went to a coffee shop in Twickenham to wait for my flatmates. I left when a guy that I used to know came up and started chatting to me, and I went to Hampton Court Palace.'

'Very nice. Why did you go there?'

'Rufus and I have a special place we like; it's called the Rose Garden. It's beautiful. We love it; it's so quiet. We can be ourselves and no one hassles us or annoys us. There's this gardener there called Frank. You can ask him. The place is lovely and I promised Rufus that I would never, ever mention to anyone where our special place was, so I didn't want to say.'

'OK.' The detective runs his hands through his short, thinning hair. He looks exasperated. I hate the fact that I'm being such a pain but if it gets out that Rufus and I love it in the Rose Garden, the place will be full of his fans and we'll never be able to go there again. 'So, tell me what really happened, from the moment you got into Henry's car to go to your friends' flat until you met your boyfriend at Heathrow airport later that night. The truth, Kelly. I need you to tell me the truth.'

'Excuse me. Can I have a word please, sir?' A tall, incredibly slim man has entered the room and stands just inside the door.

'DC Paul Campbell has just entered the room,' says Detective Swann. When the police first started doing that – mentioning everyone coming in and out for the benefit of the tape – I thought they were saying it for my benefit. I even went to stand up and introduced myself back on one occasion, but Sue urged me to sit down and suggested that introductions weren't really necessary. 'They all know who you are,' she said.

Detective Barnes stands up and walks towards DC

Campbell. They exchange a couple of words and both men leave the room.

'Are you OK?' asks my lawyer. I nod and look down at my hands. Sue starts to talk to me about breathing deeply and turning to her for help if I feel worried when the door opens and a different detective comes in, accompanied by the tall thin guy. The only good news so far today is that the terrible Barnes guy has disappeared for a while.

'I am showing Kelly Monsoon exhibit A,' says the detective, pushing a plastic bag towards me containing Rufus's dagger, the jewel–covered one that he was given after winning the Oscar.

'Do you recognise this?' asks the detective.

'Yes,' I say. 'It belongs to Rufus.'

'You are saying that this dagger belongs to your boyfriend?'

'Yes,' I repeat. 'Where did you find it?'

'In Elodie Elloissie's body,' replies the detective with a sanctimonious sneer. 'It had gone through her ribcage and into her heart. Furthermore, the DNA left on the dagger has been analysed and it's your DNA. Your blood, Kelly.'

'You couldn't have checked her DNA out so quickly,' says my lawyer, standing up confrontationally. 'It takes weeks.'

'Yes, we could,' says the new detective. 'She's on the National DNA Register. It took us an hour to get a precise match.'

Sue looks at me with coldness. 'Why are you on the DNA register?' she asks.

'I got done for drink–driving years ago,' I say.

She sits back in her seat and scribbles some notes. I'm sure I know what she's writing 'This woman is fucked.'

. . .

Police have been seen coming in and out of Rufus George's fabulous home all morning after the astonishing arrest yesterday of his girlfriend, Kelly Monsoon. Monsoon is being questioned at Richmond police station by police from the Scotland Yard murder squad in connection with the murder of leading fashion stylist Elodie Elloissie. She's been in custody overnight but it's believed that her boyfriend has not been to visit her.

'We are joined again by Ex-Detective Chief Superintendent Mike Dover. Mike, what are the police doing?'

'Well, Felicity, they'll be taking everything away that they think will help with their inquiries ... computers, discs, tapes, security footage, clothing ... anything that will help pin down whether it was Kelly Monsoon who killed Elodie Elloissie.'

'And they'll be able to tell that by looking at her clothing, will they?'

'Well, if they find the clothes she was wearing on the day that Elodie was killed, they will.'

'OK, thanks, Mike. Back to you in the studio, Bob. Remember, there's a four-hour special on tonight with Lord and Lady Simpkins, former friends of Kelly Monsoon, describing the woman they got to know, and how they always believed she was capable of murder.'

I've gone over and over and over the situation with the dagger, and how I used it to smash open the drawer. I know that for every word I say, they'll have 526,000 questions about what time it was, what angle the clouds were sitting at and how many stones there were on the gravel driveway at the time. The questions come fast, thick and furious. They barely give me time to answer one question before another one's fired at me. They don't so much do that good cop/bad cop thing, as bad cop/bad cop/bad cop. It's the new, slim detective who does most of the questioning. The others chip in whenever they feel he hasn't asked quite enough questions in quite enough detail for their liking.

'So, tell us again where the dagger was when you last saw it.'

'It was on the chair,' I say.

'Which chair? Where? What colour was the chair? How was it lying? What time was it when you saw it?'

CHAPTER 28: LYING TO THE POLICE

❦

*A*gain, there's a knock at the door. This time it's Barnes, coming back into the room. Shit. I don't like this man at all. He's convinced I'm guilty; I can see it in his eyes.

'DI Barnes has just entered the interview room,' says Detective Swann.

'Hello, Kelly,' says Detective Barnes, pulling his chair forward and leaning right across the table. My palms have gone all sweaty and my heart's racing. Perhaps I did kill Elodie? I don't know anything anymore; I feel so weak and hopeless. I stopped taking those drugs but I still feel the effects of them - I can't focus properly on anything.

'Now, where were we?' he says.

Flippin' heck. I know exactly where we bloody were. We were with him going on and on about how I have no alibi for the time of Elodie's murder, I had a reason to kill Elodie, and the murder weapon belongs to me and has my DNA on it. Even I can see that this is not looking good.

'Let's go through this once again, shall we?' he says,

looking at me like I'm some piece of dirt he's just kicked off the end of his shoe. 'Start right at the beginning ...'

There's a knock at the door before we can begin. My solicitor looks as if she's about to have a nervous breakdown. She glares at me as if it's my fault that there's a knocking sound, and I instinctively bring my hands above the table to show that it's not me.

'Can I have a moment, sir?' says a woman I haven't seen before.

'DI Barnes is leaving the interview room,' says the other detective.

I drop my head into my hands. I'm relieved not to have to go back through this whole horrible bloody story again and again, but terrified of what new information is going to 'come to light'. Every time there's a knock on that door there's some other piece of evidence that indicates that I must have done the murder after all. All we need now is for someone to appear with a photograph of me stabbing her. Then I'll know that the pills really were hallucinogenic.

We sit there for another ten minutes. It feels like about forty–seven hours then, suddenly, the door swings open and Barnes comes back in with another man. They tell the policeman who's sitting there that he's no longer needed and the two of them sit down next to Detective Swann. Barnes can barely look me in the eye. Oh Lord, what now?

'My name's DI Smith,' says the new officer, talking to me as if I were about six years old.

'Hi,' I say.

'We've just had the final pathologist's report back which gives more precise detail on the estimated time of death and more detail on the manner of the death,' he says, slowly and patiently. 'The official time of death has come in and it is different from the estimated time of death.

This can happen from time to time. The pathologist

makes an estimate of time of death in the first instance while more detailed investigations take place.'

'Oh.'

'There's a discrepancy between the original estimated time of death, thought to be between 5.30 pm and 6 pm, and the more accurate prediction. We've been told that the time of death is now considered to be 9 pm.'

'How did you get the estimated time of death so wrong?' asks Sue, standing up and leaning over the table aggressively. 'We were explicitly told that the time of death was estimated at 5.30 pm. It is a gross miscalculation to now suggest that the time of death is wrong by some three and a half hours.'

'It happens,' says the detective. 'The first estimated time of death is rarely more than half an hour out but, in this case, officers discovered that the heating was switched off at night, meaning that the body decomposed at a slower rate, thus forcing us to conclude that the time of death was actually much later in the day than we originally predicted.'

I have to admit that I'm hardly listening to the exchange. They've changed their minds about what time Elodie died. Until they change their minds about whether I killed her or not, there's not too much interest in all of this for me.

The same cannot be said for my glamorous lawyer who is up, all animated and excited and demanding to know precise details about what the official time of death is to be recorded as.

There's a conversation about the moisture levels in the vestibule where Elodie's body was found, and temperature variations through the evening.

'My client has an alibi for 9 pm,' says Sue.

Oh. Now I get it.

'She couldn't have killed Elodie. She was at the airport.'

'I know,' says the policeman, looking at me. 'Can you tell

us exactly what you were doing between the hours of 9 pm and 10 pm on the evening of Thursday 3 December?'

'That's easy,' I say. 'I was meeting my boyfriend at the airport.'

'Did anyone see you?'

'Yes. There were security officers helping me through, and there was Henry the driver and Rufus's assistant.'

'What's her name?'

'It's Christine,' I say, but Sue interrupts.

'You've spoken to her about this. She's talked at length about what she was doing at this time. There's footage from the airport. I think it's time to accept that my client couldn't possibly have committed this crime.'

The policemen both nod. 'We also have video footage of you at Hampton Court Palace, sitting in the Rose Garden talking to the elderly gentleman. We spoke to him too. Frank Gower. He confirms your time of arrival and time of departure. Why did you lie to us?'

'Rufus always told me not to tell people about our special place or everyone would want to go there. He has so many fans and they follow us everywhere. I just wanted the Rose Garden to be special – you know – for it to be our special place. It never would be if I mentioned it. It would end up in the newspapers and that would be it … my favourite place in the whole world ruined forever.'

'Can I offer you some advice?'

'Yes, sure.'

'Never lie to the police, Kelly. Even if it means your 'special place' is special no longer.'

'Yes,' I say. I'm about to explain that I was taking these diet pills and they have affected my ability to think straight, but I'm aware enough to realise that throwing a confession of drug taking into the mix at this stage would be a huge error.

. . .

Yes, thanks, Bob. That's right; you come to us live outside Richmond police station where we have just been told that Kelly Monsoon is to be released without charge. You'll remember that the girlfriend of Hollywood star Rufus George was arrested yesterday and held in police custody overnight. Well, today, in a shocking twist to this story, we hear that she is to be released later today without charge. Police have not said whether they have another suspect in mind but sources close to the police reveal that they are questioning Dr Isabella Bronks–Harrison inside the station at the moment. She's a former friend of Elodie Elloissie, but fell out with the fashionista several years ago. Police are insisting that she is just helping with inquiries but we believe that she is now the main suspect in this most incredible of murder investigations. Back to you, Bob.'

Thanks, Bindy. Now, in a change to tonight's scheduled programme Evil Women Murderers there will instead be a panel discussion on the difficulties of being accused of a crime that you did not commit. What does it feel when the world turns against you? That's tonight at 10 pm, here on Sky One and features a discussion with Lord and Lady Simpkins, the couple who have known Kelly all her life, and say they knew from the moment she was arrested that this was a huge miscarriage of justice.'

CHAPTER 29: TROUBLE IN PARADISE

*M*um stands there, holding her handbag in front of her with both hands, the strain of the past couple of days showing in her fiercely knotted knuckles. She has her heavy dark–blue coat pulled tightly around her. She looks nervous, understandably, and much older than last time I saw her. When she sees me, her eyes light up, she smiles, and loosens that fearful grip on the worn leather straps of the only handbag I've ever seen her with. Dad's there too, a puzzled look on his face as he looks out for me, trying to make sense of the events that have forced him to bring his wife to a police station in south–west London.

He relaxes too, when he sees me walking towards them and I force myself to smile and greet them warmly, pretending that nothing's wrong.

'A simple misunderstanding,' I say. 'Please don't worry. Everything's going to be OK.'

I might be more assured that everything is going to be OK if Rufus were here to meet me too, but there's no sign of him. My parents and I are led out through a heavily guarded, dark-blue back door and are moved through ranks of police officers positioned so as to hide me from the waiting paparazzi. No Rufus anywhere. Shit. I know it would be mad for a huge celebrity film star to be here. I know it would make the crowds much harder to manage, but, but ... I kind of just really wish he was here anyway.

I wish he'd sat at home and thought, I know it's mad for me to go to the police station but, sod it, I'm going anyway, I want to see Kelly.

Why isn't he here? Why didn't he visit me at the police station?

They put a blanket over my head as they lead me the final half–metre to the car; my lawyer was very insistent on this before we left the station. Sue said that pictures of me today would keep resurfacing for the rest of my life, long after the details of this case had drifted to the backs of people's minds, and though I was released without charge and thus had nothing to hide my head in shame from, it was still better that no pictures were taken of me. I didn't care. I was just looking out for Rufus, vainly peering through the gaps in the blanket at the scores of people assembled to witness my release from custody in the hope that I'd see him standing there.

A car driven by a specialist police driver takes me home. I'm told that Henry came to the police station to collect me but was sent away by police when they realised how many people were gathered at the big metal gates. It was considered to be safer for a specialist police driver to make the short journey up the Hill to my 'home'.

I sit in the back of the car, still beneath the blanket but peering out through small holes at the world as it passes. It feels as if I've been locked away for years. Time's a strange enough concept anyway – sometimes days fly past, other days drag, the minutes moving so slowly into hours that you begin to think the clock's taken leave of its senses - but when you're locked away from the signs of normal life, your sense of place and time, and your sense of yourself within that place and time disappear completely. I might as well have been locked away for a thousand years because, though it's only been two days and one night, I've come out a different person. I didn't kill Elodie and I can prove I didn't kill Elodie, but it's as if my innocence is an entirely meaningless concept. I'm still at the centre of everyone's story.

The Hill remains closed off to traffic while police analyse and interrogate to find out who killed Elodie. Their main suspect is innocent and out of custody, so I guess they start again, combing through her possessions and reading every note she ever wrote.

Mum looks round at me and smiles warmly. 'You all right, love,' she says with a smile.

'We knew this was all a terrible mistake and you could never have killed anyone. Everyone knows. I don't know what the police were thinking of,' says Mum kindly. 'We've had so many letters of support for you from people all round the world, and the staff in the house have been amazing to us. They've been telling us how much you mean to them and how kind you are. Love, we're so proud of you.'

I was arrested for murder. She's still proud. Thank God for mums.

I walk into the house flanked by Mum and Dad, and they both gasp when they see just how amazing the place is. I forget they've not been to visit yet. Dad looks around, trying to look nonchalant but I can tell he's thinking, Bloody hell! This place is amazing!

I give him a little hug. 'Nice house,' he says, gravely. 'Very nice. Better than that bloody awful flat you lived in before. Do you remember when I painted the door and the nightclub man from next door came across. God he was dreadful. You've done well here, love.'

I notice straight away that things have been moved around and that the computer is missing. It must have sent poor Rufus up the wall to have all these police crawling over the house.

'You'll be able to carry on with organising the wedding now, won't you?' says Mum. 'You won't change your mind and go for summer, will you? I'm planning a beautiful chocolate–brown coat that will really only work for an autumn or winter wedding.'

'Leave it, Jayne,' says Dad. 'I think the poor girl's been through enough this past week without you harassing her to organise a wedding.'

'Oh, but a wedding will be a lovely thing for us all,' says Mum. 'Imagine! We'll be able to show the world that the problems are all behind us and we're setting off on a new road to a bright future.'

I'm thinking that it'll take more than a bright and gorgeous wedding for the British population to forget about what's just happened. I can just see the headlines now. Instead of PRETTY BRUNETTE TO MARRY HOLLY-WOOD STAR they'll be saying MURDER SUSPECT IN SHOCK MARRIAGE TO HOLLYWOOD'S FINEST.

My fears about the future, and particularly about our proposed wedding, are not allayed by the sight of Rufus. He comes through the door from the sitting room looking twenty years older than he did when I last saw him. He practically pushes past my parents, kisses Sue Lawrence lightly on the cheek and stands in front of me. 'Welcome home,' he says, with not an ounce of conviction. I feel my heart fall through the floor and I want to scream. I feel like shouting, 'I know I did badly. I know I shouldn't have hidden things from the police, but everything I did was to protect your friend Elodie's memory and to protect our relationship from public scrutiny and public interference.'

But I don't of course. What's the point? Rufus has clearly made up his mind about me. And he's right. I have behaved ridiculously.

'Can we talk?' he says, just standing there, making no effort to touch or comfort me.

'Sure,' I say, looking back at my parents as I follow him into the den at the back of the house. Mum is smiling from ear to ear while Dad's face reflects the concern that I feel.

'Why did this happen, Kelly?' he asks. His manner and the way he is looking at me are so grave. It's like I'm back at the police station again, being grilled by those aggressive detectives.

'Because I didn't tell the police the truth. I didn't want to mention the Rose Garden to them so I said I was at the flat. They thought I was covering something up.'

'I can't believe you lied to the fucking police,' he says with such fury, that I find myself stepping back away from him.

'You told me never to mention that we go there,' I try.

'Yes, I did, Kelly. But when I said that I had no idea that you were going to be arrested for murder, did I?'

'No. But I'm not thinking all that straight at the moment. Elodie gave me these diet pills and I've just been feeling all over the place...not myself at all.'

'So, it's Elodie's fault. Elodie was stabbed to death, but it's her fault?'

'I didn't say that.'

'I'm finding all this very difficult to come to terms with. My mother's furious,' he says.

I just look at him then. He's worried about what people think. He's worried about his reputation. He couldn't give a toss about me.

'Did you think I killed her?' I say.

'Of course not. Of course not. How could you even ask that? Of course I didn't. But don't you realise how bad this looks? Do you have no idea of the impact this will have on me ... and on you?'

'Really? I had no idea there'd be any impact,' I say, loading my words with as much sarcasm as they'll carry.

'And what about going through all my things when I was in LA? What about the fact that you don't trust me?'

'I can't defend the way I behaved,' I say. 'I don't know what was wrong with me. I was awful. I shouldn't have done that.'

'The bottom line is that you didn't trust me, isn't it? All this nonsense about the carpenter coming to mend the drawer. That was because you thought I was hiding something from you.'

'Because Elodie persuaded me to ...'

'Elodie again,' he yells. 'How intriguing. Isn't it simply the fact that you didn't trust me and tried to hide that from me, and in the process lied to the police so much that you got yourself arrested for murder? You were so bloody keen to squirm your way out of things that you lied. Shit, Kelly. You lied to the police when one of our friends had been murdered. And you know what really hurts?'

Go on tell me. I've gone so beyond pain these past few days that we need a whole new word for hurt. Nothing he can do can wound me when I feel as if my heart's been blown apart.

'I spent every minute of every day in LA missing you like crazy.'

'I'm sorry,' I say, trying to catch his eye but being met by nothing but coldness and contempt, which make me feel very defensive.

'What do you expect when I find a bracelet exactly like Elodie's in the drawer?'

'It was for Mum. She's always loved Elodie's necklace – you know – the one Elodie always wears, because it was given to her by Jon. I saw the matching bracelet so bought it for Mum, for Christmas. 'When I was living in New York, Mum would always come to my house to visit before Christmas and be like a schoolgirl, trying to find presents. I thought she'd come to the house to visit when she was over for the Interior Design Awards and I thought she'd start hunting for presents, so I hid them. I taped the jewellery to the inside of the drawer; it was the only place I could think where Mum wouldn't look.

'I rushed back and proposed to you because I wanted to spend the rest of my life with you, but all you were doing was going through my things. You didn't trust me. I don't understand why.'

He carries on after that, musing vocally about the way things have panned out between us, but I'm still stuck back in the beginning of his soliloquy. The bit where he says, 'I wanted to spend the rest of my life with you ...'

'Wanted' ... past tense. It's over. He says he's organised for money to be transferred into my savings account, and practically throws my passbook over to me. He's put more money in there than I'd need in ten years. Everything he does seems to confirm my worst fears ... this relationship is over. He's making sure that I'm looked after. Or, if I'm being cynical, he's making sure I have no reason to go to the press. Either way, he wants to make sure that I don't go without, but he no longer wants to be with me.

I move into the spare room that night and sit looking at the oh-so-beautiful walls, covered in the most expensive wallpaper that money can buy, chosen by his wonderful mother with her immaculate taste and her team of perfect interior designers. And as I'm looking at all this wealth and luxury, all I can think is: God this is shit. I mean, I love Rufus so much it terrifies me sometimes, but I can't do this now. I've messed it all up. These few months here have changed me beyond recognition. No, that's not true; they've shown me who I am for the first time in my life and made me realise that what I want and what I'm getting are two very different things.

Elodie was the most stylish person I ever met, and where did it get her? She's dead now. She was dressed beautifully when she slipped down those steps and the dagger that murdered her was beautiful and priceless, like the woman herself. But she was never happy. Are any of these people happy?

Elodie had everything in abundance but in the end, it amounted to nothing at all. I want so much more than this ... I don't want fluffy carpets and expensive heating systems to keep me warm, I want someone's love. I want someone with me who loves me and understands me. I want someone who forgives me when I get things wrong. This is just crap.

CHAPTER 30: BACK HOME

'Thanks, Henry.'

'No problem,' he says. 'Let me give you a hand with your bags.'

He climbs slowly out of his seat, walks round to the boot and lifts out my luggage. I've left half of my stuff at Rufus's house. Henry says he'll bring it over later.

'Can I say something?' Henry says, looking at me nervously.

'Of course.'

'I feel bad about what happened to you. I feel bad that the police told me to recall everything you said in the car. I told them that you said you could kill Elodie. I regret that. I shouldn't have said it. Everyone knows you couldn't have killed Elodie. I just answered their questions. I wanted you to know, none of us thought for one second that you killed Elodie.'

'I think Rufus may have had his doubts.'

'No,' says Henry. 'No, that's not true.'

'Why didn't he come to the police station to see me then?

Why did he hide away and pretend none of this was anything to do with him?'

'He tried to come to the police station but the police said he couldn't. They said you had no right to visits as the prime suspect in a murder investigation. They wouldn't let him phone or visit. Christ, he was trying everything.

His legal team all told him to keep away or he'd be arrested. At one point I thought he might go and get himself arrested just to be there with you and support you through it all.'

I'm looking down at the road.

'Kelly, are you OK?' he asks.

'Yes.'

'Have you thought this through? Do you really want to go?' As he speaks, he lays the second of my three bags down onto the freezing cold pavement.

'Yes,' I say. 'I have no choice.'

'You do,' he counters, but I shake my head. I really don't think I have any choice but to stay away from Rufus and all his life represents, until I can work out what I, Kelly Monsoon, want out of life. I have so much to think about. I can't go back there. Not now, probably not ever.

It's 4 am. I had no desire to alert the world's press to my decision to leave the house, so asked Henry if he'd mind driving me. He'd taken Mum and Dad back to Hastings at midnight, so I knew he'd be around once the world had gone to bed. When I called Sophie and Mandy, they couldn't have been more supportive.

'Of course you can come back here,' they say. 'We'd love to have you back. Any time.' They even cancelled the new flatmate, due to move in on Monday.

'Henry, thank you for driving me.'

'No problem,' he says, climbing back into his car. 'We're gonna miss you, you know.'

'I'll miss you too,' I tell him and we look at each other for a brief second through the open window, a look full of sadness and understanding. It's like he acknowledges that so much has happened this week that the only way I can cope with it all is to get away.

'Come back soon,' he says and I just smile because I can't imagine how I can possibly go back after all that's happened. I can't imagine anything in the future at all, to be honest. All I know is that it's 4 am on Sunday 6 December and I'm standing outside the flat where I once lived, hoping that I don't make things too awful for Mandy and Sophie by being here. The press are bound to track me down, of course, but if I can just stay here for a while until I've sorted myself out, got my head straight and worked out what to do with my life, that would be the greatest treat of all.

I might go abroad. I don't think I could go back to my old job. My days in Richmond Theatre are definitely over. But how will I get another job? Who'd want is to employ me? The girl who went out with a movie star then got arrested for murder.

Perhaps I should 'sell my story' as I'll no doubt be urged to by tabloid editors and publishers. I'm sure I could make a fortune but, Christ, I can't think of anything worse. Having experienced first–hand what it's like to have people talking about you all the time, I'd never want to talk about other people.

I knock on the door gently. The best sound I've heard in ages is of footsteps thundering down the stairs. Mandy hurls herself through the door and hugs me tightly. Sophie's there too, pulling me close to her and letting me cry my eyes out on her big, soft, towelling dressing gown.

We all walk into the small entrance hall leading to the stairs up to our little pad. I feel so safe here. I know that's ridiculous because I was a million times 'safer', whatever that word means, in the big house in Richmond surrounded by guards and state–of–the–art security systems, but this place is safe because it's full of people like me. It's got Mandy and Sophie in it and they understand me. There are no fabulous Parisienne stylists and no women walking round with clip-boards and shouting instructions as if they were trying to take over the moon. There's no Christine to consult before I can work out whether my boyfriend wants coffee and no elderly butler awaiting instruction. I guess you get used to that way of living; Rufus certainly doesn't seem to think it's odd, but then he grew up with it. It's part of his heritage; part of who he is. No one asked him to make any changes.

I'm not criticising because it would have been daft for him to come and live in my flat, but I suppose I mean that Rufus made a mistake by expecting me to slot in and quietly get on with my new life while he travelled off to the other side of the world. I lost my job, my friends and my independence and every value I've ever known went out of the window. Nope, I love Rufus more than I've ever loved anyone in my life before, and I can't imagine life without him, but I can't do what he needs me to do. It turns out that I have more sense of myself, and sense of individuality, than I ever realised and that's got to be a good thing. Hasn't it? Has it?

We drag the bags up the stairs and I take in the dreadful peeling paint and scuff marks traced across the walls. Never noticed them before. I can get them fixed now. One of the advantages of having some money – in the short term at least – will be the ability to make this flat nice.

'Let's leave them here for now,' says Soph, letting go of the heavier of the bags that she had gallantly offered to bring up for me. I think she regretted it the minute she attempted to lift it but, kindly, she didn't say anything, just grimaced as she bobbed it up the stairs.

'The guys'll bring them in for us.'

'What g–?'

We walk into the sitting room and I see straight away what guys she's referring to. There, sitting on our madly dilapidated sofa, are Jimmy Lapdance from the terrible nightclub three doors along, and three of his biggest bouncers, all of them done up to the nines in their gold jewellery, impossibly shiny black shoes and, in one case, a matching impossibly shiny black head. Jimmy jumps up and swaggers over to me.

''Ello, doll–face,' he says. 'This is Morgan, Mather and Prentice.'

I smile at the three bouncers while Jimmy surveys them proudly. His little hairy hands rest on his fleshy hips while he taps his foot in time to an imaginary drumbeat. 'You got yourself into a bit of a trouble, didn't you?'

'Jimmy's come to help us,' says Sophie. The man doesn't look immediately like an angel of mercy, with his tub–shaped torso and ungainly swagger. He drips in jewellery, clanking and banging like a badly oiled machine with every move.

'Right, this is the thing,' he says. 'You're gonna need protecting from the paps, ain't ya?'

I love the way he calls them 'paps' like he's used to dealing with the world's media every day.

'Yes, I guess I will,' I reply.

'We're gonna have a shift system outside the flat. There'll always be a bouncer there so the paps can't get too close. No one will get past my guys.'

'That's so kind,' I say.

Jimmy stands up to go. 'Don't worry about a thing,' he says.

Once the men have left, I turn to the girls. 'Well - that's

both incredibly kind and completely asking for trouble,' I say.

They nod. 'He was impossible to stop. He really wanted to help you.'

The three of us prepare to go to sleep that night, with me promising to update them properly in the morning.

'I will take you to the Rose Garden at Hampton Court Palace tomorrow and we'll talk about it all there,' I say.

'Why would you do that?'

'Because it's the most beautiful place on earth. It was mine and Rufus's special place while we were dating, and that's what got me into trouble - because I didn't want to tell the cops about it. That's where I was the night of Elodie's death, before coming here.'

'Oh,' they both say, slightly baffled. 'But - it's an old palace and a garden. Why would anyone under 50 want to go there?'

'It's beautiful and tranquil and I'm just kind of in love with it,' I say. 'There's a guy there called Frank who Rufus knows well. I'll get him to look out for me,' I say.

CHAPTER 31: THE TRUTH EMERGES

EXCLUSIVE
By Katie Joseph Daily Post Showbiz Editor

As the story of Elodie Elloissie and the mystery over who murdered her once again dominates the headlines, Katie Joseph takes a look behind the stylish woman and reveals what life was really like for the one–time golden girl of fashion.

Elodie Elloissie was a lonely woman with few friends. She never knew her own father, never knew the love and devotion of a family around her. Her story is desperately sad. The woman who would go on to become the queen of the red-carpet dressing had humble beginnings when she was found left outside a hospital like a waif and stray from a Dickens novel. The hospital named her Elodie after the nurse who looked after her and the young girl began a life of moving from foster home to foster home until a permanent carer could be found. That permanent carer was Rosemary Brown who now works as a housekeeper for Rufus George.

Elodie's childhood was miserable, fractious and painful. She couldn't settle down to a normal life because her new adoptive mother brought her to England where young Elodie had a terrible time adjusting to the new language, new friends and new surroundings. She was isolated and alone and struggled to make any meaningful friendships.

By the time she was seventeen, she was a rebel without a cause. She had left home and moved in with a succession of disreputable men until she came across Jon Boycott, the fashion designer who died two years ago, from a drugs overdose. Elodie never recovered from the death of her great love.

It was through this boyfriend that she met and fell in love with the world of fashion. She was a natural when she went along with her boyfriend to fashion shoots and helped to style the models. She went to work on a magazine and became an instant hit. Verda Petron, former editor of French Vogue recalls, 'She was a quiet girl who just got on with the job. She was always first in the office, always last to leave. When Jon died, though, she changed. She became brittle and determined. I never saw her cry over Jon's death but she was a changed person as a result of it. She worked harder and became determined to be successful at any cost. It was almost as if she blamed herself for his death.'

Elodie was at her most successful in the 1990s when she and Jon became the golden couple of fashion. Celebrities and stars wanted her to work with them and magazine designers wanted to feature her. She was a star. The trouble with being a star in the fickle world of fashion is that it is bound to come to a sudden end. Elodie was always seen as being part of the Jon and Elodie brand, known as 'JElodie'. When Jon died and it all ended, it stung her badly.

'It was as if all the anger from the rejection she'd faced as a child re-emerged with Jon's death,' said leading psychologist Dr Matthew Stevenson. 'Elodie became a liability; lashing out at models she'd once worked with and turning up drunk at catwalk shows. She was desperate to win her place back in society and for people to look up to her again, but she was persona non grata which sent her more deeply into the cycle of depression.'

By the time she sought help, and managed to get control over

*her drinking, the world of fashion had left her behind. She was
never again the star she once had been, and that haunted her to her
dying moments, at the hands of an unknown murderer in the
exclusive Royal Institute of Fashion. The most haunting thing of all
is that the murder happened on the second anniversary of the death
of Jon Boycott.*

'I see that Katie woman has been made editor now,' I say
to Mandy and Sophie who just look at me blankly. I guess
they haven't become quite as obsessed with the machinations
of the national press as I have.

'It's just this woman who's been writing about me in the
Daily Post since she first got wind of the fact that I was
seeing Rufus. It was she who 'broke the story' as they say in
the media. Now I've become such a huge story she's got
herself a promotion on the back of it all. Well done, love:
showbiz editor. Wow, won't Mum and Dad be happy! She's
written today about Elodie's background. It's awful. I never
knew what a tough life she had.'

I lay down the paper, trying to fold it beneath the blanket
thrown across my head. The girls are silent. They hate it
when the subject of Elodie comes up because they really
don't know what to say. We're in the car on the way to
Hampton Court and it's a complete bloody farce. It's ridiculous. I need an entourage of six just to get to the Rose
Garden and sit on a bench with no name. They bundled me
out of the house with more aggression than the police ever
used and hurled me into the back of Jimmy's Mercedes, and
we went off, hurtling through the streets of Twickenham,
pursued by half the world's media.

'You're like a member of the royal family or something,'
says Mandy when she sees how many photographers there
are alongside us. 'Like Diana, the Princess of Wales, when she
was being pursued everywhere by the papers. There's a
silence in the car and I peek out at her from beneath my

woollen roof. It's not a helpful comparison to make since the Princess died in circumstances not dissimilar to this.

We phone ahead to the palace, where I speak to Frank, who has closed off the Rose Garden for an hour for 'essential pruning'. He's waiting for us when we arrive. I'm about as flustered as it's possible for a woman to be and he's sitting there, entirely at ease, saying he enjoys the quietness when the garden's closed and thinks he might work this pruning rouse more often.

'Tea?' he offers, handing me a little plastic cup that he's removed from the top of his flask. He gives it to me with hands that seem much larger than they ought for such a slight and wiry man. They're wrinkly and mud–covered. I wonder why he doesn't wear gloves.

'Let me introduce Mandy and Sophie,' I say. He wipes his hand on his trousers before realising that he can't clean them, and nods in their direction instead.

'What do you think of our lovely gardens, then?' he asks.

'I thought there would be more flowers,' says Sophie.

'In December?'

'Yeah, I guess I'm not that knowledgeable when it comes to gardens.'

'Have some tea,' he says with a smile. 'We'll get you back here in the spring and you'll be dazzled by the beauty of the place.'

I smile warmly at Frank and take a gentle sip of the tea, feeling my teeth retreating from the sugar attack. He must have about eight spoons in there. Jeez. It's nice though.

'My grandson Lawrence made the tea today,' he says proudly, and I feel myself smile. Lawrence is such a lovely guy. He works in the gardens too and is sweet and desper-ately shy. He's also huge; a great big lumbering hulk of a man. Every time I see him, I think of Mandy – he's just her type.

'Is it OK for me to come here?' I ask. 'Or is it going to make things difficult for you?'

'It's fine,' he says. 'In fact, if you don't continue to come here, you'll make an old man very sad. Just call up beforehand and speak to me, or Lawrence, and we'll shut it for an hour. No one will mind. The gardens are quiet this time of year...everyone walks round the palace in the winter, and the gardens in the summer. Call Lawrence's mobile telephone; you've got the number, haven't you? He'll pass the message on to me. I don't have a mobile myself, as you might have guessed.'

'Are you sure I can do that?'

'Of course I'm sure, love. And what'll they do if they do mind? Sack me? I'm nearly eighty and haven't been on the payroll for fifteen years so there's not a lot they can do.'

'Thanks,' I say, taking another sip of the tea.

The girls haven't fallen in love with the Rose Garden quite as much as I hoped they would, but they all agree that meeting Frank was worth the trip.

And as we sit there, all huddled up on the bench against the cold, I'm glad I brought them. Even though the rose garden isn't at its finest in December when there aren't any roses, it's still lovely and peaceful and makes me feel happy.

We head back to the flat with freezing hands and feet now tingling under the warmth of the car heater. Once again, we are forced to battle our way through photographers once we reach the flat. We've never used the fire steps at the back of the fashion institute building before, but now it seems the only way to get me in without being photographed. Mandy and Sophie enter through the front while I sneak up the back.

Once we're inside, we pile onto the sofa and switch the television on.

'No news programmes,' I shout, but the girls have already

moved on down the channel list, far from the news programmes and into the wonderful world of bad reality tv shows.

'I need to go and put an old tracksuit on for this,' I say, jumping off the sofa and rushing into my room. It's weird being back here. I wish Rufus like mad, but I feel more content here in this shabby little place, than I ever did in his mansion.

I grab my velour hoodie and throw it on top.

'Kelly. Someone to see you,' Mandy shouts through the flat before running into my bedroom.

'I don't want to see anyone,' I say to Mandy, as I've been saying to both the girls since I got here. I don't want to see anyone, talk to anyone or think about anyone. All I want to do is make my daily visit to the Rose Garden to drink tea with Frank and listen to him talking about the roses.

'Come on, quickly; it's important,' she says again.

'It's not Rufus is it?' I ask, a wave of terror running through me at the thought of him sitting out there in the flat, drinking tea from chipped mugs with Sophie.

'Of course it's not Rufus,' she says.

The bouncers won't let him anywhere near the flat. Apparently, he turned up in the early hours of this morning and has been around several times already today, and calls constantly, but the girls know that if they let him in, or hand the phone to me just once, I'll leave the flat forever, so they continue to send Rufus packing without giving him any explanation whatsoever.

'It's the police,' she says. 'That guy, Detective Inspector Barnes – the good-looking one. He wants to talk to you.'

Oh, joy.

'Hi,' I say, walking into the sitting room, and I see his eyebrows rise.

'Have you not been well?' he asks and he sounds genuinely concerned. 'You look so pale and thin.'

I know he's thinking of the glamorous woman who he met in Rufus's house - all dressed up and made up and always looking perfect. I suppose it's quite alarming to see me looking scruffy and unmade up.

'What information do you need now?'

'We've had some interesting information come to light,' he says in his police–officery way.

'Oh,' I say, sitting up and immediately paying closer attention because, despite my fragile physical and mental state, I'm as keen as anyone for them to find the person who callously murdered Elodie and bring him or her to justice. I notice that the girls are sitting forward too, looking at the detective with rather too much attention. Sophie is smiling at him like a lunatic. Does she fancy him or something? It certainly looks like it. I suppose he's attractive, really. If you go for the big and hairy look. Sophie clearly does.

'We've cleaned up the CCTV footage,' he says which is a rather baffling introduction to any sort of conversation, so we all just stare at him.

'You know, the CCTV footage from the door at the back of the building. The only logical point of entry for the assailant was that rear door, but the footage from it was very patchy. Well, it was sent off to be cleaned up and it's come back. Clean.'

'And ...'

'And,' he goes on, 'that means no one entered through the back door.'

'Oh. So, what does that mean?'

'It means the assailant must have entered through the front door. But everyone who entered through the front door had a watertight alibi for the time of the murder.'

He's got us now.

'So where did this 'assailant' come from?'

'We're not ruling out suicide at this stage.'

'Suicide?'

'Suicide,' he repeats gravely. 'I say we're not ruling it out because we haven't established it yet, but we have established that - despite our initial thoughts - it is possible for her to have stabbed herself. Scientists have looked at the angle at which the dagger entered the victim's body and the way in which it had been pushed. It's clear that she could have done it, though we're still investigating. A pathologist called Michael James is looking at the body again; he's the best in the business.

'One thing that is odd is that there's no suicide note. It's unusual for a suicide victim not to leave a note of some kind so we're going back through her possessions and final movements in the hope of finding one.'

'Oh.'

The detective looks across at us, lingering a little longer than is strictly necessary when he comes to Sophie's cleavage, then stands up to leave.

'Well, I won't keep you ladies any longer. Just wanted to keep you fully briefed. I'll call back if there are any more developments,' he says.

'Oh, please do,' says Sophie. 'Let me show you out.'

'Thanks Bob. Yes, you join us live at Richmond police station where we have just heard from the team investigating the death of Elodie Elloissie that they now believe she committed suicide. That's right; despite conducting a massive murder investigation, arresting one of Elodie's closest friends, Kelly Monsoon, and interrogating another, Isabella Bronks-Harrison, they now think the stylist took her own life. I'm joined by Katie Joseph, the senior showbiz editor of the Daily Post newspaper.

'Katie, you revealed last week that Elodie died on the anniversary of her former lover's death. Do you think that's why she committed suicide?'

'Yes, I think that's probably why. She was very cut up when he died. I don't think she ever properly got over it.'

'Thanks, Katie. For more of our exclusive interview with Katie Joseph, see www.sky.com. Now over to Brett for the weather.'

THE MYSTERY OF ELODIE'S SUICIDE BID EXCLUSIVE
By Katie Joseph Daily Post Showbiz Editor
Our woman in the know gives you the full behind the – scenes story on what happened at the heart of the police operation to convince them that Elodie Elloissie had committed suicide. EXCLUSIVELY in the Daily Post, your top newspaper for showbiz news.

It was Michael James, a pathologist working with Scotland Yard's murder squad, who found the crucial mark that would convince police detectives that Elodie Elloissie had committed suicide. A 'hilt' wound found between her thumb and index finger confirmed to them after a two-and-a-half-week operation to find a murderer, that she had taken her own life.

They investigated the shape, depth and direction of the mark, and became clear in their minds that this was not a murder after all, but the actions of a woman feeling so miserable that she wished to take her own life.

But what continued to baffle police was why there was no suicide note left. Was this a spur of the moment decision? Then, yesterday morning, while searching through files on her computer, they found a video message explaining that she planned to take her own life on the anniversary of the death of her great love, the fashion designer Jon Boycott. Daily Post believes that the video reveals that Elloissie felt she was personally responsible for the death of her boyfriend because when she found her boyfriend's body – half–dead after a night of drug– taking – she fled the flat in panic, rather than calling an ambulance. Even though she returned to the flat and rang for help, over an hour had passed – a period of time in which critical care could have been given to her boyfriend.

'I killed him as surely as if I'd plunged a knife into him myself, and that's what I plan to do today, to myself, to say sorry for what I did to Jon, and to be with him once more.'

Elloissie goes on to explain that the reason she didn't call for assistance straight away was because she worried about what the revelation might do to Jon's career. 'As soon as I calmed down, I rushed back and called an ambulance, but it was too late. I killed him.'

Police will outline their discoveries at the inquest, which is scheduled for the end of next week. It marks a tragic end to the story that has captivated millions in this lead up to Christmas. It is believed that Hollywood producers have been in discussions about making a movie about the doomed affair, which led to the death of Elloissie who was, at one time, the world's most influential stylist.

CHAPTER 32: LIFE WITH THE GIRLS

can't hear it,' says Mandy, walking round the flat and straining so much she looks as if she's about to go to the toilet. Her eyes are all screwed up and she has an intense concentration about her. 'Oh no, hang on. I can hear something. What's that? Yes, stop. I can hear it now. Nope. It's gone. You need to ring the phone again.'

'This is bloody insane,' says Sophie calling my mobile from her phone. We all fall silent, listening for the sound of ringing.

'Yes,' they both say, leaning over slightly with their heads tilted. We all wander through the flat in this bizarre, hunched over, straining with concentration manner, listening intently in the hope of hearing it ring.

'I can definitely hear something,' I say, hoping that we'll find my bloody phone after a morning of searching for it. I know I had it last night because we had a little impromptu pre–Christmas Eve drinks party, and Mum called to check I was OK. But what did I do with it then? No one knows.

The phone goes to answerphone so I hang up. 'We're never going to find this thing, are we?' I say, as the two girls peer at me through eyes that are still suffering the after-effects of last night's alcohol. 'Come on, let's have a cup of tea.'

I head in the direction of the kettle while Mandy swings open the fridge door to pull out the milk. 'Aha!!' she cries, making the two of us jump into the air. 'Guess what's in the fridge?'

'Oh God. If it was once living, please just throw it away and don't tell us about it,' I plead, fearing that she's found a dead mouse or toad or bat or something stuck in the ice at the back where we really should have defrosted.

'Nope. Nothing terrible … Da … da … da …' She holds out my phone, freezing cold, but all intact. 'Happy Christmas Eve,' she says.

'What the hell was it doing in the fridge?' I ask. She shrugs, Sophie shrugs and we all burst out laughing. 'I think that must be the end to the perfect party,' I say, because we did have a load of fun last night.

It's been over two weeks now since I left Richmond and, though not a day goes by when I don't feel my insides turning themselves inside out with the pain of not being able to see Rufus, I know I've done the right thing. I know he needs to be free to find someone who's like him and can live in that odd world of his.

Mandy and Sophie have been brilliant. We've had so many nights lying on the sofa chatting over huge pizzas (I've got money now so we have one each - not that I manage to finish mine - I've got no appetite at all these days), and we eat them with Châteauneuf–du–Pape as I explain how I developed my newfound love of wine after our wine–tasting night). I also tell them about Rufus and what it was like living with a screen god.

'The paparazzi surrounded the house, constantly,' I say. 'It was awful.'

'They surround the flat too,' counters Sophie. 'They're outside 24/7 now, afraid to leave the place unmanned since you upped and escaped at 4 am last time they took a coffee break.'

Last night at the drinks get–together, we invited Katie and Jenny who I used to work with because the girls were desperate for me to put them straight on the situation with me being given my own office. Once I ran through it all from my point of view, they got it completely. We even had a game of Malteser–throwing to celebrate the fact that everything was great with us now, but it turned out I'd lost the knack a little and hurled the Maltesers with such force and with no regard at all for direction that it's taken me half the morning to clear the chocolate– shaped dabs off the wall.

'Good fun last night, wasn't it?' asks Mandy, tipping boiling water into the mugs and watching me as I cradle my freezing cold phone.

'Yes,' I say.

'Messages from Rufus?' she asks.

'Forty–three,' I reply.

The two girls look from one to the other.

'You should talk to him you know,' says Sophie. 'You've spent eighteen days ignoring his calls, not accepting the flowers, refusing to allow him to come into the flat and not reading his letters.'

'No, I read the letters,' I tell them.

Not only do I read them, but I memorise them. Every word, every pause, every comma on the page. They are hand-written, which I love more than anything because I know he never handwrites anything. I'm still praying that's because he wants to make them as personal as possible and that's why he puts pen to paper. Half of me wonders though whether he has to handwrite them because the police haven't returned his computer yet. Let's hope not ... first option is so much more romantic.

I tell the girls that I'm over him and have moved on, but the truth is that there's not a second in the day when I don't yearn to be with him. Every night I lie there thinking of him; I go to sleep crying and I wake up crying, then I wipe my eyes and pretend everything's OK.

'Why don't you see him?' asks Mandy. 'Just go and meet him somewhere and talk to him. Do it today ... on Christmas Eve. Go on ... it has a nice romantic ring to it.'

'No, I can't,' I say, looking down at my hands and fiddling with my fingers and trying desperately not to cry. I feel like a part of me was lost when I walked away from that house. I watched a programme about a cow being separated from her new-born calf and the cry she gave made me want to weep because that's what I want to do. I feel like lying down in the street and howling like a wild animal whose new-born's just been torn away.

'I don't know why you can't see him,' Sophie says and Mandy nods in agreement. 'Look at you; you're a wreck. You're not eating, you can't think straight. You need to talk to him.'

'If I see him, it'll kill me.'

Rufus has been calling at the flat almost hourly, shouting up to my bedroom at the back from the alleyway off the street. I know the bouncers from Jimmy's help him through and make sure no one sees him but they won't let him get too close. They know the rules; I watch them sometimes through a crack in my bedroom curtains. They see him coming and smuggle him through so he can call up to me, telling me how much he loves and adores me, and saying how sorry he is that he didn't support me.

'I didn't know what to do, Kelly. This was as new to me as

it was to you. I was terrified. Absolutely terrified. Please talk to me.'

Then I see Jimmy appear, pat him on the back, and lead him away.

I wander out of the kitchen and into the bedroom to get dressed.

'Where are you going?' asks Sophie, coming and sitting on the bed while I slip on a big woolly jumper and brush my hair. I stick on a hat and my big coat and some sunglasses and tell her I'll be back later. She knows where I go every day. Lawrence was at our little party last night and he, Mandy and Sophie were tucked away in a huddle for most of it, looking over to me occasionally as I stood with Katie and Jenny explaining how difficult it was at work after I'd moved in with Rufus, and telling them about the coat incident which had upset me so much. I'm sure that in the little Lawrence huddle there was talk about me sitting with Frank in the gardens every day.

'I'm off,' I say.

'One second,' says Sophie, taking my hand in hers, and preparing to give me yet another of her talks. She's become quite the old romantic since she started seeing Detective Barnes. She denies it, of course, but I know she's been sneaking out when I've been lying in my bed. I've heard the giggles as she and Mandy get ready to go on their respective dates, and I've seen the happiness in their eyes. I'm pleased for them both, honestly I am. They deserve to be happy. I just hope she never crosses that Barnes guy because he's a bloody nightmare when you're on the wrong side of him.

'Most people spend a lifetime looking for what you've found in Rufus,' says Sophie. 'I never thought I'd say this, Kells, but you and Rufus ... well, it works. It does. You need each other. You were unlucky that you got tangled up with

Elodie, but if you take her out of the picture, there was no problem, was there?

'I can't bear to see his gaunt and pale face again, begging me to let him in just so he can see you. I can't bear to see you, getting thinner and thinner and teetering on the edge of illness constantly. And what for? No one's asking you to go back there or start the relationship again. Just talk to him, Kell. You have to.'

I smile and hug her but I know I can't do that. Every time I see a picture of him, I want to howl and scream, every time I glimpse his name or a reference to a film he once starred in, I feel this wave of unbelievable sickness rush through me. I feel light–headed and ill just being alive. I can't see him in the flesh. There's no way. I can't see him. It'll kill me.

CHAPTER 33: BACK TO THE ROSE GARDEN

*D*espite what Mandy and Sophie think, I think the Rose Garden's really pretty this time of year. Odd, because there are no flowers around, of course, just the bare thorny sticks sitting all frost–covered and jagged in the hard ground, but it's still gorgeous. There's something lovely about being in a garden all year round, seeing it change through the seasons. I'm finding myself loving every aspect of this place: not just the blooms themselves, but the whole thing about nature – working its way through its natural cycle. I love the way the hedges sit around the outside, as if placing a protective arm around the garden, and I like the way the benches lounge around the edge as if having their own imaginary conversation with one another. This place has got a life of its own; that's why I like it – because it's vibrant and real and alive.

The other great thing about this place in winter, obviously, is that hardly anyone comes here. I mean that. Most times there's me and Frank. Lawrence pops over when I'm here now, which is lovely. He was shy at first, but since he's met Mandy and knows a little more about me, he's relaxed in my company. I guess that now he realises I'm not a raving loony who's about to attack everyone and murder them, nor am I an incredibly stuck-up Hollywood type. He tells me all about the area of the grounds that is his responsibility. He took me over there once. It's magnificent with great sprawling lawns running down to the river, beautiful statues and plants. But it's not like my Rose Garden. This place is still my favourite.

My phone rings in my pocket; I should say 'vibrates' in my pocket. I switch the ring off when I'm here; it seems disrespectful to have it tinkling away when there might be people around desperately searching for a slice of solitude; time for silence to wash over them ... time to think.

I know who it will be on the phone, of course. It will be the man I'm helplessly and hopelessly in love with ... a man I'm desperate to talk to, but am terrified of coming into contact with because I know that seeing him will make me feel worse than I do now and, when that happens, I honestly don't think I'll be able to go on. I just need to forget him. I know I can do that, but I also know that it'll take time.

'OK, love?' It's Frank, dispensing his greetings and brightening up the place. 'How are you doing there, beautiful?'

'I'm fine, Frank, how are you?'

'All the better for seeing you, my dear. Mind if I join you?'

'Of course not. I even have biscuits!'

It's become quite a habit, this. He has his flask of sweet tea and I bring biscuits and we sit on the little bench with no dedication and chat about nothing in particular.

'How was the party last night?' he asks. 'Lawrence had a great time.'

'It was fun,' I say, unconvincingly.

'Sounds like you had a wild time. Lawrence says you were in bed by nine.'

'I was tired.'

Frank knows all about what's happened to me, of course. He knows about Rufus and me because it was through Rufus that I met him. I sometimes wonder whether he still sees Rufus. I doubt it. Rufus is busy. The idea of him coming down to the Rose Garden to drink heavily over-sugared tea with an octogenarian is slightly unlikely to say the least.

Frank's craggy features have settled into a smile. 'What a pickle you're in,' he says eventually. 'More tea?'

'I'm not in a pickle,' I say, thinking that 'pickle' is about as wrong a word as you could summon to describe the hash I've made of things.

'You are,' he says. 'You're madly in love with a man who's madly in love with you but you're too proud to do anything about it.'

'That's not true!' I say. 'I'm not in love with anyone.'

'OK. Fine. We'll change the subject. What are you doing for Christmas?'

'I'm going back to my parents' place in Hastings. I get the train this evening.'

'That'll be nice. Do you get on well with your parents?'

'Yeah. They're pretty cool. You'd love my dad – he's mad about gardening.'

'How about your mum?'

'She spends most of her time looking after relatives. She's lovely'

'She sounds kind.'

'Yeah. She is.'

'Like you.'

'Yeah ... hardly! I don't look after anyone.'

'You looked after Elodie pretty well. I'd say that you made a very sad, lonely and complicated girl very happy during her last weeks. You should be proud of yourself.'

'I have to say, Frank, that pride is not something I feel

when I think of Elodie. I was arrested for her murder, you know. I wrecked everything. I don't feel proud.'

'What if I said to you that you haven't wrecked anything? What if I say to you that the video the police found on her computer was recorded before she even met you? You're not responsible, Kelly. You never were. You messed up enough for the police to suspect you but that's all – it's over now. Tea?'

'Er ... yes please. Do you not think I'm completely useless for getting myself into that mess?'

'When you get to my age, dear, nothing really surprises you or horrifies you. I lost two close friends in the war – I saw them die and couldn't do anything about it. Most of my relations are dead. My wife died two years ago and my son and daughter–in–law five years before that in a horrific accident. Lawrence was thrown from the wreckage. He was in intensive care for ten months. You soon realise that the only point in life is people. Without them there is no life. If you find a special person who matters – don't let them go.'

The tears are rolling down my face as Frank talks but, to his credit, he pretends he hasn't noticed. We both look out across the thorns and branches.

'Why didn't Rufus come to the drinks party last night?' he asks suddenly.

'I didn't want him to.'

'Why not?'

I just shrug, because if I talk any more on the subject of Rufus with this kindly old man in this beautiful garden, I know I'll just drown in tears.

'Gosh you're a lady of few words this morning, aren't you?'

'I find it hard,' I say, choking on tears. 'This is a difficult day ... Christmas Eve. This is a day I always thought we'd spend together. This is a difficult place in which to sit and talk about him.'

'It seems to me that every day's a difficult day when two people are hopelessly in love but don't see one another. Even the staff at his house miss you,' he says.

'Do they?'

'Yep.'

'How on earth do you know?'

'Henry comes down here quite a lot. He's a keen gardener you know. He wanted to say 'hello' because you'd mentioned me to him. He also wanted to know whether I'd seen you, and to find out whether you were OK.'

'Tell him I am.'

'You want me to lie to him?' says Frank. 'I could do that. Or I could tell him the truth – which is that you're fading away before me because you miss Rufus so much.'

'I'm not.'

'You are, sweetheart. Did it never occur to you that you might have thrown the baby out with the bathwater?'

'What does that mean? People are always using that phrase but I don't have a baby and I take showers rather than baths. What on earth does it mean?'

'What it means is that you met someone you love dearly and have thrown him away with the lifestyle and his ridiculous friends because you didn't like the nonsense that surrounded going out with someone famous. Couldn't you just have said, 'I can't live with all this nonsense'?'

'He wouldn't have listened.'

'Bet he would.'

'You don't know him.'

'I don't know him well, but he listens to me when I talk.'

'He what?'

'He listens.'

'When?'

'He comes most days.'

'What do you mean 'he comes most days'?'

'He comes in the afternoons. Always asks whether you've been here and I always say no because that's what you want me to say. He knows I'm lying though. Yesterday he actually said as much to me.'

'You never told me he came.'

'He told me not to tell you.'

'Why are you telling me now then?'

'Because I'm sick of all of this. I'm eighty years old. I know how short life is, and I know how precious life is. The two of you need to sort this out and get back together or it'll be the biggest mistake since Hitler invaded Poland, and we don't want that, do we?'

'No,' I say.

'So, you won't mind too much if I tell you that he's here then?'

'Here?'

'Yes, he's here; I told him to wait by the maze until I'd spoken to you. Don't let an old man down, Kelly. Tell me you'll go and talk to him. It's Christmas for goodness sake.'

Fuck. I don't want to let an old man down any more than anyone else wants to let an old man down, but Jeez, I don't want to see Rufus. Really, I don't want to see him so much that the thought of doing so makes me want to weep.

'Come with me.'

'No,' I say, remaining in my seat on the bench. 'You can't do this, Frank. I don't want to see him.'

'See him. Just see him. Not date him, marry him or live with him for the rest of time. See him. Let him talk to you. If you don't, you're not being fair. I'm serious, Kelly. This is silly. There are two people whose lives are being ruined by this. It's not just about you – it's about him too. Imagine how he felt when he woke up to find you'd disappeared and wouldn't talk to him?'

My legs are like jelly when I stand up and follow the old man through the gardens and out towards the maze.

'Hello, Malcolm.'

'Morning, Ethel.'

'Hello there, Deirdre; how did Howard's operation go? Everything all right, was it?'

He seems to know everyone here.

'None of us will be here forever,' he says, turning to me. 'You either take the chances while they're there or regret not taking them once the opportunity has passed; that's the only real choice any of us has. Don't think you're being big or clever by turning down a chance of happiness, Kelly, you're not. I watched my family almost wiped out in a car crash; I watched my wife die of cancer. If I had my time again, I'd take every opportunity in the world to be with the person I loved. If you won't listen to anyone else – listen to me, Kelly. I mean it. Here we are – he's in the maze.'

At the entrance to the maze stand Morgan, Mather and Prentice. They've been joined by Lawrence, and by his side is Mandy, looking all sweet and lovely in a big duffle coat and those enormous cream mittens of hers. She taps my shoulder affectionately as I pass her. I can't believe this. The whole clan are involved. This must be what they were planning last night. The entrance to the maze is in front of me but suddenly I'm hit by a colossal fear.

'I can't go into the maze,' I say to Mandy, turning round to face her, and seeing the smile slide off her face.

'Oh, you can,' she says, with uncharacteristic firmness. 'Do you know how much bloody trouble we went to, to set this up? Get your skinny arse in there now.'

'OK.'

Left with no choice, I walk in and turn left, immediately seeing a choice of pathways to take. How is this ever going to work? I'll never find the man.

'Rufus, where are you?' I'm trembling as I speak. I can't bear this.

There's no sound. Christ, if he's expecting me to find my way into the middle he's in for a shock. I have the sense of direction of a leafy green vegetable. It's sometimes a struggle for me to find the kitchen in the mornings.

'Rufus, please. I'll never be able to find you.'

I continue walking round, praying this isn't some terrible practical joke by the girls. Hoping Rufus will be there when I find my way into the middle. 'Ruf ... are you there?'

'I'm here. Is that you? Kelly, is that you?'

'Yes, but where are you?'

'They told me to come and wait in the maze for you. Perhaps we should both head for the middle, and meet there.'

'I guess so,' I say, unconvinced of my ability to find the middle of the maze.

Suddenly the pressure of seeing him has been lifted by the silliness of us both being in a maze, trying to find one another. Finding my way to the middle has become a bigger challenge than the fear of coming face to face with Rufus.

'You could stand still,' he suggests. 'I'll come and find you. You'll have to keep talking though, so I can follow your voice.'

'OK,' I say, then I can't think what to say.

'Talk,' he insists. 'I can't work out where on earth you are if you don't talk.'

'Well, I'm here. Near the bushes, in the maze.'

'Yeah, thanks for that,' he says, and I can hear in his voice that he's smiling as he speaks. 'Near the bushes, huh? Well that's really helpful.'

'Your voice sounds like it's getting closer,' I say, and I'm suddenly filled with an overwhelming urge to see him. Where did this come from? I've spent weeks avoiding him and now I've heard his voice and can sense his presence, I'm just desperate to see him.

'Say something,' he says. 'It's impossible to know where you are if you don't say something.'

'I love you,' I say.

'Say it again.'

'I love you, Rufus. I miss you. Where are you? Come and find me, please.'

There's an almighty rustling of the bushes and clambering, pushing and a considerable amount of swearing before Rufus appears through the hedge, covered in twigs, with a small rip in his jacket and a streak of blood across his face.

'I came as quickly as I could,' he says, grabbing me and lifting me up into his arms. 'I love you, Kelly.'

And then I don't know what happens. I don't know whether it's because it's Christmas, because I've hardly eaten for nearly three weeks and am feeling very vulnerable, or because all my best friends in the world have arranged this in order to make me happy again but I say, 'I love you too.'

'I'm sorry?' he says.

'I love you too!' I shout back feeling weak with pleasure.

'And will you marry me? Can we carry on with this lovely life we were creating for ourselves?'

'Yes, yes, yes, yes, yes.'

All that remains now is for us to find our way out of this damn thing. We can hear the voices outside, but it's so incredibly difficult to work out how on earth to get to them. Then, a sighting through the twigs. Thank God it's winter so you can see a little through the branches. Not like the summer when the densely-leaved trees would have trapped us for hours. We step through the gap and suddenly we're surrounded by people – all of them cheering and clapping as they form a tunnel for us to pass through.

'I love you,' says Rufus, taking my face in his hands, but I'm beyond replying. The drama of the last few weeks has caught up with me and I collapse backwards and the whole world disappears.

CHAPTER 34: A VISITOR IN THE ROSE GARDEN

⁂

'*K*elly, Kelly. Are you OK?'

I look up and see the shimmering, vague and drifting faces of Frank, Lawrence, Mandy and Sophie, and is that Detective Barnes? Holy fuck, I hope not. There's Rufus. Oh my God, oh my …

'Come on, Kelly, sit up. Come on.'

I look up this time and it's just the girls, trying to manoeuvre me from lying to sitting for no good reason.

'What are you doing?' I ask.

'We're trying to give you water,' they say. Oh, OK

'I don't want water, I want the sweet tea that Lawrence made,' I say. 'It's in Frank's flask.'

'OK,' says Mandy. 'I'll go and get some.'

'I'm so pleased,' says Sophie when we're left on our own for a minute. 'I'm so happy for you. You and Rufus are getting married after all. Yey! It's gonna be the best Christmas ever.'

'Where's Rufus now?' I ask, as Mandy comes back with the flask.

'The guys all went to wait in the Rose Garden until you

were OK. We didn't want you to faint again. He didn't want to go but we made him. Shall I get him?'

'Thanks,' I say, and watch how she scampers off, leaving me sitting on the floor sipping sweet tea with Mandy.

It seems like seconds later that Rufus is there, striding towards me and beaming with joy.

'I'll leave you two alone,' says Mandy, standing up and backing off towards the roses.

Rufus and I walk back into the Rose Garden hand in hand, me still feeling a little queasy and leaning heavily into him at every step, him walking slowly so as to balance my weight on his hip as he moves. Both of us are so shot through with happiness that we can barely speak.

'Let's get married soon,' I whisper.

'Straight away,' he agrees.

We arrive in the garden and everyone stares. I think they're too worried about making a fuss – forming a tunnel or cheering madly – in case I collapse again. They just look and smile warmly. Frank is sitting on the bench with no inscription, looking at me with such incredible warmth and pride that I feel like bursting into tears. No, I mustn't, not now. No more drama, Kelly. Control yourself.

'I'd like to make an announcement,' says Rufus, coughing a little and turning on that actor like voice of his. 'Kelly and I are getting married. She's moving straight back into the house and we're going to get married as soon as possible.'

'But this time it's going to be different,' I say.

'Is it?'

'Yes, it is. Mandy and Sophie will come round whenever they want, we'll only employ staff who are fun, warm and kind. It's afraid there's no place for Rosemary. We should pay her off generously, but I can't live there with her.'

'She's already gone,' says Rufus.

'So, who will be the housekeeper?'

'Your choice,' he says.

'We promote Pamela and Julie,' I say straight away.

There are cheers all round then. Sophie even treats us to that quite unbelievably loud wolf whistle of hers that has us all wincing in pain.

'Now we're sorry to have to run out on you like this, but we've got a little bit of catching up to do,' he says, taking my hand and pulling me off in the direction of the exit. 'I also need to feed this girl before she fades away completely. But we look forward to seeing you all very soon and Frank ...'

Frank looks up from his seat on his favourite bench.

'Thank you,' says Rufus. 'From both of us. We're more grateful than words can ever say.'

'Bye and thanks so much to all of you,' I add, as I'm practically dragged through the gardens in the direction of Rufus's car.

'Home, Henry,' he instructs and Henry gives me the biggest broadest smile ever.

'Nice to have you back, Kelly,' he says.

Then it's my turn to smile. 'Nice to be back.'

CHAPTER 35: ME, MYSELF, I

*I*t's funny going back into the house again. This time it feels far less stressful than last time. You know, this time it feels like I should be here rather than I'm here on a temporary basis until he finds someone better suited to his needs. I'm not fresh off the bus and feeling embarrassed about every part of me. This time I'm thinking: I'm fine. If you don't like me, the problem is yours.

It's lovely to see the staff and how happy they seem. While Rufus is always friendly with them, it feels like I've reached a whole new level of rapport; we're high–fiving and smiling and I'm asking after Pamela's mum, David's sister and whether Julie ever managed to get it together with Mike, the guy from the record shop. 'Yes,' she says, excitement squeezing out of her despite her efforts to keep it in and look as smooth and unruffled as possible in front of Rufus.

'Brilliant,' I say, genuinely delighted, and we give each other a little hug. You see, I'm like these people. Before I met Rufus, so less than a year ago, I would have been out socially with the likes of Julie. I'd probably have fancied Mike from the record shop; he sounds nice. Just because I happened to meet Rufus doesn't change the fundamental constituents of my being. These are my people and the fact that they work for me and not me for them is a matter of luck, timing and circumstance, and I hope I always remember that. I think it's what most of Rufus's friends have forgotten. They're more successful than most people because they happened to have been born in a particular place to particular parents with particular views. Their schooling and upbringing gave them the push up the ladder that most people don't get, but it doesn't make them better than anyone else.

Rufus is looking at me in amazement as I hug Pamela and tell her how pretty her hair is.

'He's been miserable without you, love,' she says, and I hug her again.

'Why do the staff adore you so much?' asks Rufus as he leads me upstairs with rather more haste than is appropriate given that the staff are all watching us so closely.

'Because I talk to them,' I reply, as he swings open the bedroom door and pushes me inside. 'I talk to them as individuals and not as staff.'

I lie on the bed and feel my eyelids fold down straight away. Within minutes I'm fast asleep. I don't think it was quite the return to the house that Rufus was hoping for. When I open my eyes it's 3pm.

'You've been fast asleep,' he says.

'Haven't you been sleeping?' I ask.

'Nope. I don't sleep much anymore.' He leans up on his elbow and begins stroking my hair as he speaks. 'To be honest, I'm afraid to sleep because once, while I was asleep, the most wonderful girl I've ever met disappeared. I don't want to take that risk again.'

'Ha, ha,' I say. 'I'm not going anywhere this time.'

'So, you'll stay here for Christmas Day?'

'Oh shit! Christmas! No, I can't. I promised Mum that I'd go back home. She'll be devastated if I don't go.'

I pick up my phone to call and explain that I'm going to be later than expected.

'Grrrrrr ...' he says, kissing me on the forehead. 'Promise me you'll come straight back then. And promise me you'll let Henry drive you. I don't want you getting onto trains in the dark.'

'Thanks,' I say, because having Henry drive me there would be just amazing.

'So, before then there are a couple of things we have to do, aren't there?'

'Are there?'

'Yes. We need to book the Plaza in New York – the most famous wedding venue in the world. Nothing, my love, nothing is going to go wrong now. We'll have the best dress, the best guest list and the best venue. We'll have the time of our lives. Now, I thought, to save you having to organise the whole thing yourself, what we'd do is get Jamelia Walker to help organise it. She runs a company called Celebrity Bride. They're the best wedding planners in the universe and ... while you were fast asleep ... I called them. She can come round at 4.30 pm on the twenty–seventh. What do you think?'

Silence.

'Well, what do you think?' he asks again, all excited now.

I just snuggle up next to Rufus and breathe in his scent, soaking in the familiarity of it, and delighting in the return of it. I want to absorb the man as much as I possibly can, just in case what I'm about to say sends him running for the hills.

'Did I do good?'

'No,' I say and I see him flinch and look at me with concern and confusion.

'You haven't changed your mind. Please tell me you haven't changed your mind.'

'I haven't,' I say with honesty. 'I want to marry you more than anything. But I want this to be a marriage about us, not about the brilliance of Jamelia Walker or Celebrity Bride. How did we get back together? Was it Jamelia who set that up? Was it any of these fantastically proper and sophisticated friends that you dinner party with every night? Was it? Was it Lord and Lady Simpkins – the guys who were talking to the press about how evil I am throughout my time with the police? Do you want them to come?'

'No of course not,' he says, looking quizzical. 'I went round to see Simpkins after what he did and told him I wanted nothing to do with any theatres he was involved with. I made it very clear that if he said a word in public about you again, I'd be round there to discuss it with him personally, and it wouldn't be pleasant. Of course I don't want someone like that hovering around anywhere near our wedding day.'

'Good, because I want this wedding to be about you and me and our parents. I want it to be about Frank and Lawrence, about Mandy and Sophie. I want Katie and Jenny to come and to show everyone how good they are at Malteser-throwing now, because they are good, Rufus. They've left us way behind.

I want my friends there and I want your friends Deevers and Courty to be there, and I want them to be having fun, not worrying about how they're going to look in Hello! magazine. I want them to be able to get drunk and party all night. I want this wedding to reflect who we are, not who people think you are and who I once wanted to be. Am I making sense?'

'Yes,' he says. 'But I'm not sure what sort of wedding

you're after. I mean – we could have all those things you've just described at the Plaza.'

'I know,' I say. 'But I've never been to the Plaza. Why would I want to spend the most important day of my life there?'

'Because it's lovely.'

'No. People who've never been to the Plaza before do not suddenly decide to go there on their wedding day because 'it's lovely'. They do so because they think it makes them look good. I'm past caring how I look, Rufus. I want to marry you but I'd like us to get married my way. Will you do that?'

'I'll do anything you want,' he says. 'As long as I get to marry you at the end of it all, nothing else matters.'

'Good. Because the thing is – we're different. That doesn't need to matter at all, but you need to realise it. I have normal parents who worked hard to put a roof over my head and food in my mouth; they struggled a lot and this is my chance to say thank you and to give them a day out that's as special to them as it is to me.

I have a mad Great–Aunt Maude who's just thrilled to wake up alive every morning because she's convinced the war's still going on. When you leave the room to make tea she cries because she thinks you're never coming back. This is where I come from, Rufus. We don't have private jets and pairs of shoes for every social occasion. We eat tea not dinner, and we have one knife and one fork. If there's a starter, and to be honest I don't think there ever has been, but if there were a starter then we'd have to lick the same knife and fork clean and use them for the main course.

'We have a tiny garden and no security guards. It's been hell for Mum and Dad since I came to live with you because the photographers can get right up to the house. And before you say it – yes, they could have asked you to sort out their security for them and help them keep the papers at arm's length but they're proud people, Rufus. You don't have to have drivers, cars and multi–million-pound film contracts to be proud of who you are and what you've achieved in life. They're proud people and I love them, so – no – I won't be getting married on the other side of the world in a room full of people I don't know but who look good in the pictures.

'The wedding planners can come if they want but I won't be here to meet them. I won't be a Celebrity Bride so Jamelia can go and boil her head, as beautiful as it no doubt is. This is our wedding, it's my wedding, and it'll be me and Mum who decide what happens. For starters, everything at the wedding must match her chocolate–brown hat or the wedding doesn't happen. Do you hear me?'

'I hear you, sweets,' he says. 'Not sure whether I understand you in any way though. Did you say your mum wants to wear a hat made out of chocolate?'

'And what if she does? What if she wants all the bridesmaids' dresses made out of chocolate?'

'Then we'll have all the bridesmaids' dresses made out of chocolate. If you're happy, I'm happy. That's all I've ever wanted: for you to be happy.'

'Good. Then what are you doing for Christmas?'

'No plans,' he says. 'I tend to think I'm a bit past celebrating Christmas. I've got no desire to sit in a paper hat, reading bad jokes and eating turkey.'

'Well, that's bad news, because that's exactly what you're going to be doing. Pack your bag, sunshine. You're coming to Hastings for Christmas.'

'Right,' he says. 'But can I just ask: what's this got to do with us getting married?'

'Our wedding planner lives there,' I say. 'Her name's Jayne Monsoon, but she likes to be known as 'Mum'. Now come on, stop dawdling. Let's hit the road.'

CHAPTER 36: MUM AND DAD'S

To say Mum looks surprised to see us would be to totally misrepresent the level of shock and amazement on her face.

'My word,' she says, with that starry, mad–eyed expression that has unveiled itself to me so many times over the years – usually when she's had too much sherry or ginger wine, but sometimes when I flunked an exam or got into trouble. The look that says, 'Well, there's something I wasn't expecting, now give me a few minutes and I'll work out exactly how to deal with it.'

Her first mission on seeing us is to insist that Henry comes in. 'I won't have you driving back in the dark with no food inside you,' she announces, as Dad comes out into the hallway to greet us and nearly trips over the end of his own slippers when he sees Rufus standing there, looking bashful, clutching a box of champagne.

'Nice to see you son,' he says, patting Rufus on the back in such a friendly way that I can see Rufus relaxing instantly as he slips out of his coat and hands over the box of booze. The champagne inside it is worth more per bottle than my parents have spent on alcohol for the entire Christmas period. They wouldn't know good champagne from bad, but I'm glad Rufus has taken the trouble to bring the best for them.

'Do you mind if I come in?' Henry asks Rufus.

'Of course not,' he says. 'No, please do. You'll make Kelly's night if you come in and have something to eat.'

We're all sitting at the dining room table with mum's famous Christmas Eve pork joint sitting in the centre, taking pride of place.

'Help yourself to any more, Rufus. Shall I cut you another slice? More potatoes?'

Rufus pats his stomach appreciatively but declines the offer of a fourth serving.

'Yes, leave a little room for pudding. Good idea,' says Mum.

Rufus looks quite terrified by this thought. I don't think he's ever seen anything quite like this feast being laid before him.

'I saw the news about Elodie,' says Mum. 'Is it OK to mention?'

'Of course,' we both say. It's perfectly fine to mention it; in fact, it would be weird if it weren't mentioned. I think I'd be more worried if everyone skated around the subject and was scared to address it. The truth is that she killed herself. We should be able to talk about it.

'Did it surprise you, love?' asks Mum. 'I mean, was she the depressed sort?'

'I don't think I really knew her at all,' I say. 'She was obviously more troubled than any of us realised. I tried to find out about her and I'd ask her questions all the time – about her family and friends and home life, but she never seemed to want to talk about them. It turned out that her mum worked in the house, and Elodie had never mentioned it.'

'They found letters from Rose to Elodie,' says Rufus.

'She was persuading Elodie to try and end our relationship.'

'What?'

'Yep. It seemed that Rose liked the idea of Elodie getting together with me. Once she was installed as housekeeper, she thought she could facilitate that, then you came along.'

'Wow. So that's why she hid all my letters and messed up my phone.'

'I guess so.'

'Shall we talk about something more positive,' says mum, rather regretting bringing up the subject in the first place.'

It's a bright, clear and dry day when we wake up; in different rooms, of course, because this is Mum and Dad's family home and even if they allowed us to sleep in the same bed, I'd refuse on the grounds that it would be too embarrassing for words. Imagine coming down and sitting opposite Mum and Dad at the small dining table in the little kitchen, with them knowing what Rufus and I had been up to overnight ... No, no, no, it's all wrong. I can't imagine sleeping with him under Mum and Dad's roof when we're married, let alone now.

I can hear voices downstairs so I wander down and find Mum and Rufus standing by the patio window looking out into the garden. 'No, they're not hyacinths; those are the gladis,' she's saying, and he's pretending that he gives a toss. 'It's hard to tell them apart in winter, isn't it?'

'Morning,' I say brightly, and they spin round.

'Oh, Merry Christmas, love,' says Mum, giving me a hug. 'Let me get you a cup of tea.'

'I've just been talking to Jayne about the wedding,' says Rufus. 'I told her that you've put her in charge of it.'

'That's very thoughtful of you, dear,' says Mum, walking over with my tea in a lovely big mug. 'But I don't think I'm really the best person to ask. I mean – I know I was very keen to organise everything for you last time, but I don't think I realised just how famous you both are when I was talking about the community centre. I mean, I don't know any famous people or posh dress designers or anything like that.'

'That's why I want you to do this, Mum.'

'Well, I'd love to help,' she says warily. 'But I'd better not do it on my own. I'll need you to help me.'

'Of course I'll help you,' I say. 'We can organise the whole thing together. Mandy and Sophie will help too.'

'Oh lovely. When are you thinking of getting married?'

'Twenty–ninth of April,' Rufus and I both chorus.

'It's the day we met. Our one-year anniversary,' I explain.

'Oh dear.' Mum looks quite distraught.

'What is it?'

'Well, that's a very difficult time of year for brown,' she says. 'I've bought brown now. There's no going back.'

'Let me buy you a brand–new outfit that's perfect for April,' Rufus offers, gallantly. 'As a Christmas present.'

'OK, well maybe just a summery scarf to brighten it up,' she says. 'I don't want you spending all your money on me when you've got so much to plan and pay for. We'd like to help with the wedding though, wouldn't we, Tony?'

Mum looks over at my dad who's sitting in his favourite armchair, pushed out of the way, into the corner of the room, to make way for the Christmas tree.

'Of course,' he says. 'It's only right.'

Rufus doesn't know quite what to say. The idea of my parents digging into their pensions to pay for a wedding that Rufus could afford to cover entirely out of his small change clearly appals him, but he also recognises that Mum and Dad are proud and to deny them the chance to pay for their daughter's wedding would be plain rude.

'Right,' says Mum. 'Well, where are we going to hold it then?'

'The Hastings Community Centre,' I say with confidence. 'I thought we could get married at that pretty little church in Battle village and all go over to the community centre afterwards.'

I'm expecting her to jump up and clap her hands together in joy ... but no. She looks at me as if I'm stark, staring mad.

'Sweetheart, some of the most important people in the world will be flying in for this wedding,' she says. 'It would be much better if you got married somewhere near the airport to make it easier for them. Somewhere bigger and a bit nicer than the community centre, love. Anyway, to be honest, I don't think you'd get it now. It gets booked up months in advance, and I don't care who you are, you won't get the centre unless you're on the shortlist. Did I tell you about Marian? She's been running kids' clubs down there all year so that she can get it booked for her daughter but it's no good – the place is booked out.'

Oh God.

'Rufus, I don't want to get married in New York,' I say, just in case my husband–to–be is mentally planning the sophisticated, star–struck wedding of his mother's dreams.

'No, not New York!' cries Mum. 'No, we need somewhere lovely. Let's get our thinking caps on. Tony, are you listening over there? We need everyone with thinking caps on. We need to plan a beautiful wedding for these two and we need to do it sharpish.'

CHAPTER 37: THE PERFECT DAY

'Oh God, Kelly, you look amazing.' Sophie is standing before me with beautiful pale–pink tea roses weaved into a crown on her head. I've got them dotted through my hair, which is down, cascading over my bare shoulders as I stand in this beautiful white sheath dress. We almost did it. We almost held the wedding on 29 April, but then Frank was ill, and we knew he wanted to come, so we put it off. He's much better now, and the benefit of waiting until the beginning of July is that it's infinitely warmer, and the roses are all in bloom.

Yep, you guessed it: Rufus and I are holding our wedding ceremony in the Rose Garden at Hampton Court Palace. I couldn't be happier. He couldn't be happier. Mum and Dad couldn't be happier, and Frank? Frank looks like he just won the jackpot. He had to retire 'unofficially' as well as officially after his illness, so he's not here so much now. Neither is Lawrence, actually – we've employed him as head gardener at the house, and Frank comes once a week to check on him and to drink sweet tea with me.

'Ready for the veil?' asks Mandy, and they place the soft, long-flowing veil over my head.

'God, sweetheart, you look lovely,' says Dad, taking my arm and leading me towards the path that will lead us into the garden and to my future husband. I have four brides-maids: Sophie and Mandy are the main two, then there's Katie and Jenny in the second tier, threatening to start throwing Maltesers at me when I'm about to say 'I do'.

The band strikes up 'Here Comes the Bride', and I look towards the end of the garden where Rufus is waiting with Courty and Deeves – his two great mates who've flown over for the ceremony with their wives. They're lovely guys – such fun – and their wives will become great friends of mine; I know they will. I've made them honorary flower girls and they are standing by the exit, ready to sprinkle the ground with petals when everyone leaves. Henry, David and Lawrence are right next to them – all looking so incredibly smart.

Next to them are Rufus's staff. Sorry, my staff! They're also my friends. There's Pamela all dressed up in pale blue, and the lovely Julie looking gorgeous in a pink dress that I helped her to pick out. She, Mandy, Sophie and I went shop-ping together and had a ball picking out clothes. She's invited Mike from the record shop to come as her guest. I see him standing next to her. She's right; he's very good–looking. Christine's next to them in a shimmering coffee-coloured dress. She looks lovely. I've managed to strike up more of a friendship with her than I ever thought possible. It's amazing what being in love can do for you!

Frank is sitting on the bench with no inscription, on a velvet throw, watching patiently with a smile etched across his face.

There are four ushers here: Morgan, Mather, Prentice

and Jimmy. They stand with their sunglasses on, looking more like bouncers than they've ever looked before.

'Don't worry about security. We hired security separately,' I say, but they can't. They've spent so long watching my back that on the most important day of my life, they want to be sure that nothing bad happens. The only way to guarantee that is to stay watching.

This morning, we had to have a separate service to make the wedding vows official. Ruf and I jumped into the car and zoomed off to the Richmond Register Office, hoping to keep the whole thing low-key and go for a great big breakfast afterwards, but it wasn't to be. The press caught up with us, so we had to rush back home early. Now, we're here.

The press have been held right back. Despite an unwanted bidding war breaking out between OK and Hello!, we have no magazine deal, no journalists in attendance and no desire for any publicity.

Sophie was a little bit annoyed at the decision. 'Heat called?' she said, alarmed. 'Surely we can make an exception for them. It's Heat. I mean Heat. Surely it's OK for you to be in Heat?'

'Not today,' I said, and she let it drop. She looked confused but said she understood. I don't think she'll ever understand why I wouldn't want to be in Heat, but that's OK. A year ago, I wouldn't have understood either.

I'm right next to Rufus now, and he takes my hand as the service begins. We keep it short because the last thing we want is for everyone to be bored out of their minds. There are poems about us and poems about love. Mandy reads about roses while Lawrence looks on adoringly.

'Roses are ancient symbols of love and beauty,' she says. 'The rose was sacred to a number of goddesses, including Isis and Aphrodite, and is often used as a symbol of the Virgin Mary.'

As she talks, I just look around at all these wonderful people. Mostly, though, I look at the wonderful person next to me – Rufus. I think of the sacrifices he's made. His mother was furious when he said that the ceremony wouldn't be in New York, and at one point, she refused to come to the wedding until he persuaded her that he loved her and needed her to be there on his special day. She seems relaxed as she sits there, talking to my mum. Perhaps I'll get to like her over time.

Rufus says he's planning to dance with Great–Aunt Maude later when we have a huge party on the palace grounds, with fireworks over the river, food, drink, wine and fun. Then, we have to work out a life somehow together. I have to work out what my role in that life will be. I didn't want to be a Celebrity Bride and I don't want to be a Celebrity Wife. I want to be more than that. I'm not sure quite what yet though. Will we have kids? I hope so. I'd love that. But there's a whole lifetime before that happens. Rufus has to go to LA for the filming of the Bond movie and I've promised I'll go with him. What on earth will they make of me there? I've put the weight back on and, you know, I don't care. If they don't like me as a size 12, it's their problem. I won't diet to please them and I certainly won't lie to please them. I won't pretend to be someone that I'm not.

I look over at the bench with no name and see Frank, wearing his best suit, and smiling for all he's worth. He stands up when we approach and pulls the velvet throw aside. A shiny gold plaque gleams in the sunshine. 'A bench for lovers like Kelly and Rufus, and for all who are entranced and delighted by the magic of roses,' it reads.

'Thank you,' I say, staring deep into his soft, warm eyes. 'It's perfect.'

.   .   .

ends

If you enjoyed this, there are lots of books by Bernice Bloom that you will love.

Have you heard about her Mary Brown series of books?

This best-selling, chart-topping series is laugh-out-loud funny.

To download a FREE GUIDE to the series, input this book funnel link (below) into your computer or email us at berni cenovelist@gmail.com, and we will send you the link.

https://dl.bookfunnel.com/pqaz0ym819?fbclid=IwY2x jawEqBChleHRuA2FlbQIxMAABHQ0ONznVAEws-yDGf AWZNO99ylxditgiRvOc2zbKaBXx9hDQMDxtqxUX1Q_aem_0PCQ

All the books in the series are listed overleaf.

THANK YOU SO MUCH FOR YOUR SUPPORT x

ALSO BY BERNICE BLOOM

The order of the Mary Brown books.

THE SERIES HAS 12 BOOKS:

What's Up, Mary Brown? (Book 1)

The Adventures of Mary Brown (Book 2)

Christmas with Mary Brown: Fun, Joy & Laughter (Book 3)

Mary Brown is leaving town: (Book 4)

Mary Brown in Lockdown (Book 5)

The Mysterious Invitation (Book 6)

A friend in need, Mary Brown: A NOVELLA (Book 7)

Dog Days for Mary Brown: A NOVELLA (Book 8)

Don't Mention The Hen Weekend (Book 9)

The St. Lucia Mystery (Book 10)

We'll Always Have Paris (book 11)

She's stolen my Baby (book 12)

Thank you for your incredible support xx

Printed in Great Britain
by Amazon